HEADHUNTER

Miles Campbell

This isn't a shortlist you want to be on

Miles Campbell served as an Officer with Airborne Forces, which included operational tours around the globe. He is an SAS trained combat survival instructor and completed their resistance to interrogation training. After the army, he became a Headhunter, operating in the United Kingdom, Continental Europe, Africa, Russia and the Middle East.

People sleep peaceably in their beds at night only because rough men stand ready to do violence on their behalf.

George Orwell

Prologue

September 2008

Qatar

The bullet spat out of the sniper rifle in the hot Arabian night and the target was down.

Candidate 32 was dead.

The projectile had entered the man's forehead and there was a messy collage of blood and bone fragments on the wall behind. The target had slumped to the floor, in the entrance of the Marriott hotel and his once immaculate white thobe was gradually turning red.

David Lord surveyed his work from the hiding place and kept very still.

He could hear a woman screaming and men shouting and looking through the scope, saw a small crowd gathering around the body. Something caught his eye and taking another look through the sights, as a scientist would through a microscope, he saw another body lying beyond.

'Collateral damage' he whispered wryly.

Slowly, he crawled backwards, cradling the rifle. Removing the magazine, he pulled the cocking lever backwards, allowing the unfired round to eject into the case catcher. He placed the bullet back into the magazine and settled the spent case in the dirt next to him.

Smiling to himself, he thought of the North Korean markings etched into the metal. No harm in causing a bit of mischief. The Qataris were known to invest heavily in North Korea and perhaps the investigating authorities would think that a business deal had gone bad.

He was convinced that the police would find the spent case and his hiding place, but by then, he would be long gone. Firing off the action, he grinned when he heard the working parts race forward with a dull clunk.

Working deliberately, he removed the other rifle attachments and slid the weapon back into its sleeve, placing the magazine into the pouch.

Glancing quickly around, he was pleased with the spot that had been chosen to take the shot. It was on top of a small building and the foliage of an old date palm curled over it in umbrella fashion. The expansive leaves had provided good cover, without restricting the line of sight to the target, some seven hundred metres away.

Gathering his gear, he made his way off the roof and walked briskly back through scrubland to the car, parked in an unlit street, shaded by trees. Once he had stashed the rifle and pack, he drove off slowly, making his way to the main road and away from the scene.

Driving back towards the city, he saw police cars with flashing lights and sirens blaring, racing in the opposite direction towards the Marriott.

'It's going to be a long night for you guys,' he said aloud, watching the procession.

After a short distance, he pulled off the main road, made a few turns and drove into a partially lit parking area.

In the corner, he noticed the car of his 'assistor' on the operation, a grey Toyota Land Cruiser. Drawing up next to it, he turned off the lights and cut the engine.

'How was it?' asked Pete.

He liked Pete. He was steady, dependable and his calm demeanour made him an ideal companion during stressful times like these.

'Fine, no problems,' he replied nonchalantly. 'Saw the target clearly and he'll be meeting his maker round about now.'

'Nice one! You're a cool customer, that's for sure.'

'I don't know about that' he answered thoughtfully. 'Right, let's get busy.' Reaching into the car for the rifle case, he slid it off the seat and handed it to his friend. 'Time to get rid of the gun.'

They had agreed that the best way to hide the evidence was to throw it into the Persian Gulf some kilometres off shore. Pete had hired a speedboat a few days earlier and he would carry out the task on his own.

David was a little sad to be throwing away such a high precision instrument, but it was risky trying to get the weapon back to England. The two men shook hands and Pete placed the rifle case in the back of the Land Cruiser.

'We'll have a pint in the future to celebrate this, mate,' said David, as the assistor climbed into the driver's seat.

'I'm buying,' grinned his friend.

He drove out of the parking area and headed for the boat, moored at a sandy beach, several kilometres down the coast.

He had decided where to drop the weapon, way offshore in a deep patch of water, some forty metres down. Over time, the sand would cover the weapon and it would have disappeared off the face of the planet.

David quickly changed back into his suit, putting his 'killing clothes' into a bin liner, to be disposed of on the way back to the Hilton in West Bay. Pulling off the surgical gloves, he took a lighter from his pocket and lit them. They caught instantly and after the flame had licked half way up, he threw them onto a patch of sand off to one side and ground his foot into the ashes.

Before getting back into his car, he glanced around the parking area, to make sure there were no prying eyes nearby. Satisfied that they hadn't been observed, he headed for the corniche road, which followed an arching bay along the coast and allowed himself a smile. One more off the shortlist.

He ensured he was noticed by the hotel receptionist, by asking for a copy of *The Times* to be delivered to his room in the morning. He then made his way up to the room, taking off his tie and jacket as he entered. Leaving them on a chair by the bed, he walked over to the fridge and looked inside. Reaching for a miniature bottle of scotch, he poured it into a glass. He took a taste of the fiery liquid and immediately felt better. Glancing down at his left hand, he noticed that it was shaking slightly. He clenched it, to stop the movement and tipping back his neck, emptied the glass.

'Well, you've earned it,' he said aloud.

He reached into the fridge for another and poured it. This time, he drank it more slowly, swirling it around his mouth, relishing the oaky taste.

Turning on the Al Jazeera news, he wondered if the events of the evening had reached it yet. The state-run media organisation was strictly controlled, and he knew every story had to be checked and checked again before it was released, so it might not be till morning that the killing was aired. Also, the state might not want to even air the story, possibly seeing it as a slur on its reputation. Other Gulf countries did it all the time, he knew. He had heard of riots taking place in Bahrain, next door, and the stories didn't even appear on the news. No matter, he thought. Reuters and the international press would get hold of the story sooner or later.

He reached into the fridge again and pulled out a can of Carlsberg, pouring it gently into another glass. Glancing at his watch, he realised it was well past midnight and suddenly felt exhausted. Stretching, he undressed quickly and flopped into bed. He would be asleep sixty seconds later.

He sent a text. Afterwards, he would delete the call and message history.

It was a simple message.

'Damocles.'

Chapter One

Two years earlier

Afghanistan

The American Black Hawk began its descent into Camp Bastion, watched by hundreds of eyes. Rumour had gone around the camp about an IED strike, followed by a fierce engagement in the Sangin valley between a British patrol from the Grenadier Guards and the Taliban.

Lowering itself to the dusty desert floor, the helicopter raised a cloud of pebbles and dust. The medical team shielded their faces from the onslaught, raising their arms across their foreheads and looking down at the ground. Once the chopper touched down, they ran out to its side, bent low to avoid the rotating blades.

Inside the body of the aircraft was a scene from hell. The broken bodies of what looked like four soldiers lay on the floor, the metal coated with blood. Groans could be heard from some, but others were as quiet as the grave. The crewmen were moving from soldier to soldier, checking on their vital signs and signaling to each other what was required for each patient.

Watching the scene from afar, Captain David Lord saw stretchers being passed out of the aircraft, bearing their grim load. Men and women on each corner rushed to waiting military ambulances, for onward movement to the emergency rooms in the hospital nearby. Every second counted, he knew, when dealing with severe traumatic injuries.

He saw the vehicles screech off in a cloud of dust and hoped that his fellow countrymen would survive.

'Bastards!' he shouted in anger.

Increasingly, the Taliban were using IEDs to attack the coalition forces, knowing that they would never win by bullets alone. They were placed on roads, paths, stream banks and even on the edge of villages and would often be remotely detonated by the bomber, when a patrol went past.

The international powers had taken the decision to enter Afghanistan back in 2001, after the 9/11 attacks in America.

Many had gone before him and he was already half way through his second tour in the country.

David was 6 foot tall, slim, with blondish hair, twenty seven years old. He had a small scar on his right ear from a wayward grenade during his Platoon Commanders course in Brecon. He was originally from the Parachute Regiment, but his expertise now was in vehicle warfare and the use of support weapons. At university he had studied European languages and Arabic, and now in his spare time he was improving his Pashto, one of the main languages used in Afghanistan.

He made his way back to his unit's part of the base, noticing that the helicopter was taking off again, no doubt back to collect more victims. He was already tired of watching the same scene.

Showing his ID card to one of the sentries on the gate, he entered the camp within a camp.

He walked across a flat, hard packed area, roughly the size of half a football field, surrounded on four sides by low buildings and containers.

He headed into the Operations building. Taking off his beret, he paused at the communications room, where two wooden tables had a range of sophisticated radio equipment on them. A member of the attached signals unit was sitting with a headset on, monitoring the net. On the wall, to the side of the signaller, were a series of maps, and a soldier was standing, marking one of them with a red pen.

'Morning boss,' he greeted cheerfully.

'Hi, how are things?' asked David.

'Oh, not so bad. Only a few patrols out at the moment and they're keeping pretty quiet.'

'That's because they're hiding and keeping out of trouble.'

'Yeah, that's what I'd be doing.'

He nodded, knowing that somewhere out there, those patrols were probably watching main travel routes, or waiting in ambush for unsuspecting Taliban insurgents. They would have been out there for days, living in scrapes in the ground, or under bushes and keeping still. During the day, they had unbearable heat to contend with and often at night, freezing temperatures to rattle their bones.

'Is the OC in?' he asked.

'Yes boss, he's in the briefing room.'

Tapping on the door to his right, he walked in, noticing the OC standing in front of a briefing map.

The three other Troop Commanders, captains like himself, were sitting at a large table.

'Ah, come on in David, we were just about to get started,' welcomed the major.

He placed his beret, sandy in colour, on the table by his right hand and sat down. He glanced at the cap badge, a downward facing Excalibur sword, with flames on either side. The simple words, 'Who Dares Wins', were written underneath. To some, a beret was merely what you wore on your head when in uniform. To others, those who had earnt one like this, it was everything.

This was the Special Air Service.

The OC, or Officer Commanding of 'A' Squadron, 22 SAS, was Major Peter Shelton, aged thirty four. He was a big man, 6 foot 3 tall and from the Royal Engineers. He was a rugby man and had played for the army in his younger years. David noticed his broken nose again and marks on his face, probably from battles on the pitch. Peter had an impressive military career to date and had spent much of his time in Afghanistan and Iraq. He was always calm in a crisis and his soldiers respected him and would do anything for him.

Opposite him was James Reynolds, also from the Parachute Regiment, who had opted to join Air Troop within the SAS. He spent his spare weekends back home taking off to the Cornish coast in his beaten up camper van, to go surfing and trying to pick up local girls.

All those sat around the table, having non regulation haircuts and long sideburns, were deeply tanned from the Afghan sun and had a weather-beaten look.

He noticed the map on display was of Nimruz province, which bordered Iran, west of the province they were currently in.

'Over the last few weeks, we've been receiving intelligence on Iranian-backed bombmakers moving across the border, travelling along the Helmand River and linking up with Taliban forces. These 'specialists' are bringing Iranian technology with them, which is causing havoc to friendly forces, particularly in Helmand.'

The major paused and looked at those facing him.

'We currently have patrols from John's troop down near the Afghan/Iran border, keeping an eye on the movement of traffic. As you can imagine, it's a pretty lawless place and these bombmakers have freedom of movement, which I intend to put a stop to.'

All those around the table nodded in agreement. Peter went on to provide more intelligence and background on the IED threat, stating that the Commander of Coalition Forces in Afghanistan had it as the number one priority for Special Forces for the coming months.

'OK gents, are there any questions on the overview that I've given you?' he asked, looking enquiringly at each officer.

'I have a question' piped up Alex. Twenty nine years old with a receding hairline, he was a proud Welshman from the Royal Welsh Regiment and came from a village in the valleys. He swam like a dolphin and commanded Boat Troop, experts in amphibious and underwater warfare. David liked Alex for his relaxed personality and often played chess with him during the long evenings between operations.

'Go for it.'

'Presumably, the bombmakers are going to be reasonably well-protected when they enter Afghanistan, as they have some serious know-how and the Taliban will want to protect that knowledge?'

'Good point,' remarked the OC, 'but from what we've seen so far, our patrols down there have reported very little traffic and what there is, has not been that well guarded. The vehicles identified have been the usual mixture of pickups and beaten up four wheel drive types, with one or two people in each. So, in our estimation there is only likely to be one bodyguard at most protecting each bombmaker, as they travel along the river. In some cases, they may even be travelling on their own.'

'How many of these 'specialists' do you think there are making this trip?' enquired David.

'I would say about one a week,' replied Peter, 'although it's difficult to tell.'

There were a few other questions relating to the quality of intelligence, which all assumed had come from the 'Five Eyes' intelligence alliance, SIS in Tehran and Kabul, and other sources. The major then wrapped up the briefing.

'I'll be giving individual orders to each of you tomorrow, timings to be confirmed, but for now, inform your guys that they are on six hours' notice to move. I'll be selecting one of the troops to intercept the bombmaker or bombmakers and the other three will be given taskings elsewhere in country. Two will go to Sangin valley to raid suspected bomb factories and the remaining troop will act as reserve and additional tasks, here in Bastion. OK gents, thanks for your attention and I'll see you later at grub time.'

David found his Troop Sergeant with a few other NCOs by the side of one of the accommodation containers. A tarp had been stretched over the makeshift gym for shade and the soldiers were using a variety of weights, to increase strength to the upper body. Rock music was playing from a set of old speakers on a nearby table.

'Have you got a minute, Chris?' he asked above the noise.

'Sure boss, what's up?'

He liked Chris Jenkins. He was the consummate professional soldier, recognised by the Regiment as a rising star. Originating from the Light Infantry, he had been with the SAS for eight years, much of it spent in Afghanistan and on the counter-terrorism team back in the UK. He had a wry sense of humour and a ready smile and they worked well together.

The two walked away from the others, to be away from the noise.

'We've been given the heads up by the OC that some taskings are coming our way, so put the boys on six hours' notice to move will you?' he instructed. 'He's giving full orders tomorrow, timings to be confirmed, so you and I will go to those and then we'll have a clearer picture of what we'll be doing. It looks like the squadron is going after these IED bombmakers that are hurting the infantry guys so badly.'

The man nodded, weighing up the information and looking directly into his eyes.

'Get the boys ready as best we can and once we know our specific orders, we'll give them the full picture,' he continued.

'OK, I'll get them busy and let them know we'll be going out again.'

'Let's check zero and do some weapons training this afternoon. Also, I want Jock to take us all through the first aid drills for gunshot wounds and explosion trauma injuries again.'

Jock Cattenach, a Lance Corporal and originally from the Black Watch, was the most qualified medic in the troop and responsible for making sure the patrol medics and all other soldiers kept up to date with their skills.

'I know we did this the other week, but let's get the boys thinking straight and bang up to date. Also, can you make sure that everyone has got enough morphine, should the shit hit the fan out there?'

He glanced westwards, towards the open desert.

'Understood. I'll brief the guys and get Jock to set up the training session. Two o'clock OK for you?'

'Yeah, and let's do the rangework at four, when it's a little cooler,' said David smiling.

He had never experienced such heat as here in the desert. Even at night it was warm, but the air conditioning in the accommodation containers helped a little. In the mountains, it was a different story though. The temperature could plummet to below freezing and he always packed his down jacket and thick gloves to ward off the cold, essential when sitting in an OP for days on end.

The rest of the day followed the pattern that had been set in train with Jock taking the troop through some intensive first aid training.

David was pleased with the level of expertise that he witnessed in his soldiers and was glad that the knowledge would be fresh in their minds when they stepped off the helicopter.

The check zeroing and weapons training later that day went without a hitch and he was impressed with the skill his soldiers displayed on the range. It was hardly surprising, when they spent so much time familiarising themselves with every weapon under the sun. Ever the perfectionist, he was pleased with his own performance as well.

At the end of the range session, as the sun was beginning to dip below the far off mountains, heralding the start of the evening in Helmand province, he gathered his men together.

'Well done today, guys. As Chris will have told you, we're likely to be going out on ops again soon, so I want you to sort your kit out and have a good night's sleep tonight. Tomorrow, when we receive the OC's orders, we'll have a better idea on what we'll be doing, so for now just make sure you're ready to go. OK?'

Nods from the soldiers indicated that they understood.

'Excellent' he said. 'Have a restful night then.'

The soldiers clambered on to the trucks and Land Rovers parked nearby and headed back to camp, wrapping their shemaghs around their heads to ward off the dust.

....

The following evening, at 7.30pm, David's troop assembled at the holding area, to the rear of the Merlin helicopter. Their bergans were lined up, with body armour and belt kits in front, all waiting for the eight o'clock departure.

Some of the men gathered in small groups, with one or two taking a final drag on a cigarette, whilst others were taking more water on board.

Glancing around at his soldiers, he felt proud to be part of such an elite group. Here were the gladiators, about to enter the arena. All the hard work and sacrifice had brought him here. He only hoped that he would measure up once again to what was required of him.

'All set?' asked the sergeant.

'Err, yes, Chris, thanks. Looking forward to getting back out there.'

'Me too. It's been too long sitting around this bloody camp, waiting.'

'Yeah,' responded David. 'Time to earn that Special Forces pay!'

'Very true. Always good to get more operations under the belt and pay off the mortgage!'

It was funny, but he rarely thought much about money, out here in the middle of nowhere.

Sure, you needed money to buy bits and pieces in the little stores on camp, but you never really thought about it. Every month, his army salary was being paid into the bank account thousands of miles away, but on operations, money just didn't seem important.

'Did the guys get the extra morphine I asked for?' he enquired.

'Yes, each man has got two syrettes on him and the medic in each patrol has an extra six syrettes in his main kit, just in case.'

'That's good,' he replied, as he wandered off to the edge of the holding area, to be alone with his thoughts for a while.

Shortly before eight, the two British pilots emerged from one of the air asset buildings at the side of the Merlin and strode purposefully towards the aircraft. Seeing the movement, the soldiers moved towards the line of bergans with their weapons in hand and began to put on their belt kit and body armour. One of the pilots, on seeing him, nodded his head and he reciprocated. He knew Flight Lieutenant Doug Childs well and often went running with him around the perimeter wire at Bastion.

The pilots climbed into the aircraft and shortly afterwards the rotors began to turn, slowly at first and then building up speed, scattering dust, until they were at operating pitch. The crewman manning the machinegun at the back of the chopper signalled for the soldiers to approach and one by one they clambered up the rear ramp, depositing the packs along the line of seats. As Commander, David was last to access the aircraft, so that he would be first out when the time came to land. As he stepped on to the ramp, the smell of aircraft fumes heavy in his nostrils, he glanced over his shoulder and saw the comforting sight of two Apache helicopters hovering above. They would provide security for the troop during the flight and for a short period when they landed on the desert floor.

'No turning back now,' he said to himself, as the rear crewman gave him the thumbs up.

He responded, meaning that everyone was on board. He could see the crewman talking to the pilot on the internal radio, informing him that everyone was on the aircraft and they were ready to depart.

Soon afterwards, the occupants could feel the aircraft lift off the ground and those near to windows could see the bright lights of Camp Bastion gradually disappear below them.

The helicopter turned its nose to the south west and began its journey into the night.

Away from safety and towards uncertainty and danger.

The flight, down towards the Iranian border and lasting just over an hour, passed without incident. Some soldiers closed their eyes and allowed themselves to drift into shallow sleep, whilst others thought about their lives and loved ones. Wives, girlfriends, families, even pets, everything except the mission.

David's own thoughts wandered back to the planning session earlier that day. Sitting with the OC and Troop Sergeant for over two hours, they had looked at every issue involved in the operation and from every angle. They had pored over maps, photographs and intelligence briefings, until they knew the terrain they were going to face, and what went on down there, like the back of their hands.

The major had stressed the mission as the 'kill or capture' of the bombmaker and had smiled wryly that he preferred the latter.

They had discussed the armaments the patrol would take and the logistics that would support the men in the field, from food and water, through to additional supplies. By the end of the session, the three had agreed on the conduct of the operation and the OC had wished them the best of British luck.

Walking out of the operations room and back into the heat, Chris had patted his Troop Commander on the shoulder.

'That's a good mission, boss. The guys will be pleased, when they hear your orders.' The sergeant had smiled, shielding his eyes from the sun. 'They always are, until the enemy starts shooting at us and the plan goes to shit!'

All too quickly, he was warned by the pilot through his headset that they were ten minutes out from landing. Nudging the soldier on his right, he showed the fingers on both hands splayed apart, indicating 'ten minutes'. The soldier nodded and repeated the gesture to the trooper next to him and the process repeated itself around the aircraft, until everyone knew that they were approaching their landing zone. He could sense that the helicopter was descending and as he looked out of the back of the aircraft, he could just make out the desert floor rushing underneath them in the moonlight.

All soldiers began to turn on their night vision goggles, getting their eyes used to the eerie green glow that appeared. Those that had undone their belts on their belt kits, fastened them and everyone gripped their weapon and located their bergan in front of them. Some took a final swig of water, to clear the dust in their throats.

The call 'Two minutes!' came down on the radio and the soldiers stood up, grabbed their packs and started to shuffle slowly towards the ramp.

They were much closer to the ground now and he waited in anticipation for the pilot to level off and bring the wheels to the floor. It seemed to take an age for the rubber to hit sand, but eventually he felt the aircraft bump terra firma. He looked eagerly towards the crewman, who gave the thumps up.

'Go!' he shouted, over the noise of the aircraft and pointing to the desert.

He ran off the ramp as fast as he could, weighed down by the heavy load and went about fifty metres, before throwing himself to the ground, behind his bergan. Taking his C8, he scanned the night in front of him, his chest heaving from the exertion. He quickly glanced over his shoulder and saw the rest of the troop diving to the ground, as he had done. The soldiers formed a circle behind the aircraft in all round defence, with himself at the twelve and Chris at the six o'clock positions.

Soon, the Merlin raised itself off the ground and headed north. He felt a loss as it departed, his sanctuary gone and he felt very alone, even though he was surrounded by heavily armed comrades. He couldn't see them, but he could hear the Apaches above, their menace providing some reassurance to those on the ground.

After he had agreed their position and confirmed the bearing to the OP locations with Chris, he briefed the other Patrol Commanders, who had moved over to them.

Once he was done, he whispered to his number two.

'OK, let's move out, two minutes.'

The Troop Sergeant nodded and started going around the defensive circle, warning the soldiers that they would be leaving.

David lifted his bergan onto his shoulders and made it as comfortable as possible, as he saw the troopers forming up behind him. He bent down on one knee, scanning the ground ahead from left to right once more, his weapon following his eyes. His breathing was more consistent now and he felt sweat running down the side of his face, the drops plopping to the ground.

After a moment, he stood up and looked behind him again. He only saw the first few soldiers, whilst the rest disappeared into the green gloom beyond. Lowering his left hand to its full extension, he gave the sweeping motion, to indicate that they should start to move. Checking that he was being followed, he stepped off towards the river.

This wasn't the place to get separated from your friends. He liked to lead the first section of any patrol, to get it off to a good start and not have any mistakes. His map reading and navigational skills were exemplary and he made a point to transfer his knowledge on to others, whenever the opportunity arose. Once they had reached the first way point after a few kilometres, he would hand over the navigation to Lance Corporal Dave Hardy, his lead scout, who would take them to their final location.

They moved swiftly and silently through the night, stopping occasionally to check their navigation and security. Once or twice, he glanced up into the sky and saw the flashing lights of airliners, way above.

They'll be just starting their main course, he thought to himself, as he focused once again and scanned the terrain around him.

Carrying heavy loads over the uneven surface was a recipe for disaster, with twisted or broken ankles a real possibility, but the patrol survived the ordeal and he was pleased when he saw the Helmand River, glinting in the moonlight below him.

He called his sergeant and other Patrol Commanders forward and after the troop had been organised into a defensive position, the group moved slowly down the ridge, to recce the OP positions. Once they had scanned the area thoroughly and were satisfied that it was safe, they selected their sites and waited for the remaining soldiers to join them.

Chapter Two

A few days later, across the border in Iran, in the small town of Zahak, the bombmaker rose before dawn and washed himself. Letting himself out of the small guesthouse he was staying in, he walked the short distance to the mosque, some five minutes away. Once there, he tutted to himself about how few worshippers had made it for early morning prayers, especially the young men he had seen loafing around the town the evening before.

'They neglect their religion at their peril,' he whispered under his breath, shaking his head.

He stayed there for a while, reciting passages from the Koran and praying for a safe journey across the Afghan plains. Knowing the area they were going to travel through well, he also knew it was a lawless place. He had lost friends on the route in years gone by and asked his God for protection.

Once he had completed his prayers, he slipped out of the mosque quietly and made his way back. The sun was yet to rise in the east, but later, its rays would be beating down on the town. Opening the door to the room, he saw that his companion was up and packing a bag.

'Are you not going to prayers?' he asked accusingly in Persian.

'No. I will pray later, when there is more time. I have to make preparations.'

'Laziness!' snarled the bombmaker, scowling and walking towards his part of the room. 'I want to be across the border by seven, so we need to leave shortly.'

'I'll be ready.'

'I want to be in Rudbar before nightfall. We'll cross the border at Karanj and make our way along the river. It's a quieter route than others.'

The other nodded and continued to pack.

Once they were ready, the two stepped out of the guesthouse and walked to the car, an old Nissan pickup that had seen better days, around the corner. The bombmaker started the engine, drove onto the main road and headed east towards the border.

....

It was the third day of the troop being in position. The track had seen low levels of traffic since their arrival and apart from the odd minibus packed with people, the occasional motorbike or rusting car, there had been little to observe.

On the first morning, whilst it was still dark and after they had established themselves, David had taken the Patrol Commanders to the track, to agree the positions. Once complete, he had made it back to his OP. One trooper had taken up an observer's position, whilst the other two were already in their sleeping bags. He had pulled out his own bag and piece of foam mat and tried to make himself comfortable on the stony and uneven surface, before drifting into a light sleep. In two hours, the watch would change and a similar routine would follow for the coming days, until the ambush was sprung.

Around midday, in the blistering Afghan heat, when he was scanning the track with his binoculars, wishing for something to happen, he heard the secure radio crackle into life next to him. His signaller, trooper Tom Porter, pulled the headset tighter on to his head and brought the mic closer to his mouth. Reaching for his notepad, he steadied his biro over the page in anticipation and began to listen to the message.

'Sierra One Zero Alpha, this is Zero over,' began the signaller at Bastion.

'Sierra One Zero Alpha, send over,' replied the soldier.

'Zero, vehicle of interest crossed the border at 07:00 hours today, headed east towards your location. Two passengers. Old, white Nissan Junior pickup. Large, circular rust patch on bonnet and broken nearside headlight. Registration not known, over.'

'Roger, over.'

'ETA your location, 17:00 hours. Good hunting, out,' concluded the signaller at Bastion.

'Roger out,' replied Tom, as he looked at David with a broad grin on his face.

'Well, are we on?' he asked eagerly.

'Yes boss, it looks like we're in business,' he replied, as he began to recount the details of the message.

He mulled over the details.

'OK Tom, pass the info on to the patrols and tell them that I will give further orders at…,' looking at his watch, '…14:00 hours.'

'Roger that.'

This could be it, he thought. Time to take a bombmaker out of commission and increase their butcher's bill.

Staying in the OP, which had become an oven, had also distinctly lost its appeal.

Back at Bastion, he had already discussed his plan with his Troop Sergeant and the other Patrol Commanders, Brian Jenkins and Dave Thompson, and they had gone through the various scenarios.

Dave was a cockney with a boxer's nose, an excellent soldier and an expert in support weapons. He was a strange character though, and David had yet to warm to the man.

Brian, on the other hand, was a different story and he was pleased that he had him in his Troop. He was originally from the Gunners, where he had been an artillery spotter and forward air controller in the Commando Brigade. Many a time in Afghanistan, his skills in dropping ordinance accurately on the enemy saved the lives of those around him. Brian was one of those people who always had a joke to hand, whatever the conditions or time of day and his ability to bring humour, to even the blackest moment, was legendary in the squadron.

As it was a 'kill or capture' mission, the use of explosives was out, so it was agreed that one of the patrols, acting as the 'stopping group', would rush out onto the track and place spike strips on the ground. He had used them before and seen how effective they were in shredding tyres and causing vehicles to stop. His own patrol would be nearby.

Another patrol would be waiting further east along the track, to act as a 'cutoff group', in case the car had solid rubber tyres and managed to survive the initial encounter.

The fourth patrol would act as the early warning team and position themselves a kilometre west of the proposed ambush site.

Traffic was very light in this remote part of Afghanistan, but their role was to identify the bombmaker's vehicle correctly, allowing the rest of the troop to take up position and be ready when it arrived.

He thought about the details received from base. The bombmaker travelling during the day didn't surprise him, as there was so little traffic and he probably thought he would have a clear run up to the Sangin area, or wherever he was going. No doubt he would stop in the small villages near the river for rest, supplies and safety. Even for a bombmaker friendly with the Taliban, this was dangerous territory. There was a patchwork of armed groups and bandits here, as there had been when Alexander the Great had passed through the area two thousand years before.

Time passed quickly, and before he knew it, two o'clock had arrived. Crawling over to where his signaller was lying, he reached for the handset on the troop net, to speak to the Patrol Commanders.

'Charlie Charlie One, this is Zero Alpha, over,' he spoke quietly.

'Send over,' replied the NCOs, one by one.

'Orders to follow' he said, allowing the men to prepare themselves.

He began to confirm the plan, in line with what had been agreed at Bastion. As his commanders were clear on the location of the early warning team, the ambush site, and the cutoff team, as well as the extraction plan, the orders session passed quickly. He gave a time check and continued.

'As the vehicle is expected here around 17:00 hours, I want the early warning team in place by 15:00 hours, to give us plenty of time to get into position. Utmost stealth is required, as there have been a few vehicles on the road today. The stopping and cutoff group need to remain in their OPs for concealment and be able to get to their positions on the road by 16:00 hours, over,' he instructed softly.

The commanders confirmed that they understood.

'I want the target taken alive if possible,' he stressed, as he knew the value of the information that could be provided from the capture. 'Any questions, over?'

There were none.

'It's now 14:20 hours, so let's get the early warning group out in good time. Good luck, out.'

The NCOs signed off.

He knew that they would now begin the frantic activity of briefing their men and getting their gear ready for the ambush. Their weapons were ready, but some food and much needed water would be taken, as there would be no chance of any sustenance leading up to the ambush.

The OPs would begin to be dismantled – camo nets, pegs, scopes – all apart from the ponchos, which provided essential shade from the unforgiving sun.

He woke up the two soldiers at the back of his own position and shortly afterwards, quietly briefed everyone on the upcoming action.

They all nodded that they understood their instructions.

'Rest up as best you can, because we're going to be busy later on.' He smiled. Then he crawled back to a position next to his signaller, taking the binoculars and observing the road below. Once or twice, he glanced behind him, to check that his bergan was there, fully secured and ready to go.

....

As the Afghan afternoon settled in, David heard the trooper next to him exhale a few times, no doubt thinking about what was to come, but otherwise it was quiet. The heat was stifling and he struggled to keep the sweat out of his eyes. His beard, attracting grime and sand, had begun to itch more than usual.

He noticed a flicker of movement, not six feet to the left – an agama lizard, looking for ants or small insects. It was as long as his hand with small, distinct blue markings along its side. He studied the reptile, wondering how it survived in such a harsh environment and realised that there was probably plenty to eat here in reality, if only you knew where to find it. The lizard turned its head and looked in his direction, sensing that it had company. It scampered off over some boulders, looking for a more favourable hunting spot.

Shaking off the distraction, he resumed his watch on the road some five hundred metres away.

Looking through his binoculars, he saw the four soldiers, who were to be the early warning group, collapse their OP and start to crawl and crouch towards their new position.

They stopped frequently, listening for unusual sounds and then proceeded onwards to their lookout point. Soon, they disappeared through a small gully and he resumed his observation of the road.

A little later, his patrol collapsed their own OP and crept down towards the track, taking up defensive positions amongst some rocks, near the stopping group.

Five o'clock came and went and he felt for the soldiers in the early warning group, who had already been in the sun for a few hours. Like him, they would be hiding somewhere near the road. The temperature was still well over forty degrees.

He reflected on the calibre of the men he was working with. To endure long marches with heavy kit, to sit still in an OP for days on end, wearing belt kit and enduring 'hard routine'. To be baked out in the open with no respite and then spring into action at a moment's notice, to face tremendous danger. No wonder SAS selection was so bloody hard.

Thirty minutes passed.

Suddenly, the signaller to his right stiffened, indicating incoming traffic on the radio. The Regimental standard operating procedure, or SOP, for indicating when the enemy was close and voice could not be used safely, was three long clicks on the pressel switch.

This was what the trooper had just received and he turned to David, giving the 'thumbs down' signal with his left hand, indicating that the bombmaker's car had been spotted and was on its way.

He crawled over to his corporal, who was crouching in cover.

'Alright Brian?' he whispered.

'Yep, good to go,' the man replied quietly, as he pointed to the spike strips, placed across the road. The plan was for him, David and another trooper to stand well behind the spikes, weapons raised, forcing the car to stop. The other two troopers in his patrol would be lying prone, providing cover.

The men moved into their final positions.

'Tell the cutoff group to keep an eye out for vehicles coming the other way,' he ordered. Brian nodded and passed on the instructions.

'And it starts,' he said quietly.

'Time to earn our medals,' remarked the soldier on his right.

There was a calm now. All the preparation had been done and the men were ready. The sun was beginning to set and there was a stillness in the air.

Off to the west, he could hear a slight engine noise and then it faded.

All went quiet.

Then, he could hear it again, much closer now. He looked to his left and right, to check that everyone was ready. He glanced at Brian, who nodded back.

'Prepare for action!' he said in a forced whisper.

He heard the vehicle again, and it sounded close.

And then he saw it.

Over the brow of the road, a small dust cloud was rising, as the car bumped along the rutted track. It came into view, skylined on the crest, the late afternoon sun bathing its front in an orange red glow. Dropping down into the dip, it suddenly came to a screeching halt, as the driver saw the spike strips on the road, and the soldiers behind.

The dust began to settle around the vehicle and all was quiet, save for the engine ticking over slowly.

From his position, he looked at the passenger side first, thinking that was where the bombmaker would be sitting, and had to do a double take. Sat there was a figure in a traditional blue Afghan burkha.

His eyes flashed across to the driver's side and he saw a man aged about thirty with a full beard, wearing a dirty shirt and an off-white turban. He saw Brian make the gesture to switch off the engine, by taking his left hand of his weapon and rotating his wrist repeatedly.

Nothing happened.

Moments passed.

Brian moved swiftly to the driver's side, pointing his C8 at the driver's head.

'Stop!' he shouted, first in Persian and then Pashto.

The engine was finally turned off and the driver looked at the man blankly.

A sense of relief was palpable amongst the soldiers that the bombmaker hadn't tried to drive through the ambush and make a run for it.

Brian indicated with his rifle for the driver to step out of the car.

Again, nothing happened.

'Out!' shouted the corporal.

The door creaked open and the driver stepped warily on to the track. David kept glancing back at the passenger, who seemed to be agitated. The mesh of the burkha was moving from side to side, as if the person was trying to get a better view of the soldiers near the car.

'She's probably terrified,' he thought, as he stared inquisitively at the figure, before looking back at the driver.

Brian was signalling for the man to step away from the car and asking him to show his ID. David thought it remarkable that in this country that seemed so lawless, in this empty place, a car could be stopped at gunpoint and nobody would know. There probably wasn't a policemen for hundreds of miles. He concentrated his gaze on the driver as the man reached slowly into the folds of his clothes, staring at Brian the whole time, and withdrew a thin, brown wallet. He pulled out and handed over what appeared to be a tattered ID card.

The soldier took it and glanced at the details.

'I think we've got him, but I need to compare his ID with the details given to us by the spooks,' he said, as he glanced towards David. 'Jonny, keep a close eye on this one, whilst I get the paperwork', he ordered the trooper closest to him.

As Brian was turning to walk towards his Troop Commander, a shot was fired and there was the sound of breaking glass as the windscreen shattered. He saw Brian drop to the ground on his knees, clutching his neck, blood seeping through his fingers. David's eyes jerked from the corporal to the passenger and he saw the burkha clad figure with pistol in hand, aiming at him!

There was another shot and he felt a sharp pain in his upper left arm. It was like a red-hot chisel being driven through his skin. Another shot was fired and there was the sound of more glass impacting the bonnet.

Raising his weapon quickly with his good arm and swivelling it towards the threat, he fired twice into the chest of the figure, who slumped out of view.

Out of the corner of his eye, he could see the driver dash back the few yards to the car and reach in for something. There were two muffled shots, as a trooper fired into the back of the bent over man. The driver tried to raise himself and pulled his arm out of the car, this time brandishing a pistol. He started to point the weapon towards the soldier and there were two more shots in rapid succession, as the man was hit in the head, bright blood splattering over what was left of the windscreen.

He slumped over the seat, stone dead.

'Fuck!' shouted David, as he raced towards Brian.

'Make sure those fuckers are dead!' he instructed the troopers either side of the vehicle.

Two shots rang out in quick succession.

As he reached the corporal, who was on his knees, his heart sank as he saw him clutching his throat, moaning in pain, with blood starting to darken the ground.

'Medic!' he screamed. Then, 'Let me have a look, mate,' he said quietly to Brian, who released the pressure to reveal a gaping wound that was spurting blood down his front. Using his own hands to put pressure back on the wound, he manoeuvred his friend into a sitting position. By this time, one of the medics, Jock Cattenach, had arrived at his side.

'OK boss, I'll take over now' he said, as he laid his weapon on the ground and reached for his medical pack.

Quickly putting on blue surgical gloves, he took out a large field dressing and pushed it firmly on to the wound, wrapping the cords around the neck gently, so as to keep the airway open. The dressing rapidly turned red, as it soaked up the blood.

David looked down at his hands, which were covered in gore and he knelt down to the desert floor, scooping up some sand and gravel. He brought his hands together and tried to wipe it away, like a scene from Shakespeare's Macbeth. After a few attempts, his hands were cleaner, although some of the blood had congealed around his knuckles. He spat onto his palms and rubbed them furiously again, wanting the stain to disappear.

'How's he doing Jock?' he asked the medic, who responded by looking him straight in the eyes and shaking his head slowly.

'I'm going to put another dressing on' the medic said to Brian, who gurgled a pained acknowledgement. Reaching into his medical bag for another bandage, he took the wrapping off and placed it on top of the original dressing. It too began to darken with blood. He quickly glanced up at David and noticing the blood on his camouflaged shirt, stared in horror.

'Boss, you've been shot!' he exclaimed.

'Yeah, the bitch got me in the arm' as he winced when he tried to bend the limb.

The soldier shouted to one of the other trained medics to have a look at the arm, whilst he continued to treat Brian on the floor. As he moved off to one side of the road with the new medic, he gestured for his signaller to come to him.

'Get the early warning and cutoff groups in, as we'll probably be leaving in the next hour or so' he instructed. 'Also, get on to Bastion to send the chopper directly here, and not the extraction point, as we've been compromised and need to get Brian out of here fast!'

The signaller nodded and began speaking into the radio.

After he had taken off his belt kit and chest rig, the medic looking after him unbuttoned his shirt and pulled it off his shoulders. Placing gloves on, he held the arm high and looked at the injury closely. David could see the entry wound and noticed blood dripping down his arm, on to the ground. Glancing around, he saw that those not checking the car were taking up fire positions and watching their arcs.

'Ah, quite a clean wound this one' the medic said happily. 'The bullet has passed straight through the muscle and gone out the other side. Just as well it was low calibre, or it would have been much worse.'

'It hurts like hell,' he winced.

The soldier squirted some sterile fluid into and around the wound and dabbed it with a small bandage, then placed a larger dressing firmly onto the arm, wrapping the cords tight.

'OK, put your shirt and gear back on and we'll have a look at it in an hour and replace the dressing if needed. You'll be as right as rain when the Bastion Doctors repair the wound and stitch you up.' Once David was ready, the soldier fitted a basic sling, trying to immobilise the limb. Satisfied, he took off his gloves and packed away his gear.

Just then, he became aware of shouting behind him.

'Stay with me Brian, stay with me!' Jock was pleading.

Striding back quickly to where the corporal was sitting, he spoke to his helper.

'How is he?' he asked urgently.

'He's slipping in and out of consciousness – he's lost so much blood. I've tried to stop the bleeding, but the wound is just too bad,' he uttered in a defeated tone.

'We've got to save him!' he said through gritted teeth. 'Do everything you can!'

The medic nodded and continued his work.

'Boss, you've got see this!' shouted one of the soldiers, near the passenger door.

The soldier had pulled the figure out of the car and, suspicious about the size and shape of the body, had pulled the burkha off. Lying there on the ground was a young Afghan-looking man in grubby clothes, with bushy black beard.

The moustache area had been shaved to denote an ultraconservative Muslim. The forehead had a deep brown circular mark in the middle, from the countless times it had forcibly hit a prayer mat. He looked like some of the dead Taliban fighters he had seen in earlier encounters. There were two bullet holes in the chest, quite close together, and one to the temple. His surprised, lifeless eyes stared back at him.

'Bloody hell! This guy was the bodyguard, dressed as a woman. I suppose they thought they would have a clear run through, looking like a nice happy couple!' he added with sarcasm. 'OK, check him for ID, documents and other weapons and check the vehicle for the bomb making parts will you?'

'Will do' replied the trooper, who began the search.

He heard running along the track and looking up, saw Chris and another soldier from the cutoff group, running towards them.

'What the hell happened?' asked the sergeant, sweating with exertion.

He quickly briefed his deputy and lowered his voice about Brian.

'What's his condition?' asked Chris of the medic kneeling next to the NCO.

'He's dead,' he replied flatly, standing up. 'I couldn't save him.'

David exhaled loudly, closed his eyes and lowered his head, allowing him a moment to think.

'Right, we need to clear this mess up and get the hell out of here' he urged, looking around him. 'What's the update on the chopper?' he enquired of the signaller.

'No news yet. I've asked the Ops room at Bastion several times, who have told me that all aircraft are grounded due to a sandstorm there. I've asked if there are any spare American choppers down this way to help us out, but so far nothing.'

'Damn!' His mind was racing about the actions to take and his arm had started to develop a dull ache. He turned to the trooper checking the vehicle.

'Find anything?'

'Yep. There's an old sports holdall here, full of bomb switches, detonators and det cord,' the soldier replied, holding up a battered black bag.

'OK good. Make sure it's safe, as it's coming with us. The Intelligence boys will be very interested in this find.'

Turning to Chris, he said, 'It'll be dark soon, so let's get busy.'

The Troop Sergeant nodded.

'Take some DNA and get the bodies back in the car and drive it somewhere near to where there's a drop off from the road. Somewhere down by the river, to make it look like an accident. Make sure the stiffs are well burnt, so that if anyone finds it, they won't be able to tell that they've been shot,' he said grimly. 'Make sure your tracks are covered, as best as possible and get back as soon as you can. I'll clean up here and get everything organised for bugging out and I want to be leaving by...' David checked his watch, '...19:30 at the latest. Any input or suggestions?'

'No input boss, that's fine,' replied Chris. 'For fuck's sake though, try and get Bastion to find a chopper from somewhere, anywhere, otherwise we could be in a whole world of shit down here.'

'Yep, I'll keep on it.'

David called in the commanders that were left and briefed them on the departure plan. Looking around, he saw that they were all exhausted, but he noticed something else too. The steely resolve was still there, despite what had happened.

Ten minutes later, as he was discussing the bugout route, he heard an explosion, followed by another soon after. Looking in the direction of the river, he saw in the distance, a plume of dirty black smoke rising slowly in the still air.

'That'll be the car,' one of the soldiers muttered.

The men around him nodded in grim satisfaction.

'Chalky,' he said, turning to the signaller. 'Get on the blower and see if there's an update on the heli will you? You've got our position and tell them we're going to head east. Hopefully, they'll pick us up somewhere tonight, when we're well clear of this place.'

He turned to one of the commanders.

'Dave, your patrol will carry the body for the first section, but we'll swap around during the night. Distribute his kit, so everyone carries their share and don't leave anything behind.'

The NCO nodded.

'We leave in thirty,' he instructed, looking at his watch.

Shortly afterwards, the Troop Sergeant returned. 'Job done, boss. I put some C-4 under their arses, so they got a rocket to Allah. They'll be there much quicker now, thanks to the British taxpayer!' he chuckled.

'Sick bastard!' David grinned.

'Well, these idiots want to die in battle, so we gave them their wish and soon they'll be with their seventy two virgins, or whatever their book says.'

'Yeah, right,' smirked the Troop Commander.

'Boys ready to go?' asked the sergeant, looking around.

'Pretty much. I've briefed the commanders and they're getting things organised. Let's discuss the route out.'

The two men peered over the map, talking quietly. As they were wrapping up, the medic came over to David and asked how he was.

'Oh, not too bad. It's bloody painful, but I'll be OK.'

'Great. I think you should take some morphine though, as we may have a long walk out.'

'Maybe you're right. What do you think, Chris?' he asked his sergeant.

'Up to you. Take it if you need it. I'm happy on the route and can lead us out for the first bit, if you want to take a breather.'

'Thanks,' he replied and turning to the medic, said 'Bang some in then, would you?'

The man took out one of the syrettes from the medic pouch.

'Sorry boss, but you're going to have to drop your trousers.' Hovering with the syrette over his thigh, the soldier banged it down hard into the muscle. He then pinned it to the lapel of the patient's shirt, indicating that morphine had been given.

'How's that?' he asked, a slight grin on his face.

'That's good shit!' he replied smiling and beginning to feel light headed. The drug began to take effect and he felt a warmth enveloping him, taking away the pain.

'You can stick with me, up at the front,' offered Chris, 'and we can get this show on the road.'

He nodded his head slowly and stood up, shakily at first, until he had found his feet.

The sergeant called in the other patrols on the radio and once he was satisfied that they were ready, headed east into the night.

Chapter Three

The first part of the march out was tough, over rocky ridges and loose rocks and once or twice, David lost his footing and fell over, landing hard on his side. He didn't feel anything because of the morphine and trudged on, the sergeant guiding him. Every thirty minutes or so, they stopped to change over the body-carrying duties, as they continued on under a sky of winking stars.

At around midnight, during a brief pause, he tapped Chris on the back.

'Any news on the chopper?' he whispered.

'No, not yet. Chalky asked for an update about an hour ago and was told that the sandstorm is still raging at Bastion.'

'OK. Let's crack on and we can rest up in cover tomorrow, for one to arrive.'

He gave the order to move off, and the men stood up and trudged on wearily behind him. They walked through the night, the temperature still warm, and the terrain gradually began to change, from rocky ridges to undulating hills and desert. In the hour before first light, he halted the patrol and briefed his commanders. He was feeling tired, but much better and the effects of the morphine had all but faded.

Positioning the troop into all round defence, he observed the terrain through his night vision goggles, whispering to his sergeant that apart from the ridge behind them, it was gently undulating.

He then took his commanders out and sited their laying up positions for the day, selecting dips in the ground where the men could hide and rest up, each about a hundred metres from one another.

His own position was in a hollow in the ground, the size of a squash court, and central to the other positions. He worked with the soldiers to create a makeshift hide, where the bergans were the corner posts, overlaid with ponchos and camouflage nets. Once he was satisfied, having checked it from a few angles, he instructed his men to get into routine, with one man on sentry and the other three resting. He knew they were dog-tired and wanted to give them plenty of rest, not knowing when they would be extracted.

David took the first sentry and within minutes he could hear heavy breathing emanating from the soldiers asleep behind him. Before he knew it, two hours had passed and he was shaking awake the trooper nearest to him to take over. After briefing him, he moved to the corner of the hide, lay on his back and fell into a fitful sleep.

When he awoke, it was late morning and baking hot. The poncho and netting above his head provided excellent shade, but underneath, it still felt like an oven. He was rested, but his arm was still sore and he noticed that blood had soaked into his shirt more as he slept. Removing the sling and pulling open the garment, he removed the old field dressing. He then selected a new one from his kit, and tightened it around the wound. Buttoning up his shirt, he grabbed his weapon and slid over to the trooper on watch.

'Anything happening?' he whispered.

'Nah. Nothing of interest. It's like the end of the world out there.'

Taking his binoculars, he scanned the terrain in front of him. The trooper was right, he thought. In front was stony, undulating, barren desert, with no sign of life. Looking to his left, he saw part of the ridges that they had struggled over during the night, now looking like a row of dirty and misshapen teeth. Glancing at the hides of the other patrols, he hoped their camouflage would suffice until the chopper came.

'See you later,' he whispered, as he slid back to his resting place, and laid his back against the bergan.

Working quickly, he unloaded and stripped his weapon down and gave it a clean, noticing the muck and grit it had picked up. He got rid of as much as he could with his flannelette and, giving it a light oil, reassembled the C8 and cocked it with a knowing smile. Then, he reached for his sidearm, the Sig Sauer P226. After unloading it and cleaning it thoroughly, he pushed the weapon back into the holster, wondering if it would be needed.

Taking the water bottle from his belt kit he took a decent swig, conscious that they were running low, then reached into one of his pouches for some food. Tearing open the silver packet, and pulling a spoon out of his pocket, he delved into the bacon and beans mix, relishing every mouthful.

……….

Later in the day, after he had been on sentry once more, he was resting at the back of the hide and about to fall asleep again, when he felt a tap on his leg.

Opening his eyes, he saw a trooper looking at him, with his hand in the 'thumbs down' signal, indicating enemy.

Grabbing his C8, David slid over to the man.

'Guy on a motorbike, about a kilometre away over there,' the soldier whispered.

He pulled up his binos and saw dust spiralling into the air and, following it downwards, an Afghan man on a motorbike, moving left to right. He was travelling slowly and difficult to make out in the searing heat.

'Warn the others!' he instructed, continuing to watch, as the trooper got on the radio.

The figure seemed to be looking for something. Every now and then, he would stop and look at the ground around him and then into the distance in front.

'Where the hell did he come from?' he murmured to the soldier.

'Don't know, boss. I picked him up a minute before I woke you. I saw his dust trail then tracked him moving across our front. Do you think he's a spotter?'

'Yep, I think so. We're miles from the river and any habitation and there's nothing out here, but snakes, spiders and dust. Let's hope he gets bored and moves off.'

But the Afghan didn't get bored and move off. He kept riding slowly and deliberately across the plain, closer and closer towards the hides.

'How far out is he now?' he asked.

The trooper aimed his laser range finder on the bike and whispered out the readings, as the figure came closer.

'638 metres...............631 metres...................627 metres.'

'Fuck!' he cursed, getting on the radio to his sergeant. 'Have you seen it, Chris?'

'Yeah, I see him. Seems to be getting closer.'

'Thoughts?'

'Well, hopefully he'll ride on by and not see the hides. If he gets too close though, we'll have to slot him.'

'Agreed. Looks like he's coming in my direction, so I'll take him, if he gets too close.'

'Roger,' confirmed the sergeant.

'What range now?' asked David.

'587 metres...............581 metres................576 metres,' whispered the man.

Pulling his weapon into the shoulder slowly, he moved into a stable position. Looking through the sight picture, he picked the figure up straight away. He saw the man clearly now. He looked old and his dirty clothes helped him to blend in with the surroundings. The motorbike looked ancient and battered too, probably older than himself, but he knew that bikes in the region were kept going for decades.

'How far?'

'554 metres.............545 metres................532 metres.'

'Fuck! He's getting too close,' he whispered, keeping the man's image in his scope.

'Do you think he's seen us?' asked the trooper nervously.

'No, not yet. But he's here for a reason. I think they've found the car and assumed we've legged it in this direction. They've probably got spotters north and south of us.'

Watching the bike edge closer to the hide, he whispered again.

'I'm going to have to take a shot, if he gets much closer, as he might give away our position. Spot for me would you?'

'Roger that.'

'How far?'

'518 metres……………..507 metres…..' and then more urgently '496 metres…….'

'OK,' he acknowledged, adjusting his sights. 'Watch for splash.'

'Roger.'

The figure stopped suddenly, side on now and clearer. The Afghan placed both feet on the ground and looked in David's general direction, his eyes sweeping over where the other hides were located. He saw him reach for something tied to the handlebars and realised that it was a radio of some kind.

As he settled his breathing, he noticed a dust spiral spinning to the left of the man.

Moving slowly and trying not to put too much weight on his injured arm, he placed the figure in the centre of his sight picture. When he was satisfied, he fired. The bullet drilled out of the C8 and he was surprised a moment later, to see that the figure was still sitting on the bike. Maybe it was the fatigue, the heat, or perhaps the wind, he wasn't sure. Either way, he was annoyed with himself.

'Splash way beyond figure. You've gone just over his head' reported the soldier, who gave corrections.

Making the adjustments, he viewed the figure once more. The Afghan seemed unfazed by the first shot, or hadn't heard it, because of the suppressor. He had picked up the radio, slowly pulling out the antenna. Settling his breathing, he aimed at the man.

The second shot was released and he saw the figure crumple to the ground.

'On target,' whispered the trooper.

Exiting the hide, he got on the radio and told his sergeant to meet him with a medic at the downed bike, as he broke into a trot. He ran towards the kill, noticing that the sun had begun to dip behind the mountains and he knew they had only an hour or so of light left.

He reached the bike first and saw the Afghan lying on his back, groaning, behind it. The round had hit him in the chest and a bloodied patch had formed on his dirty shirt. He patted the man down, checking for weapons but found none, only the radio that was lying in the dust beside him. The man was murmuring something and his glazed eyes, pointing skyward, belied his pain.

Chris arrived at the scene, followed by the medic and both looked down at the man.

'Did he get a message off, do you think?' asked the sergeant.

'Hard to tell. Even if he did, he didn't have time to say much.'

The Afghan began to breathe heavily, his chest rising and falling in rapid motion.

'Give him morphine' instructed David.

'Eh?' queried the soldier, looking sideways at his Troop Commander.

'I said give him morphine!' he shouted. 'It's the least we can do. The guy is dying, so let's make his last moments on earth painless ones.'

'Fine' replied the medic, setting his pack down and pulling out a syrette.

He thumped the device through the man's leggings and shortly afterwards, the groaning stopped. The man's eyes fluttered and almost shut as the drug took effect and the breathing calmed.

'Good call,' said Chris, looking down at the Afghan. 'It's what makes us different from them. They would torture us as we lay dying.'

David took a moment to gather his thoughts, walking a short distance away from the bike.

'Chris, over here' he said.

The sergeant followed, cradling his weapon and looking towards the dipping sun.

'I reckon we should bug out after last light, head east about 10k's and set up hides again. If the guy got a message off, his friends will be coming. Let's make it hard for them to find us. I think we're owed a bit of luck now with the chopper.'

He walked back to where the Afghan was lying and noticed he wasn't moving. He looked at the soldier next to the body, who shook his head slowly.

'He's gone.'

Breathing out deeply, he looked at the body and closed his eyes. Snapping out of it, he turned to the sergeant.

'OK, we need to close things down here. Get some guys to bury the body, a shallow grave will do, and destroy the bike. I'll close down the hides and plot a route out.'

'Sure boss,' replied Chris, glancing down at the corpse.

He nodded and turned back towards the hides, running through in his mind the actions needed. He felt tiredness creeping up on him again and he longed for a shower, decent food and a comfortable bed.

His mind wandered back to Brian and how he died, as his footsteps crunched through the grit and sand. He would miss him sorely and, although it was painful, ran through the events of the ambush again, asking himself if he could have done better.

Suddenly, there was a single shot, followed by many others and he threw himself instinctively to the ground.

'Contact rear!' he heard someone shout from one of the hides.

Looking around for cover, he saw a small berm to his right and sprinted over to it, covering himself in sand as he threw himself to the floor once more.

'What have you got?' he shouted on the radio to the corporal back in the hides.

There was a pause as more gunfire echoed out and he peered over the lip to try to see what was going on. The fizz of incoming rounds, like angry wasps, passed just above his head and he crawled to another position of safety, further along the berm.

'Figures, about ten, on the slope directly behind us,' replied the NCO. 'They're just above that dark band of rock running left to right. Four hundred metres from my position.'

'OK. I'm coming back to get a better look. Let the guys know would you, so they can give covering fire?'

'Will do'.

Peering out of cover again, he saw movement in the position that the corporal had described. A figure with a dark turban was running to a position of cover. More figures showed themselves above the band and began shooting again in the direction of the hides. Glancing behind him, he saw that Chris and the medic had taken cover behind the bike and were taking long sniping shots at the distant figures. He took one last glance towards the threat, noticing that the insurgents were moving gradually down the slope towards them. Taking a few aimed shots at the figures, he sprinted as fast as he could back to his own hide, where the troopers were firing from.

'Fucking Terry Taliban have turned up again, boss!' one of them shouted wryly between shots.

'Yeah. Can't seem to shake them,' he replied, as he took up a firing position at the back of the hide. He placed his sights over a spot where he had last seen movement, steadied his breathing and waited.

Another turbaned head appeared out of cover as the man tried to get a better view and David fired. The head flopped backwards and an arc of blood splattered the rocks behind it.

'Great shot!' one of the troopers yelled.

Assessing the situation quickly, he spoke to Chris on the radio telling him what he was going to do and requested more harassment fire from them. He then called Dave the corporal and ordered him to take his patrol and flank from the right, as the rest of the troop provided covering fire.

'Roger that. Leaving in two minutes.'

'Utrinque Paratus!' David shouted into the radio in encouragement, reminding the NCO of his proud Parachute Regiment heritage.

He controlled the fire from the hides as the corporal ran to cover with his patrol and began to skirmish up the slope towards the belligerents.

'RPG!' someone shouted, followed by an explosion close to the hide.

The soldiers were covered in a cloud of grit and dust and he felt a sharp pain on his cheek. More Taliban rounds rained down on the hides, with the sound of ricochets pinging off nearby rocks.

'Fuck, I've been hit!' shouted the trooper next to him.

Feeling his own cheek, David touched wet skin and saw blood on his fingers. 'Bollocks!' he said irritably to himself as he wiped away the gore and crawled over to the injured soldier. 'How bad?' he asked.

'Shoulder, boss. Must have taken a piece of shrapnel from the RPG.'

'OK, I'll sort you out,' he replied as he reached into the man's pouch for a field dressing.

Bullets continued to thud into the ground nearby, as the SAS men returned fire.

When he was satisfied with his handiwork, he looked up at the ridge and saw that Dave's patrol had made good ground.

As they got closer, David increased the fire from the rest of the troop to keep the Taliban heads down which worked well, as the assaulting soldiers were on top of them before they had time to fully react. There was a period of rapid fire from them and the sound of grenades exploding, followed by single shots and then it was all over. As if it had never happened.

A few minutes passed and the radio crackled into life.

'Boss, we've got seven enemy dead and one injured prisoner up here. He'll be alright as he only took a round in the arm.'

'Nice work! I'll send some guys to help you out. Leave the bodies, just take DNA and check them for docs, before pushing them out of sight. Patch up the injured guy and bring the weapons back here. We're leaving in an hour!'

....

They had been walking for over two hours, making good progress, when the signaller asked David to pause for a moment.

'Good news, boss. We've got a chopper! They reckon thirty minutes and are asking for our location.'

Pulling out his GPS, he allowed the system to acquire satellites.

'What's up?' asked Chris, as he reached his position.

'Chopper inbound!'

'Oh, thank God!'

'Yeah, good news. Make sure everyone knows would you?'

He heard it way off to the north as it approached. His arm was hurting again from carrying the pack and he thought about taking some more morphine, but decided against it, in case the heli had a problem. His cut cheek was still sore, but the medic had cleaned and plastered it well and the bleeding had all but stopped. Eventually, lying next to the signaller, he was informed that the pilot had seen them through his night vision goggles and was preparing to land.

'Thank Christ!' he whispered to himself.

They had endured a rough few days and he knew that those under him were keen to get back to the safety of Camp Bastion. He looked up and saw the small but bright flashing red lights on the aircraft and knew they were safe.

It landed fifty metres away from them and once the crewman had given them the signal to approach, the patrols jogged over, shielding their eyes from the debris being scattered by the downdraft.

Once Brian, in the body bag, had been pulled aboard, he stepped on to the chopper as last man.

He patted the rear gunner on the shoulder.

'Thanks for coming!' he shouted above the noise, before taking a seat at the rear.

Within seconds, the aircraft lifted into the sky and he felt it bank to the left, level out and then steam towards Bastion and home.

Chapter Four

The next day, after he had been under the Surgeon's knife to repair his arm and had his cheek stitched up, had some food and slept a few hours, David made his way over to the operations room.

He found the OC peering over some maps with John Taylor, one of the other Troop Commanders. John was about the same age as him, a man of big build, originally from the Royal Tank Regiment. A great climber, he was an obvious choice for Mountain Troop, who were experts in climbing and Arctic warfare. In his short climbing career, he had summited a number of peaks well over seven thousand metres and one day hoped to climb Everest.

On seeing him, the major came over quickly.

'Thanks for getting the guys home. Sounds like you had a time of it!'

'You could say that.'

The OC turned to the other Troop Commander. 'OK John, we'll leave this for now and finish up later.'

'Sure' John replied. Turning to David, he playfully punched him in the chest. 'Good to see you in one piece, mate.' Smiling, he rolled up the maps and walked out of the room.

After he had gone, the OC placed his hand on David's shoulder.

'Very sorry to hear about Brian,' he said, looking at the floor. 'One of the best soldiers here.'

'He was.'

'I'll be writing to his wife, but it'll be small comfort to her I know. The Families Officer will be visiting her sometime today as well. How's the arm? You must have been in a lot of pain out there.'

'The Doc says it should heal nicely. The painkillers he gave me are like horse pills, so if I look a bit out of it, you'll know why.'

'Great news! We'll get you back out there soon. No point in moping around camp and I'm sure your lads will want another go at the Taliban. The injured guy you brought back had some interesting snippets to give us by the way, so we'll be acting on those shortly.'

He nodded, his face impassive.

'You'll be wanting to fully debrief your men. Get the patrol report to me tomorrow if you can?'

....

A few days later, he sat with the other Troop Commanders in the operations room, listening to the OC giving an update on the latest intelligence. His mind wandered back to the road, out in the barren landscape. He heard the shots ring out and relived the moment when he had been shot.

The OC was speaking.

'So, gentlemen. We are seeing an increased use of IED's in theatre, making it almost impossible to go anywhere by vehicle.'

'Intelligence is telling us that more bombmakers are coming through from Iran, so we'll be focusing heavily on that threat from now on. David here is a good source of information on the area, so be sure to pick his brains.'

After an hour, the major brought the meeting to a close, not before talking about the volleyball match with the Americans later in the week. As the captains gathered their notes and maps, the OC asked him to stay behind.

'It was a wonderful thing you did, getting the men out safely,' he said, sitting down.

'It was nothing really. They were a great team and helped me out a lot,' he replied, taking a seat opposite.

'I've been speaking with Chris. He says what you did out there was outstanding. How you led things, even when you'd been shot. About how you got them out of danger, from the ambush site and then again when you took out the spotter and saw off the attackers in the desert.'

'Well, any Troop Commander would have done the same.'

'I don't think so and neither do you, if you're being honest.'

David looked at the man blankly.

'So, I'm taking you and the troop off operations for a few days. Give you all time to grieve for a while and rest up.'

'That's very good of you.'

'You all deserve it. You're a pretty understated character I can tell, but you don't need to be so modest.' The major stroked his chin and looked hard at him. 'David, you're the best officer I've got. One of the best I've seen in Special Forces and you'll go far. You're a thinker, but you're also a killer,' he said forcefully, clenching his fist and baring his teeth. 'Not all your fellow officers in the Regiment are like that.'

....

'All set, boss?' asked his sergeant, as they sat near the silent helicopter that would take them to their next area of operations.

A regime of sessions in the gym, proper food and plenty of rest meant David's arm was much better. The cut on his cheek had also healed well, thanks to the precision stiches that had been applied. His troop had been on several operations without him, one where they had captured a bombmaker in a compound just outside the town of Gereshk in Sangin province. They had struck in the early hours, when the occupants were asleep and had returned to Bastion with their prize, as well as useful documents to be analysed by the intelligence people. Another operation, near Malgir, had targeted a Taliban quartermaster and his supplies of bomb-making materials and other ordnance. They had found their man and destroyed his arsenal, the explosions heard many kilometres away. He was pleased that luck had gone their way and they hadn't suffered any casualties.

He hoped they really were making a difference, but feared for the country long term, when coalition forces would eventually leave. He was frustrated by what they were doing, trying to bring modern Western ideas to a country that seemed reluctant to change.

This time they were going to Deshu, a small village on the Helmand River, way south of where coalition forces normally operated. Their target was a mid-level Taliban leader who had escaped from an Afghan police cell in Garmsir weeks before.

'Yeah. Ready to go' he replied, looking up into the darkening sky.

'We need to catch this bastard!' said Chris, through gritted teeth. 'A nasty piece of work by all accounts. He's responsible for multiple coalition deaths in the Sangin valley and enjoys torturing those he captures, over days and sometimes weeks.'

'Yes, we need to put him away. It's a 'kill or capture' operation though, remember?'

'Yeah, of course!' he sneered.

The two men saw the pilots walk out from their operations room towards the aircraft and stood up, pulling on their gear and picking up their weapons.

'Time to go. Get the men ready would you?'

'Will do,' replied Chris. He half turned and then looked hard at David. 'You know, these blokes would follow you to the gates of hell.'

'That's good to know, but I'm not intending to take them that far…'

The man nodded thoughtfully, turned and began walking over to the rest of the troop.

'Did I tell you the one about the Afghan, the Jew and the Christian, arriving at the gates of heaven?' he shouted to the retreating figure.

'It'll have to wait!' yelled the sergeant in reply.

He watched him go and then, pulling out his torch and map, studied the area around Deshu one last time. It was like so many villages along the Helmand River, with walled compounds scattered around a track. Their whole life revolved around that piece of dirt in the middle of nowhere. Apart from the few buildings, there would be a small mosque, but no clinic, or evidence of outside help. They lived and died in that village and few would travel more than a few kilometres away from it in their lifetimes.

....

A day later, back in Bastion, David was nursing his right hand in his room. He had caught some shrapnel on the top of his hand, cutting deep into the tissue and grazing a tendon.

Two soldiers in his troop were not so lucky.

One had died when he stepped on an IED at the entrance to the Taliban leader's compound and the other, a trooper just behind him, had lost a leg below the knee.

Getting up from his bed, he tried to clench his fist a few times to see what movement he had, but stopped after a few tries because it was just too painful. Grabbing his beret, he headed for the operations room, kicking the stones in his way as he walked.

He found the OC in the briefing room, reading some reports, and asked if he had a moment.

'Sure David. How's the hand?'

'Oh, not too bad. The medics have done a pretty good job, again, and the doctor said there wasn't any permanent damage.'

'That's good. Nasty business, that,' the major said. 'One soldier dead and another crippled for life. What a tragedy!'

'If only the bugger had been there. We could have had him and been back in Bastion within a few hours, laughing and joking in the chopper on the way back.'

The compound had been deserted. Apart from finding a rusty AK-47 and a few rounds, the operation had been a disaster. He wondered why it had gone so spectacularly wrong and blamed himself. The intelligence had sounded so good. The OC had put it down to bad luck as the soldiers had made their way back to their rooms, licking their wounds.

'Yes, it's very sad. Two of our best soldiers out of action, permanently,' replied the OC, shaking his head. 'Anyway, how can I help?'

David looked at him blankly.

'I wish to resign my commission, sir.'

'What!' the OC exclaimed. 'You can't be serious?'

'Deadly serious.'

'What on earth has made you decide that?'

'I've been thinking about it since Brian died. The events of yesterday have merely hardened my resolve.'

'But David, you're one of the best Troop Commanders in the Regiment. Probably the best! In a few years, you could be leading an SAS Squadron, possibly this one. Why would you want to throw all that away?'

'It's not throwing anything away, Peter. I've had enough.'

'Look, we have to expect losses from time to time. That's the game we're in.'

'Yeah, well I don't want to suffer 'losses' anymore. I'm fed up with it. There are bits of me scattered out there,' he said, pointing to the desert, 'and I want to get out while I can. I've seen enough dead bodies and crippled soldiers to last a lifetime.'

The major looked him in the eyes and shook his head.

'You're going through a bad patch. Why don't you think about your decision overnight and speak to me tomorrow?'

'My mind is made up. Further thought will not change my decision. I'll bring you my resignation letter tomorrow.'

'If that's what you want?'

'Yes, it is. I want to go somewhere I can make a difference.'

The OC looked at him with sad and tired eyes.

'OK. I'll speak to the CO, who I know will be disappointed. You'll have to serve out your time here of course and I ask you to keep this to yourself for now. Where are you going to go?'

David broke into a grin.

'Far away from all this.'

Chapter Five

Six months later

Zambia

David stepped off the plane at Livingstone and walked down the steps, the sweat already starting to soak into his shirt. In the arrivals hall he joined the queue in front of the immigration desks. Photos of Zambia's national parks adorned the walls, showing the magnificence of its nature. He handed his passport to a bored looking official, who glanced at the personal details page and stamped the document with a thud, before handing it back.

Amazed to be through immigration so quickly, he found the baggage carousel and waited for his bag to arrive. Although it was winter in Zambia and only ten in the morning, the heat was beginning to build and the poor air conditioning and sluggish fans made it feel far hotter than it was. He checked his watch. Ten thirty and still the carousel wasn't moving.

An older American woman, wearing out of the packet safari gear and puffing in the heat, sidled up to him.

'Excuse me, do you think they have toilet paper in the hotels here?'

'They'll have paper,' he replied convincingly.

'Oh, good. I just thought in these underdeveloped places, that they may not, you know, look after the needs of developed peoples.'

Already irritated by the woman that he had known for barely twenty seconds, and sensing that she was going to ask another inane question, he looked over her head and feigned a wave.

'Ah, there's my companion' he said, walking around her and across the hall to be on his own again. Another ten minutes passed and he was pleased to see his carousel begin to move.

He wiped his brow, as the bags began to appear.

Thankful that his seemingly indestructible duffle bag had come into view, he grabbed it, threw it over his shoulder and made his way out into the sunshine, where tour leaders with their company signs looked out anxiously for their guests.

'Excuse me, are you David?' he heard from behind him.

Turning around, he saw an attractive, deeply tanned, slim girl in her mid-twenties. She was dressed in faded khaki shirt and shorts and smiling broadly at him.

'Err, yes. I'm David,' he replied.

'Great!' she said, holding out her hand. 'I'm Sandra. I work with Dennis at the Sioma Ngwezi Park. Welcome to Zambia!'

'Good to meet you Sandra!' he responded, wondering if all the white girls in the country looked as good as she did.

'Dennis sends his apologies. He was going to pick you up, but we had some poaching in the Park last night and he's trying to track the culprits into Angola.'

'Ah, no problem. You can tell me all about it on the way there.'

'Sure! Happy to,' she said, flashing him a brilliant white smile.

Without invitation, she pulled the bag off his shoulder and instructed him to follow her. They walked across the car park, shaded in trees, until they reached a battered and old open-top Land Rover, covered in dust.

'Do you think it'll make it?' he asked jokingly.

'Sure, she'll make it. She always does,' grinned his escort, throwing his bag into the back. 'Hop in and we'll get going. It's a fair old drive, about five hours, and the roads are a bit ropey for the last bit, but I'll get you there in one piece, I promise!'

She drove out of the car park, paying the attendant on exit and after a few turns, joined the M10 heading west.

There were locals on ancient bicycles, struggling in the heat to balance the heavy sacks of what looked like grain and rice strapped to the back. Further out of town, women were walking by the side of the road carrying on their heads huge bundles of firewood, lashed together with twine.

After they were on their way and had already exchanged small talk, she turned to him, her sun bleached hair ruffled by the wind.

'Is this your first time to Zambia?' she asked.

'Yes, first time. I've been to other parts of Africa, on short trips, but never Zambia. I've always wanted to work out here for a longish spell.'

'You're in for a treat then! It's a beautiful country and the wildlife is amazing! It's politically stable, unlike our friends next door, so it's peaceful as well.'

'Glad to hear it,' he said and smiled back at her, as he noticed a large dead dog lying on its side by the road. Flies were swarming around the eyes and mouth and he wondered if it had been hit in the night. 'What about the poaching?'

'Yeah, that's a problem for us and the other Parks. Where there's a market for ivory and rhino horns, there will always be poachers sadly,' she answered. 'Anyway, that's what you're here for isn't it?'

'Well, I'll do my best,' he assured her. Changing the subject, he asked 'How long have you been out here?'

'Ah, most of my life really. My father is a doctor, based in Lusaka. He came out with my mother from England before I was born and they fell in love with the place. Been here ever since.'

'Have you been to England much?'

'Yes, a few times. I went to university in Sheffield and I suppose I could have stayed there, but the sights and smells of this country were too strong to keep me away.'

He knew he would like Sandra. Her easy going attitude and love of Africa were endearing to him and he looked forward to learning more about her.

They chatted on throughout the journey, stopping once for fuel and to stretch their legs. The countryside was flat, covered in pale, dry scrub and small trees and they passed through small villages and hamlets, eking an existence from the surrounding countryside.

There was evidence of small scale farming and he saw enclosures holding goats and sheep, thin with the lack of decent pasture. Hens pecked around the houses in groups, looking for anything worthy to eat, followed by chicks, destined for short and uneventful lives.

Eventually, they reached a sign by the side of the road, saying 'Welcome to Sioma Ngwezi National Park' in big letters and underneath, it read 'Protecting our animals for the future'.

'It's about thirty minutes from here,' she said smiling, taking a well-used track. 'We should start to see some animals if we're lucky.'

'Wonderful!' he replied, scanning the countryside.

They drove on into the Park, the dusty track throwing up fine particles into the air and leaving a cloud behind them.

'Look there!' she urged, pointing to the left.

He looked and saw some warthogs on their knees, grey with dust, digging into the ground near some bushes, looking for roots. Sandra slowed the car, drawing level with the animals and put a finger to her lips.

'Need to be quiet,' she whispered, 'or they'll get spooked.'

He glanced over at Sandra, who was studying the creatures intently through binos. He looked down at her slender, sun bronzed legs, covered in dust now, but no less alluring. Diverting his eyes quickly, he looked back at the warthogs.

'We get lots of these. Lions and leopards go after them, but they breed quickly, so their numbers remain stable. Anyway, we'd better get on,' she said, driving away slowly.

They reached a small stream and drove through it, disturbing some impala off to the side. Rising up the bank, he saw another sign ahead.

'Ranger Station' it read, with black paint on a pale green background.

After sweetly greeting the ranger at the entrance, she drove through, the gate closing loudly behind them.

'We need the gate to keep the animals out,' she explained. 'Early on, when we were setting up the camp, we had lions and hyenas wandering through here, which made a trip to the loo at night very interesting!' she giggled.

'I bet they miss all the fun, now there's a fence!'

Chuckling, she parked up in front of a low, wooden building painted in dark green, and cut the engine.

'Right, we're here! C'mon, I'll show you where you'll be sleeping.'

She reached again for his bag despite his protestations and walked, humming as she went.

He looked around the square compound, about a hundred metres on each side, surrounded by a sturdy wire fence. To the right was a line of large, olive green tents, deeply faded by the sun. At the end, furthest from the gate, was a small building which looked like a washing room and beyond that, another structure of a similar size, with a red cross on the door.

The building that they had parked in front of looked like administration and had another Land Rover parked outside. To the left was another low structure, also of red brick with windows along the side, and a small, newer looking brick building with a large padlock on the door, perhaps an armoury. Flat-topped acacia trees were dotted around, enhancing the setting.

She pushed open the door of the low building and walked in, followed by David closely behind.

'OK, you're in here. Room three. Dennis is in one, I'm in two and Peter, the Head Ranger is in four. Room five is spare at the moment, so we use it to store kit. The rangers sleep in the tents that you saw on the way in. We'll be building them an accommodation block, as soon as we have the funds. The bathroom is shared and next to room five at the end' she said, pointing down the corridor. 'Why don't you unpack your stuff and have a wash if you like and we can meet up for some tea in the main building? I can show you the rest of the camp after that.'

She smiled and as she turned for the door, she looked at him.

'It's good to have you here, David. I think you'll be able to help us.'

'Thanks for looking after me. What a great location!'

She grinned at him again, tapped him on the shoulder affectionately and walked out, back towards the vehicles.

He glanced around the room. It was basic, but functional. There was a large window in the back wall, covered with mesh, which overlooked the savannah beyond.

In the corner to the right, was a single metal bed, with a pillow and blankets resting on top. To the left, was a small wardrobe. A bare light bulb hung from the ceiling forlornly and he broke into a smile.

'Home sweet home' he said aloud, as he began to unpack his kit.

....

A little while later, he walked over to the main building and found a dining room at the end of the corridor. What looked like a small bar was in one corner, beer glasses stacked in neat rows on a shelf behind. Sandra was sitting at one of the tables, drinking tea with a ranger with a bandage on his hand.

Seeing him, she waved.

'Ah, there you are. Meet Daniel,' she said.

Walking over, David greeted the man. 'Looks like you've been in the wars. What happened?'

'Oh, I got stung by a scorpion in the washhouse yesterday, and had to go to the clinic.' He smiled meekly.

'How is it?'

'Fine now, but it was very painful when it happened! I'm still on painkillers.'

'Are there many scorpions around here?'

'Oh yes, they're everywhere! You must take care, as they hide in the most unlikely places,' he warned. 'Shoes, cupboards, sinks....'

'I'll remember to check my shorts properly each morning, then. Thanks for the warning!'

She poured him some tea, added milk and slid over a small plastic container holding sugar. The three chatted away, discussing the Park and the animals, when he heard vehicles entering the camp, followed by metal doors banging shut. Footsteps thumped along the corridor.

'David!' shouted Dennis happily, as he strode into the room. 'Great to see you at last!'

After he'd left the army, David had been a little lost, not sure what he wanted to do. Ever since he had contacted Dennis, he had been excited about the prospect of putting his military skills to good use and fulfilling his dream of working in Africa, if only for a short time.

The Chief Warden was a studious looking man of about forty. His once brown hair was turning grey at the sides and his face was deeply tanned, the colour of seasoned oak. Slimmer and taller than David by a few inches, he moved purposefully like a big cat. His sandy coloured trousers, brown boots and green shirt were covered in dirt.

The two men shook hands enthusiastically. Rangers were starting to walk into the dining room and Dennis introduced them, as they filed up to charge their mugs. In the main, they were relatively young, in their early twenties, he guessed. They all looked fit and strong, with intelligent faces. Another, older African in ranger gear came in and walked towards them.

'Come and meet our new arrival, Peter!' said Dennis happily.

The man took his hand and shook it warmly.

'Peter is our Head Ranger here and has been with us for years' he explained.

'I'll be able to learn much from you,' nodded David.

Once he had met everyone, he settled back down in his chair and listened to Dennis talk about the adventures of the last twenty four hours. They were patrolling the western edge of the Park when they spotted suspicious vehicle tracks. They found blood trails close by and had followed the impressions left in the dirt for hours. Later on, they had heard shots way in the distance to the north and raced in that direction, where the track allowed. They found further blood marks near the road. They had driven around all night, occasionally hearing shots in the dark, but always many miles away. In the morning, as they drove back towards camp, they had found new blood markings, but there was no sign of the vehicle.

'They got away this time,' said the Warden dejectedly, 'but next time, we'll get them.'

'Who do you think they were?' he asked.

'Difficult to say. Could have been rich hunters from America, shooting up the place, or it could have been corrupt officials from Lusaka, pillaging the land they are supposed to be protecting. Who knows?'

David nodded his head, realising that this was going to be a tougher contract than he had thought. 'I'm so glad I contacted you about the job,' he said. 'Now that I'm here, I know this is where I want to be for a while.'

'That's good to hear. You could have a big impact.'

Chapter Six

David was woken by the roar of lions in the early hours.

Later in the morning, he met up as planned with the Chief Warden in the briefing room, to learn about the Park. Sandra was already there, leafing through some papers. It was a basic room, with chairs and tables laid out and maps on the wall, also posters showing the variety of wildlife to be found and some of the highlights of the area.

'Did you hear the lions?' asked Sandra, as he settled himself.

'Yeah. They beat my alarm clock by a few hours.'

'They're beautiful creatures,' remarked Dennis. 'But get on the wrong side of them, or underestimate them and you're in trouble. You need to be careful around hyenas too.'

'Very true. I was with the Paras in Kenya, up on the Archers Post ranges and one of the guys fell asleep, with his head poking out of his basha. A hyena came along in the night and bit half his face off.'

'Ugh' shivered Sandra, 'what a horrible thing to happen.'

'He'd only been in the army for just over a year and had to leave because of his injuries. Two years of reconstructive surgery patched him up a bit, but let's just say he's not top of the list in the looks department anymore.'

'Last year, some crazy Dutchman attempted to walk across the Park for charity,' said Sandra. 'Sadly, he didn't get very far and his remains were found near to some resting lions, a day or so after he set off.'

Dennis cleared his throat.

'So, let's get on shall we? Sioma Ngwezi Park is about five thousand square kilometres in size,' he explained, showing David on the map, 'the third largest in Zambia, and is bordered with Angola to the west and Namibia to the south. It's quite a remote Park and although we like to see tourists here, its primary aim is to nurture the wildlife and introduce rare species that can develop and thrive, away from public scrutiny. But over the last few years, as the Park has become better known, we have been the victim of poaching and illegal hunting.

'The poachers come in to take animals mainly for food, and the hunters come in to satisfy their blood lust, in killing whatever they can find. If they're from outside the country, someone has sold them a package to come and shoot here. Sandra has caught poachers on several occasions and a number are in jail.'

'Now, as you may know, the rhino has been targeted heavily over the last few decades, to satisfy a myth in the Far East that the horn has some medicinal power. Total nonsense of course, but it hasn't stopped the slaughter of these wonderful beasts. Sadly, Zambia hasn't had any endemic rhinos for a few years now. They are mainly found in Kenya, Tanzania, Zimbabwe and South Africa, but the populations are declining. A few years ago, it was decided to reintroduce the rhino to Zambia and I'm pleased to say that our Park was chosen to take them.'

'We had four rhinos, one male and three females, relocated to us from Kruger National Park.'

'A great honour!' smiled David.

'Indeed. They stayed in a pen out back for a few weeks, to get over the relocation and then we set them free. We see them occasionally. The male tends to stick by himself, but the females keep together. They seem to prefer the northern end to the park, probably because it's bushier up there and more grazing available. So you see, as well as the other animals here, we also have those beauties to shadow and look after and it's a huge responsibility.'

They talked for a little while longer, then after lunch, a steaming hot beef stew and potatoes, Dennis took him over to the armoury to take a look at the weapons. Unlocking the padlock on the steel door, he pulled it open and switched on the light. David caught a smell of cordite, oil and old cardboard and saw rifles in a rack on the opposite wall. A small metal cupboard was to the right.

'We have AK-47s here, one for every ranger, plus a few spares and five Browning pistols. We also have four sets of basic night vision goggles.'

'Not bad' he said, looking around. He picked up one of the rifles, pulled the working parts back and looked inside. It was in reasonable condition, although heavily worn and he noticed small flecks of rust on the muzzle. Picking up another and carrying out the same action, he saw a weapon in a similar state. A third weapon was in a similar condition, usable but worn.

'What about ammunition?' he asked, continuing to check the weapons.

'Well, we have about a hundred rounds for each of the AKs and about thirty rounds for each of the Brownings.'

'Can you get more? I want to see these guys on a range.'

'Sure, but it'll take time. Weeks probably. It has to be sent from the National Parks Headquarters in Lusaka and they just love their red tape.'

'Order some more today would you? Another two hundred rounds for each of the AKs should be fine and while you're at it, another twenty rounds per Browning'.

'Do you want to have a look at our range?' asked the Warden.

'Sure, where is it?'

'Round the back.' He led him out of the main gate and around the side of the camp.

They came to a flat, open and rocky area and he could see a firing point, with some sand bags laid out and targets set up about fifty metres away. There was no backstop and he could see spent cases lying on the ground nearby.

'What do you think?' asked Dennis, looking around him.

'Not bad, but with no backstop, we may kill or injure any animals that wander behind the targets. These AK-47 rounds can travel some distance, you know.'

'Good point. Well, I'll leave it to you, if you want to find an alternative. Peter set this one up years ago and I'm sure he'll appreciate your expertise.'

He nodded, continuing to look around him.

'Tell me about him?'

'Well, I inherited him when my predecessor left a few years ago. I think he's alright, but he can be a little lazy and I wonder sometimes if he covers the ground that he says he does. I've had one or two arguments with him over the years, but all in all he's OK.'

'Only OK? Your Head Ranger needs to be at the top of his game and inspire the other rangers. I've seen the state of the weapons and this so called 'range', but to be honest, I'm not impressed.'

'And that's why you're here, David!' he said, patting him on the shoulder and smiling.

....

For the next few days, David went out on vehicle patrols, sometimes with Dennis but more often with Sandra. He enjoyed her company and she clearly loved working in the Park.

He turned to look at her, the early morning sun shining bright through her hair and the sweat glistening on her forehead. Her infectious smile was there again and she looked happy with the world.

Driving east towards the Zambezi River, they stopped at a large water hole being enjoyed by a family of elephants, resting in the cool waters.

'Magnificent aren't they?' she whispered, transfixed by the scene.

Two young ones were playing in the shallows, flaring their ears and chasing water birds. The matriarch eyed the vehicle warily, but seemed content to let it stay.

The other females were rolling in the muddy liquid, enjoying the sensation of water on their dry and dusty skin.

Suddenly there was a shot, followed by another, not more than a kilometre away and the tranquillity of the scene was destroyed. The elephants splashed to the water's edge, gathered behind the matriarch and ran into the bush, trumpeting angrily.

'Quick, head in that direction,' he instructed, pointing towards a track. 'They can't be that far away.'

Sandra gunned the engine and manoeuvred the vehicle away from the pool and towards the gunshots. She saw her companion reach behind him, grab a rifle and insert a magazine seamlessly. Taking his lead, whilst holding the wheel with one hand, she reached into the bag beside her and pulled out a Browning, resting it on the floor by her feet.

Bouncing along, acacia trees and thorny scrub flashing past, he pulled the binos up to his eyes, scanning the distance. The foliage was quite thick and he had trouble seeing more than a hundred metres in front. A group of impala off to his left scattered in panic, and he wondered if they were running from their jeep, or the hunters.

They came over a rise and he spotted two vehicles ahead, parked to the side of the track.

'Park behind them,' he shouted to her, as he placed the binos in the bag between them.

The vehicles, one white and the other grey, were new looking Suzuki off-roaders, both covered in grime.

As they drove closer, he saw a small group of men crouching over something and laughing. He also saw at least two of the men holding hunting rifles, the butts resting on the ground.

'OK, grab the pistol and watch the drivers, whilst I go and see what the hell is going on,' he instructed. 'Keep the weapon pointing downwards, I don't want to spook them.'

She nodded and brought the car to a screeching stop. They both jumped out. Holding the rifle by the pistol grip, he strode purposefully towards the men, watching them closely. There were three black Africans, with two dressed in bush gear holding the rifles and the other dressed in chinos and a polo shirt. They were crouching over what looked like a kudu, its horns laying forlornly in the dirt.

'Put the weapons on the ground,' barked David as he approached.

An older man, seemingly affronted, puffed out his chest.

'Who do you think you are, ordering me about?' he shouted.

The other hunter, now standing, scowled and began to slowly raise the barrel of his rifle.

'I wouldn't do that if I were you,' he warned, bringing the AK-47 level to emphasise his point. 'Now, put the weapons on the ground!'

'Now look here!' bellowed the African, raising himself to his full height. 'I have a permit to hunt here, so you can push off and leave us in peace. Who are you anyway?'

'We're part of the ranger service here,' he replied calmly. 'For the third and final time, put your weapons on the ground!'

Reluctantly, the men did as they were told and glared hard at him. He looked back unmoved and instructed for the drivers to join them, with Sandra shadowing them from behind.

'Now that we're all calm, please tell me who you are,' asked David.

The older man spoke up.

'I am Patrick Mulonga, a businessman from Lusaka and this is Joshua Tafika, an associate of mine. This other man is our guide,' he said, sweeping his arm towards the figure. 'We are here with permission to hunt, so you should go on your way!' he growled.

'What permission? This is a National Park and there is no hunting permitted here!'

'I have a letter from the Chief Ranger in Lusaka,' said the African pompously.

'Show me,' he instructed, thrusting out his hand.

'Ah, the letter is not with me at the moment,' the man said, patting his pockets. 'It must be at home.'

'Sandra. Get their IDs and make a note of their details. Also take the vehicle registrations.'

She did as instructed, while he watched the men closely.

The other hunter, Joshua, a few years younger than his friend, with a round face and pearl white teeth, spoke up.

'Listen. There is a misunderstanding here. Let us go, throw away our details and we can all forget this unfortunate incident.'

'I don't think the kudu will forget it, Mr Tafika' he said sourly. 'You've killed a wild animal on National Park land and that's an offence in Zambia.'

He looked at the men with contempt.

'Now, this is what we're going to do. I am confiscating the weapons and the animal and we'll drive back to our camp, where we'll hand you over to the police. Do you understand?'

Patrick, the older man, stepped forward. 'I'm sure we can come to an agreement about this episode,' he said smiling. 'We have had 'arrangements' with rangers in the past.'

'What arrangements?' he demanded. 'Who have you paid?'

'Let's just say that some of your rangers are better off for letting us go,' he said defiantly.

'Well, you can tell all that to the police when you see them. Oh, and if I ever see you in the Park again, I'll destroy your vehicles and make you walk out on foot. I wonder how far you'd get?' he snarled, meaning every word.

He called Sandra over and whispered in her ear.

'Get on the radio would you, and tell Dennis what has happened and that we're bringing these people back to camp? Also, ask him to get the police to come.'

She did as instructed and nodded to him when she returned.

Taking the hunting rifles, he instructed the men, still scowling at him, to carry the kudu to his own vehicle. Once complete, he instructed Mulonga to join him and told the others to follow him back to the ranger camp.

He was relieved when they got back to see a police car was already there. After he had given a statement, the hunters and their vehicles were escorted off the Park.

'Well done!' said Dennis, patting them both on the back. 'Now, you two have had a hell of a day, so how about a few drinks before dinner?'

'Good plan,' replied David, smiling. 'I've been looking forward to a cold beer all day.' And the three walked into the main building, heading for the bar.

Later, after dinner, when most of the dining room and bar area had emptied, David asked his companions if they wanted another drink. Sandra declined, but Dennis gave a thumbs up, so he walked to the fridge, took out two Mosi lagers and returned to the table.

'You know, it really annoys me that people think they can bribe their way out of trouble' David said.

'It's outrageous' growled the warden.

A veteran of animal conversation in Africa, he had experienced much in his career – beauty, success, death, failure and greed. 'Here we are, trying to protect the nation's wildlife and some our own rangers are allowing them to be slaughtered.'

'We don't know when this happened, but I suggest that you talk to the guys tomorrow and tell them that we've heard stories about bribe-taking. Tell them that anyone caught taking money will be thrown out of camp.'

Sandra nodded.

'Good idea,' agreed the warden. I'll talk to them and lay down the law. You have now seen with your own eyes, what we're up against.'

David nodded his head thoughtfully, wondering if one man was enough to turn the tide. Sandra had left soon after, saying she was dog tired and the two men chatted long into the night about Africa and its woes. The empty bottles of Mosi lager built up on the table and clutching his glass, Dennis turned to him, his eyes bleary from the booze.

'TIA. We have a saying on this continent, David. 'This is Africa!' It means that this is the way it is, this is what happens here and we should get used to it.'

'I've heard of the saying,' he replied, slurring his words. 'Maybe it's time that a few of us started to change things. In our little corner of Zambia, maybe we can make a difference and not accept TIA!'

'You're right, my friend. We'll make a difference here and I see only good things to come' he said, burping. A minute or so of silence passed. 'Anyway, if we're to make that change, maybe this is a good time to hit the sack!'

....

Seven thousand kilometres north, near the isolated oasis town of Tazirbu in southern Libya, the men in the camp rose for early morning prayers. The night had been cold in the middle of the desert and they were looking forward to seeing dawn and feeling the warmth from the first rays of sun.

The terrorist training camp, like many others in the country, had been set up in the 1990s by the despotic leader, Colonel Gaddafi, and had seen thousands of fighters pass through over the years. The location had been specially selected, far out into the desert, in an attempt to thwart the prying eyes of spy planes and satellites.

The camp was a basic affair comprised mainly of off-white tents, apart from a small stone built mosque off to one side. The living quarters, three randomly spaced tents, had camp beds for eight people in each. The kitchen and dining area, also under canvas, was close by, near to some low lying evergreen bushes. There was a larger, camel coloured tent to hide and service the old Bedford truck, used to transport trainees and collect rations from the town. Additional tents for classroom training were set up in dunes nearby.

The men washed themselves as best they could and ambled to the mosque in small groups, to be met by the stand-in Imam, who was also one of the trainers. They prayed and heard his fiery words, preaching jihad against the unbelievers. Once it was over, they returned to their camp beds to rest.

As the sun was beginning to rise over the dunes to the east, one of the trainers from Egypt ordered the men outside for the fitness session. Lining up in two ranks and dressed in trainers, shorts and singlet, the group of fifteen set off at a steady pace, led by the instructors. They ran for over an hour, stopping now and again to complete press ups, sit ups and fireman's lifts with each other.

Returning to the camp sweaty and tired, they changed into boots, trousers and shirts and made their way to the dining area for a basic breakfast of unleavened bread, figs, hard boiled eggs and tea. Sounds of chatter circled around the tables, as the trainees ate the food and savoured the respite from training.

An instructor from Algeria, with mean eyes and a deep scar across of his nose, strode in and snarled at the group.

'Enough eating!' he shouted in Arabic. 'It's time to improve your weapon handling. Be outside and ready in five minutes.'

The trainees reluctantly finished their breakfast, cleaned their plates and went back to their tents, to grab what they needed for the morning.

They reassembled and the instructor walked them over to the makeshift firing range, a short distance away. Laid out on the firing point was a line of AK-47s resting on half-filled sandbags, a full magazine next to each. The Algerian explained the nature of the session and selected firers to stand behind a weapon. The remainder were told to observe from the rear.

For the next few hours, before it got too hot, the trainees fired the weapons from a variety of positions. After each practice, they ran to the targets a hundred metres away to check on their accuracy and paste over the holes with old newspaper. Those who annoyed the instructor with careless shots or handling errors were ordered to crawl back to the firing point, complete press ups and crawl back to the targets.

At the end of the session, the instructor gathered the men together.

'My brothers, I see some improvement, but I expect more from you when next we meet. If you are to carry out the will of Allah, you will need to shoot straight and become one with your rifle.'

The men looked sheepishly around and the trainer paused, before uttering a Koranic verse.

'Soon shall we cast terror into the hearts of the Unbelievers…'

The trainees smiled at the reference and vowed to improve. The Algerian walked around the group, looking meaningfully at each man, before instructing them to carry the targets and other equipment back to camp. Once there, they returned to their tents, drank warm water from their canteens and began to strip and clean the weapons.

'I'll be glad when this is over,' muttered Yasin, pulling through his rifle.

Mohamed, an older man sitting nearby, turned angrily to him.

'Why do you think we are here?' he shouted. 'For a holiday?'

The man stared back blankly, surprised by the response. 'Every day we do the same thing, eating the same shit and roasting in these ovens they call tents,' he replied.

The older man smiled benignly at his friend. 'Yasin. All this training and pain will be worthwhile when we return to Germany, to carry out our Jihad!' he said through gritted teeth. 'Be patient here and endure, for Allah will reward you when the time comes.'

'Thank you Mohamed, you're right. I should suffer out here, knowing that paradise awaits.'

The older man rose from his bed, strode over to his charge and patted him on the back.

'Inshallah,' he said softly.

Just then, the Algerian strode in and asked to see the weapons. Checking every part of the rifles for cleanliness, he kept the men busy for the next hour, never seeming satisfied with what he was shown. Eventually, after inspecting them several times, he was happy and told the men to rest, before the next bout of training.

The trainees gathered together again later in one of the classroom tents. Lying on a wooden table in front of the Egyptian instructor were all manner of bomb-making materials. Det cord, plastic explosive, batteries, detonators, timers, a small bag of fertiliser and circuit boards. The trainer taught the men how to construct basic IEDs, explaining how the items fitted together and warning them of the risks.

'Take care when you handle these things. Only last year, a brother from Chechnya was injured at this very spot, when building a basic device,' he warned. 'Because of his foolishness, he has trouble wiping his arse with his left hand these days!'

Titters went around the group.

'But seriously, you must take care, particularly with the detonators, as they're not toys,' he stressed.

The men looked around anxiously, nodding their heads and settling their eyes once more on the Egyptian.

For a further hour, they watched and listened, until finally they saw him construct a basic IED. They were instructed to follow him outside, to some tree stumps and an old bedframe on the other side of a dune. Carefully, he placed the device next to metal and wood, setting the timer and instructing the students to walk a safe distance back. Minutes later, there was a loud bang and bright flash, as debris from the explosion went skywards. The men clapped and whistled at the display and the trainer grinned at his audience.

'When you construct these bombs in your own countries, make sure you have a similar effect, only bigger!' he smiled.

The men, impressed by the sight, slowly made their way back to their tents, laughing and joking as they walked. After lunch, the trainees learnt how to carry out an operation, from selecting a target, carrying out a reconnaissance, through to the event itself.

They rested until it was cooler and assembled once more for physical exercise. Their instructor from southern Tunisia, a thin, wiry man missing an eye, led them on a run into the dunes for over an hour. After some time and finding a suitable spot, he took the trainees through a series of tasks. First, they took turns in carrying each other across the sandy surface, followed by sprints up and down one of the taller dunes, until their lungs were bursting. Finally, before the slow trudge back to camp, the instructor marked out several circles in the sand and made the men wrestle, until he was satisfied with their efforts.

Arriving back, the trainees washed and tried to get the sand out of their ears, noses and hair.

Suitable cleansed, they made their way to the dining area, to enjoy an evening meal of lamb, rice, pitta bread and lemon drink. It was a Friday, when the best food of the week was served. After evening prayers the men, without exception, collapsed into bed, the snores rumbling around the tents.

The following day was similar in tone, followed by the next day and the one after. After a week, their fitness began to improve and their weapon handling was safer, with their aim greatly improved. Their knowledge of explosives was more refined and they could each construct a workable bomb, the marks on the tree trunks testimony to their new found skill.

On one afternoon, as they headed to the range again, a white Land Cruiser appeared in camp. As the trainees fired their weapons, the visitor, dressed in flowing white thobe, watched them from the rear. The man had disappeared before the end of the session and speculation ran around the group as to who he might be.

'Maybe a benefactor?' suggested Yasin later, when they were back in their tent.

'Perhaps,' acknowledged Mohamed, 'but if he wanted us to know him, he would have stayed.'

On the final evening, before dinner, Mohamed led his friends away from the noise of camp, out to a spot near an old fort.

'Brothers, we have all done well these last weeks and are now ready to return to Germany to prepare for the operation,' he said.

'Do you know what it is?' asked Abdullah eagerly, glancing at the older man.

'No, not yet. I will be informed soon and notify you both when that happens.'

'That will be a glorious day!' smirked Yasin.

'Yes, it will,' agreed Mohamed. 'Our sponsor in Qatar will be pleased that he has invested wisely in us.'

'Do you know who he is?' asked Abdullah.

'No. His name is a mystery to me, as it should be, but I understand that he heads one of the rich families there. Maybe the visitor we had is part of the family?'

The two younger men, content for the first time in weeks, nodded their heads slowly, as they watched the sun start to disappear behind distant dunes.

....

David woke to the sound of bickering songbirds outside his window. He smiled, remembering where he was and rose from the bed unsteadily, placing his feet on the floor. Putting a hand on his temple, he tried to soothe the throbbing headache and reached for the bottle of water next to his bed. Taking a long gulp of the reviving fluid, followed by another, he stretched and made his way to the shower room down the hall.

Suitably revived, he walked over to the main building and into the dining room. He looked at his watch and was shocked to see that it was past nine. Reaching for the large teapot, he touched the side to check how hot it was and recoiled when his senses told him that it was scalding. Shaking his hand, he let the pain subside and poured himself a cup, adding plenty of milk of sugar.

Hearing footsteps in the corridor, he looked up to see Sandra in the doorway.

'Ah, there you are,' she smiled. 'We thought you'd gone AWOL!'

'No, no. Just suffering a bit from too much booze last night. Much happening today?'

'Yes, there is actually,' she said, helping herself to tea. 'We have some foot patrols on the Angolan border and a vehicle patrol up in the north. The police are dropping in later as well as they've got some follow up questions about the incident yesterday, but it looks like they're going to charge the buggers.'

'That's great news. We did well!' he said, looking up from the table and staring into her eyes.

'Yes, we did,' she replied, returning the compliment. He looked at her, realising again how beautiful she was.

'You must get a little lonely out here?'

'Not at all. I spend my days doing what I love in one of the most beautiful parts of Africa. Who knows though, one day I might be whisked away by a knight in shining armour!'

David chuckled, noticing the look her face.

After a pause, she spoke again.

'Anyway, Dennis wants to see you when you've finished your breakfast. He wants to talk about the training you'll be giving the rangers.'

'Sure, no problem.'

She smiled again, finished her tea and walked to the sink, to swill out her cup.

His headache had eased, but he allowed himself another cup of tea before walking down to the briefing room. Dennis was tapping away at his laptop by the window and looking up, asked him how he was feeling.

'A bit fragile, but I'll survive' he said, grinning.

'Glad to hear it'. Looking back at his laptop, he said, 'I thought it would a good time to talk about the training plan. Now, tell me what your thoughts are?'

Standing up and walking to the whiteboard, David selected a pen and drew a vertical line with the headings 'David' and 'Dennis/Sandra' on either side.

Under his own name he wrote weapons training, rules of engagement, patrol skills (movement, stalking, OPs, harbour areas, night routine), first aid, comms and vehicles. Under 'Dennis/Sandra' he wrote animal welfare, animal transfers, visitor management, law and ethics.

'So' he began. 'I think there is more than the military related aspect here, so that's why I think you and Sandra need to be involved. The topics for you both, are self-explanatory and outside my expertise anyway. Following yesterday's incident about possible bribes, I think it will be good for them to learn about ethics and about a zero tolerance approach in taking bribes. Let's make sure they understand the consequences.'

'Totally agree. We need to make sure they're on our side. As with the other subjects, I like your overall approach.'

'OK, good' he continued.

'Now, on the military related side, I'm assuming they're reasonably proficient, particularly with weapons handling, but I'll take them through a full training package, to bring everyone up to a good standard. I think if we're going to catch poachers and hunters, we need to operate like soldiers and use concealment and observation as primary tools. Walking through the Park and driving around in vehicles is all very well, but we also need to hide and observe, to build up a picture of what's going on out there.'

The warden nodded thoughtfully.

'The other skills are fairly obvious as well. First aid is a no brainer. Comms skills and vehicle maintenance are also important.'

'I like it!' said Dennis. 'How do you want to proceed? Our topics can be done in the evenings, once the day's work is done.'

'My programme is going to take a few months, at least, and we need to make sure everyone goes through it, whilst fitting around the patrol schedule. What I intend to do, is to go out on foot patrol with Peter and some of the other rangers, so that I can assess their level and take it from there. Spending a few days with them, will tell me everything I need to know.'

Chapter Seven

The patrol was ready to leave by seven. They would travel along the border with Angola, for a distance of over forty kilometres. There would be seven in the patrol, including David and he was looking forward to stretching his legs. They pulled out of camp in two vehicles and turned right, away from the rising sun.

'How long have you been a ranger?' he asked the driver, a young Zambian with a permanent smile.

'Oh, two years, sir. Before that, I worked in a shop in Sesheke, about fifty kilometres from here. I was bored for most of the time and wanted to do something different, so I came here.'

'This is much more interesting, I bet?'

'Oh, yes. Before, as well as other things, I was advising women on what wig to buy! Now, I can enjoy it here and see the animals every day.'

'A better career choice!' he agreed, smiling and looking into the bush.

After about forty minutes, they came to a flat area above a large bend in the Kwando River, marking the border between the two countries. The men got out of the vehicles and walked towards the edge with their kit and weapons.

'Nice spot for a morning dip!' he joked.

'No sir, not here,' warned one of the rangers. 'Tis very dangerous,' and to prove his point, a large crocodile, sunning itself, slid off the bank below them and disappeared into the murky depths of the river.

'You're right!' he replied, patting the man on the shoulder. 'Not such a good place after all,' he added as the rest of the rangers sniggered.

Looking over his shoulder, he saw Peter talking to the drivers, presumably discussing the pickup point and he looked around, enjoying the feeling of being out in the wild again.

'OK, let's go!' shouted the ranger, as he turned and started walking north.

The men followed him in single file, about five metres between each. Shouldering his pack and cradling his weapon, he followed, one ranger behind him. They walked along a dusty animal trail, just above the river and he wondered if they would see much wildlife. It seemed a bountiful life here for the herbivores, plenty of grazing, cool rivers and pools to drink from, but with the bounty came the possibility of death at any moment.

They were fast, most of these animals and as long as they stayed fit, they could look forward to a long life. Get injured, old or unlucky and the predators were waiting. Lions would be the main threat, due to their numbers in the Park, but he also knew that leopards roamed the area.

The sun was rising now and he could feel it burning his skin. Pulling his collar up to protect himself, he also eased his floppy hat lower onto his head.

Glancing to his right, he saw a small herd of waterbuck, grazing near some mopane trees. When they saw the patrol, they all froze, looking towards the men with icy stares. Their ears pointed forward, picking up every sound. Satisfied that the strangers weren't a threat, the animals resumed feeding, but raised their heads frequently just to be sure.

A while later, still on the animal trail, he looked along the river and saw a group of hippos lounging in the water. Dennis had told him about rangers being charged in the past, particularly when young ones were about.

'Never get between a hippo and the river,' he had warned. 'They'll run straight into you as if you weren't there.'

As the rangers drew level with the pod, the animals watched the men warily, grunting to each other in support. One or two of the giant beasts dropped below the surface without a ripple and he saw a large male turn to face them, its red eyes glaring in dark menace.

A few hours later, the patrol paused under a large acacia tree by the river, to take a snack and some much needed water. The heat by now was blistering. Taking off his pack, he retrieved his water bottle and a packet of hard tack biscuits and settled down to sustain himself, the other rangers doing the same.

He saw Peter walk cautiously down to the river, peering down at the ground with interest, then move towards the water's edge, touching the ground delicately with his fingers. Turning around and walking towards the bank, he indicated for David to join him.

'You should see this,' the Head Ranger said, when he reached him.

'What is it?'

'Tracks!' he replied, pointing at the ground.

Looking closely, he could see shoe prints in the dirt, heading away from the river and into the bush. Walking closer to the river, he saw a 'V' wedge in the mud, caused by the bow of a small boat hitting the shore. 'How many do you reckon?'

'There are three different sets of prints here. They came by a small boat last night,' he said, looking at the ground.

'What are they after?' he asked.

'They come for meat. Kudu, impala, zebra, you name it. They cross the river from Angola, walk into the bush, kill some animals and then carry them back. We've seen it many times,' he said, shaking his head.

'So what's the plan, it's your patrol?'

'I think we should follow the tracks away from the river and see if we can catch them.'

The two made it back onto the bank and he was surprised to see the ranger walking into the bush and signalling for his men to follow, without briefing them. The sun was relentless and he could feel the sweat drenching his shirt. Moving eastwards, away from the river, he could clearly see the tracks in the dust, left by the poachers. Every so often, the tracks seemed to stop, with the shoe prints facing in different directions.

'They're using binos to look for prey,' he muttered to himself, looking around.

The group stopped for a rest an hour later, under a large mopane tree, grateful for the shade.

'What do you think, Peter?' he asked. 'They seem to be a long way from the river now.'

'Yes, it's strange,' replied the Zambian. 'It's such a long way to carry game back to the boat, unless…'

'Unless what?'

'Unless they are not here for the game. Perhaps they're here for the rhinos.'

'Oh God, no!' uttered the Englishman.

'I don't know. Maybe they've come to try to find them, and will call in a helicopter to get the horns?' he said, squinting into the plain.

They followed the tracks for another hour, still eastwards, until he saw Peter put up his right arm and show a fist. The rangers crouched down, listening and watching, waiting for their leader's instructions. He saw him move forward towards a copse and look intently at the ground. The patrol was signalled to join him and the men moved cautiously towards him. On reaching the trees, they saw the remains of a fire and scratched out areas in the dirt.

'This is where they stayed last night,' whispered the ranger. 'Two sleeping places and one of them on guard, over there.'

'Yep,' he nodded, glancing around. 'So they're hours ahead of us then?'

'Yes, they may be back at the river by now. See the tracks curling off to the right?'

David nodded.

'So, we can follow them, or continue on the original route,' Peter said thoughtfully. He looked around the discarded camp and sighed to himself. After a few moments, he spoke. 'Let's head back towards the river and join it further up. Those poachers will be long gone.'

'Fair enough,' he agreed.

Everyone took gulps of water and some bit into the hard tack biscuits they carried. Peter and David checked their maps and took bearings back to the river and the group began moving again.

They reached some rapids by the river a few hours later, grateful to be able to fill up their water bottles and splash their faces. The intense heat of the day had started to fade and the men started to slump down on the ground, resting their weary bones for a while.

'Before you get too comfortable, we need to move further up the river and find a spot for the night,' shouted Peter.

The rangers nodded wearily and began to stand up again, waiting to move off.

'I know a better place,' said the Head Ranger. 'Somewhere safer than this.'

Nodding, David resumed his place towards the rear. A short time later, as the group was walking along a thin animal path, something caught his eye.

'Stop!' he shouted.

The rangers froze and glanced uneasily back.

'Thomas. Take a step back towards me, very slowly,' he instructed.

The ranger seemed unsure.

'Just do it, Thomas.'

He did as instructed and came level with him.

He pointed to a small bush, to the right of the path. The ranger squinted for a moment and seemed to go paler. Curled up in the vegetation was a short, fat snake, which began to hiss loudly.

'It's a puff adder, as I'm sure you know, Thomas. Treading near that, would be like stepping on a landmine. I only saw it at the last minute.'

'Thank you, sir' whispered the ranger. 'That would not have been good.'

'No, not good at all. A bite from that beauty, would put you in hospital for weeks, maybe longer. Good to let your eyes scan the ground, when you're walking through brush.'

'What is it?' shouted Peter irritably from the front.

He shouted back what it was and the men walked gingerly towards the bush, gathering a safe distance from it. By now, Thomas had picked up a stick lying nearby and strode towards the serpent, which hissed again and began to unfurl its coils. The ranger lifted the weapon high and brought it down on the snake's head with a dull thud. He then hit it repeatedly, until he was sure it was dead. The other rangers looked on sombrely, realising that they had all walked within inches of the danger.

'A good lesson!' said Peter, looking from man to man. 'Take care where you place your feet. Let's keep moving.'

The patrol walked on for another few kilometres, each man checking the ground constantly, until there was a signal to stop. They were near a thicket of small trees, a short distance from the river and it had superb views over the surrounding savannah. He could see evidence of previous fires and to one side, spikey branches and bushes, used to protect the rangers from big cats.

'Where do you want us?' he asked, looking around him.

'Go anywhere you like' answered the Head Ranger, sweeping his arm around the copse.

He spotted a small tree that he could lean up against. The men switched into harbour routine, taking off their packs, pulling out mosquito nets and selecting what food they might have. Some lit fires, some walked to the river to collect more water and some rested, closing their eyes and lowering their heads onto their packs. He was surprised at the casual scene in front of him, but bit his tongue and settled into the flow of the camp, taking note of where everyone was settling down.

The sun dipped on the horizon and the light began to fade, reminding him how lucky he was to be there. He knew he had already led an interesting life, but nothing could beat the majesty of the scene in front of him. In the plain, a mixed group of impala and kudu made their way towards the river, thirsty after a days' grazing on the baked earth. Over to his right, he noticed a troop of baboons playing in the trees, a few hundred metres away, enjoying the last rays of the sun's warmth.

A little later, after the sun had disappeared and darkness began to set in, he prepared himself for the night.

Selecting a stick near him and scraping away the twigs and leaf litter, he prepared his rest site. Next, he pulled out his mosquito net and laid it on top of his pack, which he rested against the tree for back support. Unzipping one of the side pouches, he retrieved his night vision goggles and placed them by his side. Leaning against the pack he settled in.

He was thankful that the mosquitos and biting insects hadn't made an appearance and wondered if they were feasting on the animals by the river instead. He was roused out of his thoughts when he saw a lighter flare up and someone lit a cigarette, the embers glowing brightly in the still night. Every so often, the cigarette would flare, when the ranger took another drag and he could smell the burnt tobacco, as it wafted slowly past him.

The temperature began to dip and he pulled the collar around his chin and wrapped his arms around his body for warmth.

He was supposed to be on guard at midnight, but no one came to handover to him. He smiled to himself and nodded his head, as he realised that everyone was asleep. In a land of man-eaters, they were certainly rolling the dice. He sat for a further thirty minutes and then, walking stealthily around the camp, he checked on each of the rangers. They were all fast asleep, lying on their backs or sides, oblivious to the world. Moving back to his own position, he sat down and made himself as comfortable as possible, knowing that the safety of the men was in his hands.

....

Dawn came as a relief, as the mosquitos had discovered the camp in the early hours and David had been forced to drape the mosquito net over his body. He couldn't get rid of the whining sound in his ears though, as the insects tried to gain entry into his sanctuary. He rose, pulling the net off and stretched himself in the early morning coolness. He noticed one or two of the men stir and do the same, scratching themselves where they had been bitten in the night.

He took a long drink of water, retrieved some dried beef and raisins from his pack and settled down to breakfast. Looking over the plain, he watched a mixed group of zebra and wildebeest head into the bush, no doubt drinking their fill from the river in the early hours. Slowly, the rangers began to organise themselves, packing away unwanted kit.

Peter walked over to him. 'How did you sleep?'

'Not bad. I was supposed to be on guard at midnight, but nobody came.'

'Really? I shall speak to the men. This is unacceptable!' he said, striding away.

A little before eight, the Head Ranger gathered everyone together and indicated on a map the route for the day. They were going to continue to patrol along the river, stop for lunch by a large bend and then push on through the afternoon and make camp by some large pools at the end of the day. Satisfied that they were ready to go, he set off northwards, with the rangers falling in behind.

The morning heat was relentless and the rangers trudged on, stopping every few hours to refill their water bottles from the river.

David noticed that apart from a few isolated groups, the game was quite sparse. The group stopped for a lunch break and sought shade where they could find it. He noticed large crocodiles lurking on river's surface, watching and waiting.

They set off after the break, well rested from the morning's trek. An hour or so later, he caught some movement in a thicket, a few hundred metres away. Walking forward to the man in front of him, he signalled for the rest of the patrol to stop. With the naked eye, he could see some fawn coloured shapes in the shade and then noticed a tail lift nonchalantly off the ground and flop back on to the dirt.

Lions.

He walked slowly up the line to where Peter was and whispered to him.

The ranger took out his binos and studied the animals.

'Lucky you spotted them. They could have charged us.'

'What's the plan?' he asked, taking the safety catch off his weapon and thrilled to be so close to the beasts.

'We'll just walk by slowly and leave them in peace. Ah, their bellies are full. That's why they're not interested in us!'

Handing the binos to him, he could see their full stomachs, almost bursting. He noticed the carcass of a zebra nearby, with only the head, ribcage, some bones and skin remaining.

'They can eat over fifty pounds of meat in a single sitting' whispered the ranger. 'That zebra has filled their stomachs for the day, so they'll rest up and go out hunting again when it's cooler.'

Suddenly, one of the large females sat up, sensing the intrusion for the first time. She looked at the men and growled, baring her stained and deadly teeth. The others sat up quickly and eyed the men suspiciously, flicking their tails.

'We'd better go' warned Peter.

Later in the day, they reached the pools that would be their stop for the night.

Looking around, he was pleased with the location, although he wondered if the proximity to water would invite biting insects all night. They had filled up their bottles at the last river spot, so there was no need to touch the water.

Not a good idea anyway, he thought. Every animal for miles around had probably walked in it, pissed in it and worse.

Peter called the men in and briefed them about the night's activities. They had already encountered lions and he reminded them that leopards and hyena would be close by too. The men acknowledged his words and strolled casually back to their sleeping places as darkness descended.

David, due to be on guard at midnight again, prepared himself as he had done the evening before. As he hadn't slept, he did feel tired, but although he allowed himself the luxury of closing his eyes, the SAS had taught him well and he didn't keep his eyes shut for long.

Stretching his muscles and blinking repeatedly stopped him from settling in a comfortable position. He kept his mind active, thinking about the events of the day and the possibilities of tomorrow and he felt at peace with the world.

As with the night before, he saw the rangers completely disregard night discipline. The pair closest to him chatted for over an hour. He noticed that it was past midnight and he hoped that someone would tap him on the shoulder, but nothing happened. Ten minutes later, realising that no one was going to come, he picked up his rifle and stood up silently. Listening carefully and satisfied that all was quiet, he crept to the rangers closest to him. He checked that they were fully asleep, and then reached down and picked up each of their rifles, unloading them and placing the magazines down on the ground nearby. He walked around the camp slowly, doing the same to each weapon.

Satisfied that he had reached everyone, he returned to his resting place, pulled the mosquito net back over himself and watched over the rangers till dawn.

....

In the morning, as it grew light and the rangers began to stir, David heard one of them ask his neighbour if he had unloaded his weapon during the night. He then heard others talking about it and chuckled to himself.

'Cruel to be kind,' he whispered to himself.

He looked over at Peter, who was also trying to understand how his weapon had been unloaded during the dark hours, without him knowing about it.

'I did it' he said plainly, as he walked over.

The ranger looked hard at him.

'Why man? Why have you unloaded our weapons?'

'To teach you all a lesson, my friend. You can't patrol this Park properly and look after the animals, if you can't even look after yourselves! What I've seen is a shambles. This is the first time I've been out with you guys and on both nights, your men have fallen asleep and left everyone at risk. You're lucky I stayed awake, to look after you all. What do you think the armed poachers would do, if they caught you asleep?'

'You shouldn't have done it!' snarled the man.

'Your role is to get everyone to the meeting point with the vehicles and we can discuss it further, back at camp if you wish?'

'Yes, we can,' replied Peter flatly, collecting up his gear. 'OK, everyone. I want to move out in thirty minutes, so make sure you're ready!' he shouted.

The men began to busy themselves, packing up their gear and grabbing a hasty breakfast. They set off for the final part of the patrol, David reckoning it to be about ten kilometres. The light and heat were gentle at this time of day, as he saw some kudu scatter in front of them, spooked by their arrival. They walked throughout the morning, only stopping once to look at the remains of a giraffe and take a drink, before they arrived at the pickup point. The two vehicles were parked up on a small hillock, overlooking a flat stretch of the river and he could see hippos enjoying the cooling waters in the distance.

Peter, without looking at his nemesis, ordered the rangers to mount up and they were on their way within minutes. They drove away from the river and back towards camp.

Arriving back, the dusty men unloaded their gear and walked to the armoury to hand in their weapons. David strode towards the main building. Peering into the briefing room, he saw his friends with cups in their hands, chatting by the window.

'Is it lunchtime yet, I'm famished?' he asked.

'Welcome home stranger!' teased Sandra, looking him up and down.

'Good to see you,' said Dennis. 'Come on in and have some tea.'

'Thanks, I could use a cup,' he replied, laying his pack and rifle down on a table.

She poured him a drink and handed it to him, a big grin on her face.

'Better not get too close. I haven't washed for a few days,' he joked, sipping the tea and sitting down.

'So, how were they?' the Warden asked.

'Not too bad. A few things to work on, but nothing we can't fix,' he replied tactfully. 'I'll give you a full report once we've done the patrol debrief and I've cleaned myself up. Oh, there is one thing though,' he said, recounting the events of the previous evening.

'Thanks for telling me. No doubt he'll be in here later, telling me all about it.'

Hurriedly finishing his tea, David made his way to the armoury.

'Are we doing the debrief?' he asked Peter.

'We'll do it later, when the men have sorted themselves out,' replied the Head Ranger, not looking up.

Biting his tongue, used to debriefing straight after a patrol or operation, David spoke calmly. 'OK, let me know when' and he made his way back to his room, to clean his weapon and take a much needed shower.

A little later, fully revived and dressed in clean clothes, he wandered over to the rangers' tents. Seeing flaps open and walking along the line, he noticed that the men were lying on their cots, fully dressed and fast asleep, some already snoring.

Turning, he set out to find the Head Ranger. He found him in the dining hall, cup in hand, joking with one of the kitchen ladies.

'Have you got a minute?' he asked.

When they were seated, David looked at the man.

'I know you're annoyed about what I did last night, but I did it for a good reason.'

'You shouldn't have done it' glared the ranger. 'You made us all look stupid!'

'Well, I'm sorry if I hurt any feelings, but things need to change around here.'

'This is how we work here. We keep it relaxed and we do our jobs,' remarked the ranger coldly.

'Not anymore. Now, before we speak to the men, I'm going to run through that patrol with you. I suggest you get a pen and paper.'

When he returned, the Englishman debriefed him.

Peter was quiet throughout, his face impassive.

Chapter Eight

One night, when David was fast asleep after a heavy day, there was a banging on his door followed by urgent shouting. Waking with a start, he rolled out of bed and snapped the light on.

'Shots fired out in the park,' exclaimed Dennis, when he opened the door.

'Oh, Christ!' he replied, suddenly fully awake. 'Where?'

'Eastern side, a few kilometres from the old ranger's hut. There's a patrol out there that has just called in.'

'I know it. Get everyone together in the briefing room in five minutes and we'll organise a response.'

Thirty minutes later, with everyone briefed, armed and fired up, the convoy of two Land Rovers pulled out of the camp and raced towards the ranger's hut twenty kilometres away.

Bouncing along the dusty track, he glanced across at Sandra and patted her knee.

'We'll be OK,' he said reassuringly.

'It's not me I'm worried about,' she replied calmly. 'It's what they've hit.'

Rounding a corner, he had to brake suddenly when a small herd of zebra showed up in his headlights, blocking the way.

'Come on guys, out of the way!' he shouted irritably.

The equids eyed the vehicle with disdain, before slowly moving into the bush.

A little later, they reached the hut and after a quick discussion with the rangers there, set off again, away from the track, in the direction of the reported shots.

Switching to sidelights, he slowed the convoy and drove carefully around the trees and thorny bushes, scanning for signs. As they started to come over a slight rise, he spotted some light in the distance and stopped the vehicle, killing his own lights. Gathering everyone together, he pointed towards the threat and they moved slowly towards it, fanning out across the bush.

When they were a few hundred metres away, he halted the rangers and whispered his instructions on the radio. Taking the night vision goggles, he crept slowly forward with Sandra to study the scene.

Peering into the gloom, he saw a large elephant on its side and a few men standing nearby. They were carrying weapons, which could have been AK-47s, but he wasn't sure. Another man, on his knees, was sawing laboriously at one of the tusks. Close by was a pale off-roader, parked next to a tree. The men had set up two lights, casting broad beams over the animal.

He handed the goggles to Sandra, who studied the scene.

She grabbed his arm.

'Bastards!' she whispered bitterly.

He nodded, then led her back to the waiting rangers.

Briefing them quickly, the group moved in formation towards the lights.

With his weapon pointing towards one of the standing men, David stepped out of the darkness and shouted.

'Put your weapons on the ground, now!'

One of the men brought his weapon up sharply and he fired, dropping him to the floor.

The other turned and started to run in the opposite direction, into the darkness. A shot rang out from the right and the figure staggered, before limping away.

Running over to the man with the saw, he grabbed him by the throat and threw him into the dirt.

'Who are you?' he shouted angrily.

'My, my name is Jacob Liseli,' he stuttered.

'And the buyer is?'

'I don't know, sir. We were to take the tusks to Kadoma, near Harare.'

'Guard him,' he instructed one of the rangers nearby. 'I'm going after the other one. Sandra and you two with me.'

They moved off and just beyond the elephant, where the man had been shot, there was a splatter of blood on the ground and taking out his torch, he shone it into the darkness.

'Let's go,' he instructed and the small group followed.

He scanned the ground, seeing blood in the dust every few metres and used the goggles to check for danger ahead. They had been going for a few minutes, when he spotted a shape at the base of an acacia tree.

Peering closer, he saw a figure slumped against the trunk, his head resting on his chest. Instructing the group to fan out and cover the body, he crept forward.

'Push the weapon away from you and put your hands up,' he shouted at the poacher.

Slowly, the man did as instructed and the rangers moved in.

Approaching the African, he saw in the torchlight that he had been hit in the upper leg. His trousers were soaked in blood and his breathing was shallow and laboured.

'Tell me about the buyer?' he snarled.

The man looked up at him with weary eyes and slowly shook his head.

Stepping forward, he kicked the injured leg.

The man howled and forced his eyes shut in pain.

'They'll kill me if I snitch,' pleaded the man.

'I'll kill you myself if you don't,' he warned. 'Or rather, the animals out here will.'

The man closed his eyes and lowered his head. Knowing what lurked in the darkness, he didn't take long to respond.

'OK. The buyer is from China and we're due to meet him in Kadoma tomorrow night, at this place,' he said resignedly, reaching into his pocket and pulling out a slip of paper.

David took the address and ordered the man to hand over his phone.

Telling one of the rangers to treat the injured man, he walked a few paces away from the group and called Dennis to update him. Giving the details of the buyer, he instructed the warden to inform the Zimbabwean authorities to try to arrest him.

Back at the site of the slaughter, he asked Sandra to take some photos of the kill, with the poachers and their weapons sat next to it. Once complete, he instructed the rangers to collect firewood and to lay it on top and around the creature.

Taking a jerrycan from one of the vehicles, he doused the elephant with fuel, concentrating on the tusks. When the pyre was ready, he lit a torch of dry grass and handed it to her. Touching it to the carcass, flames shot up into the air as her body rocked with sobs and tears streamed down her face.

....

A month later, after lunch, David was sitting with Dennis in the main briefing room, enjoying a cup of tea after a busy morning. His skin was heavily tanned now and his hair was fairer, bleached by the sun. He was thinner and leaner too and had never been happier.

The training had gone well and although reluctant to embrace new ideas at first, the rangers had accepted that changes were needed and their skills had improved enormously. It had taken them a while to operate effectively at night, but through practice after practice on the little training area by the camp, they had proved themselves worthy to be called rangers.

Apart from one more incident of hunting, where the perpetrators were caught, the level of attacks on the wildlife had decreased. He had put it down to the extra vehicle patrols he had organised along the western and eastern borders of the Park.

'Shame about Peter,' remarked the Warden.

'Yes, but as you saw, he was stuck in the past and you were right to let him go.'

'Thomas seems to be doing well as his replacement.'

'Yes, now that he's out of Peter's shadow. I think you can rely on him for many years.'

Hearing footsteps behind him, he saw Sandra enter the room.

'There you are!' she said cheerily. 'What are you two up to?'

'Oh, just talking about the changes around here,' said Dennis, smiling.

'We couldn't have done it without you!' she said, patting David on the shoulder. 'I thought we might go on a drive tomorrow David, if you're free? To see if we can find the rhinos. They haven't been spotted for a few weeks now and I thought you might enjoy a trip out?'

'Good idea!' said Dennis, answering for hm. 'You've spent a lot of time around camp these last few weeks and it would be good for you to blow out the cobwebs!'

'Err, yes Sandra. Great idea! What do you have in mind?'

'Well, I thought we could leave nice and early and drive up to the northern edge. They seem to like it up there because there's plenty of grazing and it's furthest away from people.'

'OK,' he said smiling, looking at his watch. 'I'd better organise things. See you both later!'

After he'd gone, the Warden turned to her.

'He's an excellent chap and has done great things here. I'll be sorry to see him go.'

'Why, is he going?' she asked, a confused look on her face.

'Well, he's not going to stay forever is he? Men like that, with those skills, never hang around in one place for long.'

'Well, I hope he does stay. We've all got a bit attached to him, since he's been here' she said, glancing at the door.

Early the next morning, the two set off in the open top Land Rover wearing fleece jackets over safari shirts, with gear and provisions for twenty four hours. For the first hour, their headlights picked up the eyeshine of grazing animals, enjoying the coolness of the morning.

Rounding a corner, they found a family of elephants walking away from them on the track, the youngsters shielded in the centre. David slowed the vehicle so they could watch the animals, with one or two occasionally leaving a deposit in the dirt. He drove slowly past them, looking for the youngsters.

'I see four little ones, three adolescents and six adults,' he said. 'Better get that in the book and take a GPS fix.'

She took the details down and hummed a local song to herself, which he had heard the men singing back at camp.

They drove on northwards and a little later saw a large group of buffalo grazing a few hundred metres from the track.

'Now, those you have to be careful around,' she warned, studying them through the binos. 'In the old days, when hunting was more common in Africa, wounded buffalo would charge their pursuers and gore them with their horns.'

'Nasty!' he whispered, enthralled by the sight.

'Yes, very,' she agreed. 'Not something you would get up from. That's why they are part of the "Big Five", the most dangerous animals to hunt.'

He accepted the binos from her and studied the heavy horns, curling inwards, their tips like daggers. The whole head seemed to fill his view and he imagined being hit by it and shuddered. Looking closer, he also noticed the small pale birds sitting on their backs, pecking for insects and ticks, grateful for the bounty.

One of the animals, possibly a male, stepped towards the car and glared. It seemed to give a signal to the rest of the group, who stopped feeding and looked towards the disturbance.

'Should I drive on?' he asked.

'No, we'll be OK,' she replied, 'as long as we don't approach them on foot. They've seen plenty of vehicles before and don't see them as a threat.'

They watched for a while longer and sensing that danger had passed, the herd moved off further into the bush.

They drove on into the morning, heading more west than north and hit the river a few hours later. The water glistened in the sunlight and the two smiled at each other.

'Not a bad spot is it?' she asked.

'No, it's quite magnificent,' he replied, savouring the moment. 'I would go for a swim, but I've seen what lives there.'

They moved off along the bank and came to a bushy area with an abundance of acacia trees.

'Stop the car!' she whispered, grabbing her binos and peering at the undergrowth.

Pulling in behind some thick scrub, he looked straight ahead, wondering what she had seen.

At first, he saw nothing, just bush and trees. He panned his eyes slightly to the left and looking closer saw a grey, rounded shape, almost hidden by foliage.

'Guess what we've found?' she whispered, holding her breath.

'A rhino?' he asked, hoping it was.

'Yes, it's one of the black rhinos we brought here last year. Their eyesight isn't great, but their hearing is excellent, so we have to be quiet.'

After a few minutes, the beast strolled out into the open, unaware of the human presence.

Looking through the binos, he could clearly see the pointed lip that distinguished the species from its white cousins. It had two horns, the one at the front much longer than the one at the rear. Its ears, twitching to deter insects, were raised and pointing away from the car. The tough hide, like armour plating, was grey and covered in dirt from the dust baths they took to get rid of pests.

'Isn't she beautiful?' she murmured.

Suddenly, there was a movement in the bushes close to the animal and he caught another flash of grey.

'It's a baby!' she cried, gripping his arm.

Slowly, the little rhino walked out of the bushes and rubbed itself up against its mother, enjoying the reassurance. It rolled in the dirt, ran around excitedly for a few moments and then began grazing next to its protector.

'They must have bred soon after coming here,' she whispered. 'It only looks a few months old.'

'That's excellent news. Maybe there can be a new sanctuary for them here, after all?'

'Let's hope so!' she replied, never taking her eyes off the find.

They watched the animals in awe for a while longer, not wanting the encounter to end. Reaching into his pack, he retrieved his camera and took a few careful photos, until the mother moved off slowly into thicker bush, followed by the little one.

They waited for a few more minutes, to see if the animals would reappear, and sensing that it was unlikely, he started the car and moved off slowly.

Sandra took a GPS fix and wrote down what they had seen in her notebook.

When they were well out of earshot, she turned to him.

'Wow!' she shrieked, her eyes sparkling. 'That was incredible!'

'Fantastic!' he agreed. 'They were so close. Dennis will be pleased.'

'Oh yes! I think this deserves a celebration' she replied. 'Let's stop at the Mutemwa pools on the way back to camp.'

They drove on through the heat of the day, arriving at the pools an hour before sunset. He pulled up near to a group of wildebeest, quenching their thirst. Jumping out, Sandra walked to the back of the vehicle and returned with a cool box and a blanket, grinning.

'Where did you manage to hide that?' he asked.

'Oh, under some blankets,' she teased over her shoulder, as she walked down to the water's edge.

David followed, laughing.

They lay the blanket on the ground and sat down next to each other, marvelling at the stunning location.

There were three jade coloured pools curving off to the right. Two of them were the size of a large swimming pool and the other about half the size. Off to one side were a number of large towering baobab trees in a clump, each showing the ravages of elephant tusks.

Further back, stretching as far as the eye could see, acacia trees and thorny scrub filled the landscape.

On the other side of the pools, following the curve of the water, stood a rocky kopje with small green bushes sprouting out of the darkness. Birds of every description and size were paddling in the shallows, flying overhead or squabbling in the branches.

'Shall I do the honours?' he asked, pulling the coolbox towards him and opening the lid.

'Sure, go ahead.'

He peered inside and saw some bottles of lager sitting in a pool of water, from where the ice had melted. Opening the bottles, he passed one to her.

'Cheers!' he said, tapping his own bottle with hers. They chatted about the Park and what its future looked like and the improvements that could be made.

Near to one of the distant pools, he saw a troop of baboons taking a grateful drink, no doubt after spending hours on the plain. A few youngsters were playing with each other, running around a larger animal and bumping clumsily into it.

'So, what lies in your future, David?' she asked, turning to face him.

'Oh, I don't know. I'm quite enjoying life here for the moment, to think too far ahead.'

'Will you extend your contract?' she murmured, looking into his eyes.

'I'm thinking about it,' he replied, glancing towards the baboons.

'Because I'd like you to stay,' she said.

Taking the bottle from him and placing it on the ground, she leant over and kissed him, gently at first, but then more passionately. They stayed in the embrace for some time, enjoying the intimacy that had never surfaced before, but somehow had always been there. He stroked her hair and smelt her skin and wondered if he could really make a life there.

'As much as I'd like to stay here all evening with you, I think we'd better get back, or the camp may be worried.'

'You're right,' she murmured, standing up. 'We'll have to celebrate more often!'

'Yes, we will,' he answered, smiling and accepting her hand to pull himself up.

They walked back to the car hand in hand, and moved off as the light began to fade.

That night, as David was drifting off to sleep, he heard a tap on his door, followed by the sound of it opening slowly. Raising himself on one elbow, he tried to see what was going on and saw a figure in a white slip come through the door, close it gently and walk towards the bed.

He felt the warmth of her body next to his skin and wrapped his arms around her in longing.

....

A few weeks later, returning from a gruelling foot patrol on the eastern edge of the Park, David settled on his bed to rest. Postponing sleep for a moment, he reached across to the table and grabbed his laptop.

Turning the machine on, he scrolled through the seventy-four new emails that had arrived since he last checked, a week before. Most of the messages were spam. 'Learn Spanish in just one week!' one message boasted and another claimed, 'Carpets good enough for Royalty'.

He wondered how they had got his email address and was sad that the internet was clogged with so much rubbish. He deleted as he went down the list and an email from an old girlfriend caught his eye. Opening it, he wondered what he would find. It was a photo of the girl, lying topless on a tropical beach somewhere. The words 'Come and get it big boy!' were written underneath, making him smile.

'Julie!' he grinned.

They had enjoyed some good times, back when he was starting out in the Paras. He remembered, with a smile, sneaking her into the officers' mess after hours. She had a great body. Slim, tall, small breasts and a little blonde bob cut. He was sad that the relationship had come to an end, but the endless exercises in the UK and abroad had scuttled the romance after only a few months.

Continuing down the list, his eyes latched onto the name 'Simon Chester.'

'Christ, what does he want?' he said aloud.

Simon was his former Commanding Officer, from 22nd Special Air Service Regiment.

He smiled at the brevity of the note, remembering his CO fondly as a man of action and not words. David had given him his email address when he left the army, never expecting to hear from him again.

Hello David

I hope all is well and that you have found what you were looking for?

We miss you in the Regiment and I in particular was sorry to see you go.

I know that you may have other things on at the moment, but I'd like you to meet a friend of mine, when you are next back in the UK. You won't regret it, I'm sure.

All the best

Simon

PS. Who Dares Wins

Reading and re-reading the note several times, he wondered what it could mean. He certainly wasn't going back to the Regiment, that was for sure. His life as a full-time soldier was over. But something was nagging him. Simon would only contact him about something important. He wasn't the kind of man to waste time on frivolities. Turning off the laptop and placing it back on the table, his mind churned over. Much later, he drifted off to sleep.

The next morning, as he woke and prepared for the day ahead, the contents of the note swirled around his head and he couldn't think of anything else.

'How did you sleep?' asked Sandra at breakfast, grinning at him broadly.

Her visits to his bed had become almost a nightly occurrence, although she had left him alone the previous night.

'Oh, pretty good,' he replied unconvincingly, wiping the sleep out of his eyes. 'And you?'

'I was out tracking lions until the early hours!' she said, taking a sip of her tea and placing her hand on top of his.

After a moment, he withdrew his hand slowly and looked at her fondly. 'I'm going to get some more tea. Do you want some?'

Just then, Dennis came in with an anxious look on his face. 'We've just had news from one of the patrols about an injured elephant in the middle of the Park. Can one or both of you go out there and take a look? I've warned off the vet, who is getting his gear together now.'

'I've got to stay here,' he replied. 'There's some key training organised for later.'

'I'll go,' said Sandra enthusiastically, standing up.

'Try to leave as soon as you can.'

'Will do. See you both later,' she said, walking quickly out of the room.

As her footsteps receded, David turned to the warden.

'I was thinking of going back to the UK in a month or so,' he began. 'My contract is coming to an end with you and with Christmas coming up, I thought I'd pop home and see friends and family and take stock.'

'Good idea. You should go. It'll be good for you to get away from here for a while and recharge your batteries,' smiled the Warden. 'But I want you to come back, do you hear?'

'I hear you!'

'There is still so much to do. It looks like Kruger are going to send us a few more rhinos next year and one of the Parks in Tanzania have offered to give us a decent number of African wild dogs, to boost our numbers. And if you do come back, I'm sure we can get you a contract for a year and maybe a bit more money?'

'Thanks Dennis. You've been good to me and I'm grateful for the experience. I'll think about things and let you know.'

'OK, that's fair enough,' replied the Warden, slapping him on the back.

A month later, Sandra drove him to Livingstone airport in the early morning sunshine.

'Seems a long time since we were going in the opposite direction,' joked David, as they passed through Cholola.

'Yes,' she replied thoughtfully, glancing across at him. 'A lot of water under the bridge since then.'

They drove on in relative silence and he realised how much he loved the country. The wildlife, the scenery, the climate, the people. He wondered if he would return and looking at her now, he hoped he would.

Eventually, they arrived at the airport and he reached for his bags.

'Please come back. We, I need you here!' she pleaded.

'Let's see,' he replied. 'I need to sort out a few things back in the UK and I'll let you both know what my plans are.' As an afterthought, and he regretted saying it straight away, he offered, 'Whatever happens, I'll treasure the moments we had.'

Tears began to form in her eyes and, looking at the ground, she began to sob gently. Reaching for her, he clutched her in his arms, trying to offer comfort. He stroked her hair and kissed her on the cheek, telling her it was going to be alright. She clung to him, not wanting to let him go, it seemed.

After a while, she kissed him and spoke quietly.

'I love you, David. I always will. You know where I am.'

He nodded slowly.

She smiled weakly at him, tears streaking down her face.

'Have a good trip,' she said flatly. Then she turned, jumped back in the vehicle and pulled away, never looking back.

He watched her leave with a lump in his throat and a tear in his eye and wondered if he would ever see her again. After he lost sight of the car through the trees, he sighed heavily, picked up his bags and walked towards the terminal building.

Chapter Nine

London, England

David crossed St James's Square, his footsteps crunching through the overnight snow, the collar of his coat turned up to shield against the cold. His breath condensed as it hit the air.

'I'm here to see Simon Chester,' he said to the girl behind reception at the Special Forces Club.

'One moment, sir,' she replied, picking up the phone and dialling a number. She gave his details to the person on the other end of the phone and asked him to take a seat.

He had thought of joining the club whilst with the SAS. Spending so much time away, he had decided against it, but looking around now, he saw the appeal. It was a perfect place to meet up with people and very confidential. There are no idiots or chancers in here, he thought to himself. He'd come across plenty of them in the army, outside Special Forces, where in some units there was more bluster than brawn.

Soon, he heard footsteps on the staircase and looking up, saw his ex CO.

'Hello David!' he said, shaking him firmly by the hand. 'How the devil are you?'

'I'm good Simon. I see you've laid the cold weather on for me! And you?'

'Oh, had a busy Christmas seeing everyone, but now peace has been restored.' Heading for the wide staircase, he said, 'Thanks for getting in touch. This chap I want you to meet, James Walker, is an old friend of mine and he has been keen to meet you for some time. Listen to what he has to say and make your own mind up.'

'I will Simon, thank you'.

They reached the top of the stairs and the lieutenant colonel directed him towards a door. 'Meeting Room Two' was written above it in black letters.

He tapped the door lightly and they entered. Sitting at a table was a man in a blue business suit and a Guards tie, reading a copy of *The Times*. He had a full head of neatly cut brown hair, speckled with grey, and piercing blue eyes.

'David, I would like to introduce James Walker,' said his former CO.

When he stood up, David saw that he was of slim build and tall, well over six foot.

They exchanged pleasantries and ordered some coffee, and Simon soon excused himself and left them alone to talk.

After some discussion, James rested his hands on the table.

'So, you like to fight for a cause do you?'

Thinking about his answer, David looked at him.

'Yes, I suppose I do. I want my life to mean something,' he replied honestly.

'Very good, very good,' nodded the man slowly. 'Simon told me your MC came through for service in Afghanistan. Very impressive!'

He allowed his mind, just for a moment, to wander back to the harsh realities of the country.

'Thanks. The guys who were with me share that award.'

The man nodded his head slowly in understanding before speaking.

'Now, I may have an opportunity for you. I belong to a small group, within a secret organisation, comprised mainly of ex SAS people like yourself. We are funded through SIS, but are a very deep subset within their structure. Few know about us: the Director General, the operatives themselves and one or two others, but officially we don't exist and that's exactly how we like it. For years, journalists and investigators have been convinced that there is a hit squad that goes around the world killing people who are a threat to the UK.'

He paused, looking directly at his guest.

'The fact is, they're right.' The former colonel brought his fingertips together and continued.

'In the past, during the Cold War and afterwards, these overseas sanctions went on and no one really took any notice. They were run through mainstream SIS then of course.'

He paused, glancing thoughtfully out of the window.

'In recent times though, because of Britain's 'Ethical Foreign Policy' and the huge oversight that operates at the heart of government in this country, these operations have had to be buried and buried deep. SIS rarely dirties its hands with sanctions overseas. It's more interested in intelligence gathering than killing. So, a hush-hush outfit had to be created. Those journalists and investigators stumbled on some of our previous incarnations: 'Group 13', the 'Increment', the 'Det' and others. Those peeping toms were encouraged to stop investigating, and pretty much they did. Apart from the odd one, that needed extra encouragement,' he said coldly. 'They were told to look elsewhere for their stories and thankfully they have.'

'And so now, we don't have a name. We felt that would help to keep us buried and so far...' James tapped the table, '...it's worked well.'

'So, you're funded through SIS, but that funding is off the books and you carry out sanctions for Her Majesty's Government?'

'Yes,' he confirmed. 'Most of the sanctions are conducted overseas: Africa, the Middle East, South America, the Far East. Occasionally though, we might be asked to carry out a sanction on a foreign national living in this country, but it's very rare. Normally, justice would take its course and the bad apple would be extradited to their own country, or go to jail here for fifteen to twenty years. So, they would have to be a very bad apple for us to get involved.'

'What about British nationals?'

'We rarely target them, but there have been cases,' James replied.

He nodded. 'Sounds interesting. Please go on.'

'You would have two lives. Your first life would be for the Crown, helping to defend this country's interests overseas. Where required, you would be asked to eliminate those individuals who are deemed to be a threat to this country, or are considered to be *persona non grata*. Simon tells me you're a good shot,' he noted, changing the subject. 'A trained sniper, no less.'

'That's right. Officers don't normally train as snipers, as you know, but he allowed me to do it. It's a long story.'

'You can tell me all about it, if you do join us,' the man smiled. 'Your second life would be to work as a headhunter, in my firm, Coldridge Partners. This would be the perfect cover for you when you go overseas, as meeting clients and candidates will help to mask the real reason for you being in that country. If you are ever stopped or questioned and checks are made on you, your cover will always be watertight, as you really are a headhunter and operating as one. There are some procedures to go through. Signing the updated Official Secrets Act, making a will, being fully vetted, that kind of thing. Also, as well as being briefed on our modus operandi and completing the tradecraft course, you would also undergo our own resistance to interrogation training.'

He looked up in surprise.

'I know that you did RTI at Hereford, but we have learnt over time that additional training in this area is a good insurance policy for all of us. And besides, you'll get to spend a lovely week in the Welsh countryside again! You would also be fully trained as a headhunter. For a bright chap like you, that will take about six months to learn the basics. On the subject of money, you'll be well rewarded.'

He ran through the figures as David studied him intently.

When he was finished, he reached into a pocket and handed him a smart looking business card.

'Reflect on it all and let me know in a few days. Now, if you have time for lunch, you'll be in for a treat. The fish in the club was delivered fresh from the coast this morning.'

....

Number fifteen St James Square, SW1, was in a smart part of London, near to St James's Park, Piccadilly, Regent Street and close to the Houses of Parliament, the seat of government. Grand Georgian buildings surrounded the open area, home to a number of international companies and a favoured location for gentlemen's clubs. There was a garden in the middle of the square, with footpaths bisecting it and a grand bronze statue of William III on horseback, dominating the centre.

The main reception for the building was on the left and after David had checked in and clearance had been given, he proceeded into the heart of the building.

Past the reception area was a choke point that channelled the visitor through a metal detector, manned by a security guard who checked access passes.

It was a week since the meeting and taking the lift to the third floor, brought him to the offices of Coldridge Partners. On entering, there was a smart, airy reception and a comfortable seating area for visitors. A selection of newspapers and business journals lay neatly on top of a glass table.

He walked over to reception, smiled at the girl and introduced himself. Shortly afterwards, he heard a beep and a door opening and glancing up, saw a woman in her mid-thirties with fiery red hair walking towards him.

'Hello David,' she said, shaking his hand, 'I'm Margaret Ashton, James's PA. Please come with me.'

She turned and headed back towards the door. They passed a number of small offices where he heard snatched conversations.

Eventually, they came to a large corner office, surrounded on two sides with glass panelling and blinds brought partially down. He could see James through the glass, sitting at a large oak desk, working on a laptop in front of him.

The PA tapped gently on the door and leant in.

'David is here to see you, James,' she said casually.

'Ah, excellent!'

'Good to see you again!' he said warmly, as he walked around the desk. 'Found us alright then?'

'Yes,' he nodded, looking around. 'How could I miss such a wonderful place?'

James invited him to sit, gesturing towards two antique chairs.

Taking a moment to glance around, he noticed that everything was of good taste and probably expensive.

In the corner, was a small bookcase, which looked to have various business related texts in it, as well as an old Bible on the top shelf.

To his right was a set of oak filing cabinets, with one of the drawers opened, revealing hundreds of blue covered files.

On the walls were several paintings, one a depiction of a Waterloo era battle, another of an English country scene, possibly from the 1800s and another of a Naval battle, probably from World War Two, he guessed.

'Are you sure this is what you want to do?' James questioned after a short discussion, studying him closely.

'Yes, this is what I want.'

'Good. I think you'll do well. I know we went through a lot of the detail when we met, but I'm going to run through the key aspects with you again, so that you're clear how this is going to work. Crystal clear.'

....

After they finished, James welcomed him to Coldridge Partners with a firm handshake. The rest of the morning was spent meeting the other partners who were in the office, as well as the other consultants and support staff, and his appointed mentor. Penny Simpson was a stylish, slim young woman of about thirty and of medium height, with shoulder length blonde hair that suited her thin, flawless face. She had a slight tan and her makeup was minimal, just a little lipstick in a light pink. She wore an expensive-looking peach coloured skirt, just above the knee and a pure white blouse, buttoned just above the cleavage.

'You have an easy day today, David, so make the most of it!' she said. 'A few of us are taking you out to lunch on Jermyn Street, so I'll see you at 12.30.'

His office was quite small but adequate for his needs. It had modern furniture, desk, chair and bookshelf and it overlooked a line of buildings that led into the square. On the desk was a laptop, a mouse mat with the Coldridge Partners logo and a modern phone. The beige carpet was a little worn under the chair and by the door. On the wall, there was a solitary picture of some fruit in a terracotta bowl.

There was a tap on his open door and he looked up to see Suzie, who he had met earlier. She was Penny's researcher and right hand woman. A plain looking girl of medium height, she was fairly slim like Penny, her short brown hair cut in a modern style.

'I've brought you some reading material about the firm, what its specialisms are and what markets and sectors it operates in,' she said. 'Don't worry, we'll be spending a lot of time on this over the coming weeks.'

'Thanks, Suzie. I can see you're going to keep me busy!' he said, smiling, taking the material from her and flicking through it.

He looked down at the documents she had left him and selected one entitled 'Where We Operate'. The list included the Middle East, primarily Saudi Arabia, Qatar, Kuwait, the United Arab Emirates and Oman. He welcomed the opportunity to use his Arabic again.

He had trained with the Parachute Regiment in Oman and knew the country reasonably well, remembering the vast desert of the Empty Quarter and the rocky southern coast with fondness. With less fondness, he recalled Dubai in the UAE, where he had once gone with a girlfriend on a Christmas trip.

She had been such fun early in the relationship, but the trip had been a disaster because she had wanted to spend each and every day walking around the vast malls that plagued the country. He had suggested that he might go skydiving at the local parachute school, or scuba diving on one of the wrecks a few miles offshore, but she didn't want to be on her own and the rest of the three day trip just crumbled. They hardly spoke, the sex dried up and the last he saw of her was getting into a taxi at Heathrow, crying.

He was disturbed from his reminiscences by a tap on the door and looking up saw Penny framing the doorway.

'A penny for them?' she joked.

'Ah, I was just thinking about a trip to Dubai centuries ago,' he smiled. 'Have you been?'

'Yes, I went with a friend some years ago, but we didn't enjoy it really. Too hot,' she replied guardedly. 'Anyway, time for lunch! Are you hungry?'

'Starving!' he replied, as he picked up his jacket from the back of the chair and followed her out.

....

When they returned, Penny turned to him as they were walking past reception.

'I have some candidate interviews this afternoon, so I'll leave you in the capable hands of Suzie. She'll start to take you through the research process and begin to tell you how we find candidates. It's quite complicated sometimes. You'll then have some time on your own and you can read through the material.'

By this point, they had reached her office, which was similar to his own, but somehow smarter, he noticed.

'And tomorrow, I'll take you through your training plan for the next few weeks, as we like our new joiners to know what they will be doing, segment by segment.'

'Can't wait to get started!' he responded enthusiastically.

She smiled at him and stepped into the office. Making his way back to his own desk and before he had a chance to settle into his chair, he saw Suzie standing in the doorway with her laptop under one arm and a sheaf of papers and a notebook under the other.

'Ready to go?' she asked. 'I've got one of the small meeting rooms for us.'

He spent the next few hours with Suzie showing him the variety of social media options available and how to work with each. She was a good teacher, clear, precise, thorough and he was pleased she had been assigned to him. Towards the end of the day, as his head was beginning to throb, she looked at him sympathetically.

'That's probably enough for today. We'll have plenty of time over the coming weeks to practice this, until you can find your own candidates.' she smiled. 'Prepare for some long nights!'

'I will,' he said, winking at her, and she blushed.

After a month with the firm, as David was coming towards the end of a long training day, he received a call from Margaret, James's PA, asking him to pop round.

When he arrived, he could see him through the glass, talking on the phone and beckoning him to enter. James was making calming statements to whoever was at the other end.

It ended with him promising to look into the matter and getting back to the caller within twenty four hours.

'Amazing. We've been providing services to that client in Saudi for years and every time we work with them, there is an issue or a problem. Every time!' he shouted irritably.

He scribbled something down on a pad and looked up at him, smiling.

'Anyway, enough of that, you'll find out soon enough how tough clients can be!' he laughed. 'So, how are you getting on?'

He hadn't seen much of his boss in the first month, apart from the odd snatched conversation in the lift or corridor.

'Really good!' he enthused. 'I'm enjoying working with Penny and the gang and the work that you do is starting to make sense.'

'Excellent! She speaks highly of you, which is rare for her. She thinks most new joiners are a waste of rations!'

'I'm getting into my stride now.'

'A lot to learn, though. Some people overcomplicate this industry, but actually it's very simple. We approach people about a new job and persuade them to take the offer, if it comes. Now, I wanted to bring you up to speed, on aspects of your first life.'

David breathed in and exhaled slowly, concentrating all the time on James's face.

Just then, there was a tap on the door and Margaret poked her head in.

'I was wondering if you needed me for anything?' she asked.

By now, it was past 7pm and he noticed the dark sky outside.

'No Margaret, thank you. I'm pretty much done for the day myself, so you can get yourself home,' he replied.

She smiled and closed the door quietly.

James looked at his watch and then back at his guest.

'I'm going to tell you about the 'sanction lists' that we operate,' he resumed. 'Basically, there are four lists in use and in order of priority, I'll take you through each one. The first list, normally about ten names, are for the high value and accessible targets. The second list, of about twenty names, is for the high value, but inaccessible targets.'

'Inaccessible?'

'Those individuals in countries off the beaten track, like North Korea, Somalia or Yemen, or the individual in question may be in jail somewhere. They might also have disappeared and SIS is in the process of trying to locate them. We rarely go after people in the 'inaccessible' category, but if there is a strong case, then we'll do it,' James remarked, looking at him gravely.

'The third list, also about twenty names, is for lower value and accessible targets and the fourth list, of around thirty names, is for lower value, inaccessible targets. You'll be mainly concentrating on the third list for now, until we see the true measure of you.'

It wasn't particularly hot in the room, but he could start to feel the sweat running down his back, making his shirt damp. This was becoming very real, he thought to himself.

'When I say 'accessible', I'm talking about how easy it is to get to an individual. Now, the truth of the matter is that few of them are easy to target,' the man grinned, 'as it's unlikely you'll be taking people out in their back gardens, but who knows, you might be fortunate one day. Don't worry though, you're not on your own. I'm not going to tell you how many other primary operatives there are, but let's just say a handful. You won't ever meet them, for OPSEC reasons, but just know that there are others like you, looking after the interests of the British government.'

David nodded, sure this was going to give him the challenge and purpose he had been seeking since leaving the SAS. He felt exhilarated at the prospect and wanted to be part of this group of men, who sanctioned those that were deemed fit for being put down.

'As you are now in the headhunting profession, your targets will be referred to as 'candidates'.

The man paused for a moment.

'There is another task we occasionally perform. Sometimes, extreme violence is not the only way to resolve an issue. There may be times when we send you to speak to an individual, for them to see the error of their ways. Clearly though, if it doesn't do the trick, then we may send you back for a more permanent solution.'

James checked his watch.

'Right, that's probably enough for one evening. We'll do other sessions like this every few weeks, so that your understanding grows and you see how you fit in to the big picture. Reflect on what I've said,' he said sternly. 'This is no small task you're taking on and if at any time you want to quit, let me know and I'll understand. You can walk away when you like, no questions asked.'

Chapter Ten

The next day, as David walked from Piccadilly Circus station to the office, he was still thinking about the conversation the previous evening. He wondered why he had been selected and if it was as easy to quit as James had suggested. Always good to have an exit strategy.

Even when he was in the Special Air Service and living life to the fullest, he always knew that he would leave at some point. He knew himself too well and admitted that he was never going to climb up the ladder in the army, to command a regiment and beyond. He was always looking for new challenges, new adventures. Perhaps the work that he had discussed with James would fit the bill for a few years, maybe longer?

He reached the square and glanced up at the statue of William III, glinting in the morning sunshine, before crossing to the other side and making his way to the front door. Kate and Ella were on reception and seeing him, they cheerily welcomed him in unison.

Passing the kitchen area, he smelt freshly brewed coffee and began to savour his first cup of the day. Penny was already in and, passing her door, he waved in greeting when he saw that she was on the phone. He fired up his laptop, put his phone on charge and glanced out of the window, then his emails. The first one was from Penny, which she must have just sent.

'Hi David. On the phone now, but can you pop in after about fifteen minutes?'

When he got there, he could see that she was still on the phone. She waved him in and pointed to one of the chairs in front of her. She was taking copious notes and asking questions about required skills, qualifications and experience. Once or twice, she glanced at him, rolling her eyes. He grinned back, acknowledging her frustration.

He took a moment to look at her, whilst she was on the phone. She was surely an attractive woman. Today she was wearing an ivory coloured top and a pearl necklace. Surreptitiously, he glanced at her neck, letting his eyes wander downwards.

She had buttoned her top lower than normal and he could just make out the curve of her breast. He looked away, lowered his eyes back down to the daybook. Busying himself, he read through the notes he had made over previous weeks.

'Thank you for briefing me on the role, Ahmed' she said. 'I'll draw up the role profile, based on our discussion and email you that along with our contract, in line with the terms we have agreed. I'll call you in a few days, to see if you have any questions. I hope to see you as well, when I'm next in Kuwait. Thanks again and enjoy the rest of your day.' She placed the handset back into its cradle.

'Phew!' she exhaled, smiling at him. 'This guy, Ahmed, was referred to me by another client in Kuwait, who we've worked with for many years. They are one of the main family businesses there, with fingers in many pies. Ahmed is friendly with one of the sons in that business and he's setting up a construction company there, which will have interests all around the Gulf. He's looking for expat talent and the son referred him to us.'

'That's generous of him,' he offered.

'Well yes, but these roles are always a bugger to fill. When we began speaking, Ahmed said he just wanted a 'finance guy'. But as I drilled down, what he actually wants is a western CFO, ACCA qualified, through one of the big accounting firms, twenty years' experience, ten of which must have been in the Gulf, in the construction sector and knowledge of setting up SAP!' she said, exasperated. 'Oh, and he only wants to pay three and a half thousand Kuwaiti dinar a month, plus benefits. That's about ten grand, sterling!' she laughed. 'Good CFO's in that part of the world can earn twice that. Anyway, we'll give it our best shot and try to fill it. Actually, this would be a good role for you to cut your teeth on,' she said thoughtfully, as he looked at her. 'Yes, I'll get Suzie to lead on it, for candidate generation, but you can help her, based on what she has taught you so far.'

'Nice to start with an easy one!'

'Anyway, let's grab a coffee before we discuss what I wanted to speak to you about.'

Rising from her chair, she led the way towards the kitchen.

'OK, so I wanted to talk to you about a client meeting that I would like you to come to tomorrow. This is an old client of ours, who gives us their senior and some mid-tier roles and it'll be good for you to meet some of the people there. I'm talking about Portland Chalmers, the investment bank' she explained.

He had heard of the bank, but was no expert on their activities. He knew they had thousands of employees and a presence in the major cities of the globe.

'What I would like you to do, for a few hours today, in between your sessions with Suzie, is to prepare for that meeting. I'd like you to research them on the web and read up on the backgrounds of some of the people we are going to meet.'

She handed him a list with names on it.

'Have a look at what the press is saying about them and just get a feel about the organisation if you can. I'll lead the meetings, but I'd like you to watch what I do and learn from it. In this business, you have to develop your own style, but it's good to learn the styles of others. At some point, I'd also like you to go on client meetings with other consultants, but for now you can observe me!' she said, grinning widely.

I'd be very happy to observe you, he thought.

'Hopefully, we'll pick up one or two roles when we visit them, but let's wait and see. I haven't seen them for a few months or so and even if they don't have work for us, it's always good to keep close to the key players there' she said.

They left promptly the next morning.

The office for Portland Chalmers was at number ten, Leadenhall Street in the City, a stone's throw from the Bank of England. After paying the taxi driver, David followed Penny into the building, a glass and steel affair that towered over them. Once they had signed in, the two walked over to the seating area and sat down on brown leather sofas. He picked up a copy of the *Financial Times*, lying on the table.

'Great client this' she whispered.

'Oh?'

'Yes, they pay the best fees, thirty-three per cent, and are quick to make decisions once they've found the candidate they like.'

She smiled and looked around the reception area, watching who was coming in and going out. They heard footsteps clicking some way off and looking up, saw a middle aged woman in a dark business suit, coming towards them.

'It's Jane, the COO's PA,' she whispered, from the side of her mouth.

They made their way to the lifts and climbed skywards, the two women making small talk. Waving to a girl behind the reception desk, Jane led them along a brightly lit corridor, with solid wooden doors on either side. Brass plaques on each denoted the occupants.

'Here we are,' said the PA, as they reached a door marked 'COO'.

Stepping inside, she picked up a notebook from her desk and walked over to another door, tapping on it gently.

'Come!' boomed the voice inside and opening the door, she led them in.

It was a large office with an excellent view over the city, David noticed. The décor was expensive, with pictures of racing horses and country sports adorning the walls and a sizable carpet, probably from Asia, on the floor. Behind a substantial, stained oak desk sat a man of about forty with rosy cheeks, a bald head and considerable girth.

'Penny!' he bawled, getting up from his desk and shaking her warmly by the hand. 'I haven't seen you in ages. How have you been?'

'Good, thanks John. Apologies for not dropping in for a bit, but I've been so enormously busy,' she said, fluttering her eyelashes.

'Splendid! We've been pretty busy ourselves. Had a bit of a restructure you know, but things have settled down now.'

'May I introduce David?' she asked, putting her hand on the shoulder of her companion. 'He's working with me on some my assignments and is ready for any roles that you may have.'

'Excellent!' replied the banker and thrusting out his hand, said 'Welcome to our temple of commercialism!'

'Pleased to meet you,' he replied, getting the measure of the man.

After some coffee and an exchange of pleasantries, the man sank back in his chair and pulled some documents towards him.

'That restructure we had, has opened up a few vacancies in our IT department. Some dead wood in there to be sure! We were hoping that the person we promoted to CIO would do well, but alas, he's struggling and we need to replace him.'

'OK John, what are you looking for in the new candidate?' she asked, leaning towards the desk.

'Here's the job description' he said, passing her some pages of A4. 'All the usual stuff is in there. Computer graduate and twenty years plus of experience in the banking sector. International exposure and a good understanding of banking systems and processes, a knowledge of cybercrime, etc, etc. There is something else though. What we want is a leader. The last one had no control over the department and the replacement has turned out to be a mouse! What we want, is someone who is going to grip that function by the balls and get it delivering for the bank.'

'Fair enough' she replied, seemingly unfazed by his language. 'How about I read through and send you over a proposal in the next few days. Usual fees and terms alright with you?'

'Yes, but speed is of the essence here, Penny. We're implementing a new system next year and I want your candidate to be here to lead it.'

'We can get cracking on it next week, once you've signed the documents and paid the retainer. Hopefully, we can have the shortlist in front of you by the end of the month.'

'Excellent! Let's get this role underway and then I'll get you back in, to discuss some other positions in that department. Lower down, but still quite senior.'

'That would be kind. We'll get started and I'll call you in a few weeks, to set up a meeting.'

'Look forward to it,' smirked the banker, getting up and shaking them both solidly by the hand. Turning to Penny, as they were about to leave and lowering his voice, he said, 'And we still need to have that dinner!'

'Oh, yes,' she replied, suddenly blushing. 'Let's do something when we've kick-started this assignment?'

The man patted her on the back affectionately.

'My diary is waiting!'

She smiled and led David out of the office.

'What was all that about?' he grinned, once they were out of earshot.

'He's been trying it on with me for years,' she replied, exasperated. 'He doesn't seem to get the hint. I have dinner with him now and again, to keep the business relationship going, but he always tries it on. Once, when we were in a bar, he ran his hand along my thigh, can you believe it?'

'Yes, I can. Does he have a wife?'

'Oh, yes. She lives in Kent somewhere, I think. He has a flat in Kensington, where he stays during the week, before going home to wifey at the weekends. God knows what he gets up to on his own from Monday to Friday!'

'I shudder to think,' he replied.

....

'Ah, there you are.'

Turning, he saw James. 'I haven't seen you for a while. How are you?'

'Oh, fine. I've been travelling a fair bit these past few weeks, to the Far East mainly. Could you pop in to my office later, around five o'clock? There is something that I wanted to discuss.'

The rest of the day seemed to drag, even though he was busy and his schedule was full. After three months with the firm, he was busy finding CFO candidates for Jason, one of the other consultants. Hungry for more information, he wanted to know more about his first life and what it would entail.

Eventually, the clock on his laptop showed that it was a few minutes before five and pulling on his jacket, he headed down the corridor.

After being offered a seat and discussing the vagaries of the industry for a several minutes, James glanced at him thoughtfully.

'Now, you may recall that you need to complete an enhanced resistance to interrogation course with us?' he asked. 'Well, we need to get you through that, before you go into the field. Think of it as our insurance policy.'

'I'm happy to,' he responded convincingly, even though he remembered doing RTI on his SAS selection course and it hadn't been pleasant. He had enjoyed the initial phase of escape and evasion, navigating across the countryside for days, trying to live off the land, sleeping in ditches and evading the Hunter Force, who were out to capture him and his coursemates. What he hadn't enjoyed was when that part of the exercise ended and everyone was herded into trucks and driven to a training camp near Hereford to start the interrogation phase. He shuddered at the memory.

'We've put on something for you, starting in a fortnight in Wales. You'll need to be up there on Saturday and you'll return home the following weekend. The first day will be for prep and briefing, followed by a few days on the run.'

'Then, the main event, RTI for a few days, ending up with the final day for cleanup and debriefing,' he said with a smile. 'You'll need to come up with a cover story of course, for your colleagues here, as to why you are away. Just tell them you have a sick relative in Cardiff, or something.'

'I'll think up something imaginative,' he replied, trying to sound enthusiastic and already thinking about how to prepare.

James studied him carefully, before continuing.

'The other topic I wanted to brief you on, is how we typically operate, when carrying out sanctions.'

'OK' he replied, looking across the desk.

'As we are such a small 'outfit,' he paused, smiling broadly, 'we operate in very small groups. Typically, there is a 'shooter' which is you and there is an 'assistor,' who is there to help you. The role of the shooter is obvious. You'll go in there, carry out the sanction and get out. The role of the assistor, who sometimes resides in that country, is to help you with logistics, weapons, briefings, escape plan and so on. If they don't reside in the country, they will go out a week or so before the shooter, primarily to obtain or receive the weapon and recce the site where the kill is going to take place.'

'Understood.'

'The assistor,' James continued, 'is critical to your success. Normally, you will only meet them a day or so before the sanction, so you must gel quickly with that person and take as much information from them as you can in a short space of time.'

'You'll know their first name only and you are not there to make friends, for OPSEC reasons. Occasionally, there may be two assistors on a job, if it is deemed more complicated, or is in a country where additional support is required. The assistor will have the latest details on the individual being sanctioned and will have chosen the best routes in and out, for the operation. Apart from the briefings they give you, one of their most important roles is to dispose of the weapon. We rarely use diplomatic bags to bring a weapon back these days. It's very risky and incriminates the UK government, if discovered.'

'That all makes sense.'

'We keep the teams small and try to eliminate any risks, where we can.'

James spent some time talking about logistics, weapons and escape plans if the sanction went bad or problems arose. He explained why the 'second life' of operatives was so important, as he wanted people to move seamlessly in to and out of countries, using their business backgrounds as cover.

'I don't want thugs to carry out these missions' he stated. 'I want thinking killers, who can blend into the business environment, have business meetings and sensible conversations with senior people. Using a business background helps our people to go unseen, carry out the operation and then disappear, before anyone can work out what happened.'

The older man leant across the desk and paused before speaking.

'Have you ever been to Qatar?' he asked casually.

'No, never been.'

'That's good. I'm going to send you out there in a month or so, for a recce. There's an individual on the third list that will be a good starter for you. This candidate has been a pain in the arse for years, sending money to jihadist groups in the region, including Iraq, Afghanistan and Gaza. Some of his money has ultimately resulted in the deaths of British soldiers and aid workers.'

The man paused and looked David in the eyes.

'What I want you to do is go out there and have a good look around. I'll arrange for you to meet our assistor and he can show you the sights, so to speak. The next time you'll meet is when you're there to kill!'

'Sounds good.'

Nodding his head, James continued.

'Take this opportunity to learn how things work, David. Normally, you won't have the luxury of a full recce.'

Chapter Eleven

Wales

David lay prone at the edge of the wood, observing the village below. Dawn was approaching and the songbirds were starting to find their tune. The mist was beginning to clear, but where it hung around the village, the yellow streetlights created a ghostly glow. It was May, but the night had been bitterly cold, made worse by the lack of cloud cover.

He had been walking all night, from where they had thrown him out of a truck, north of Tregaron and his feet were sore. Pulling out the sketch map they had provided, he worked out that he had covered about twenty kilometres.

'Only another fifty to go,' he whispered wryly to himself.

They had given him some bread and an onion on the truck, which he had wolfed down, but he hadn't eaten since then and his stomach was beginning to rumble. He would lay some snares in the wood soon, in the hope of catching a rabbit, whose sign he had already spotted. He knew he had to eat something a few times a day, otherwise he wouldn't have the energy to cover the distance.

He glanced wearily down at the gear he was in.

Army boots, old service trousers tied together with string, a green T shirt, an old army shirt and a tatty greatcoat with all the buttons missing. He looked like a tramp. His water bottle, tied to paracord, draped over his shoulder, bandolier style.

'Just like SAS selection,' he smiled, although this time he was on his own and had to survive using his own wits and cunning.

They had also given him a survival tin, with fish hooks, fishing line, snares, a button compass, a small torch, some water purification tablets, safety pins, matches, a razor blade and a few other items.

He hadn't come across his pursuers during the night, but he knew they were out there, watching and waiting. They would have set up observation posts on the high ground, hoping to catch him if he dared stray from cover.

'Who are the pursuers?' he wondered.

Blindfolded on the truck, he hadn't got a look at them, but he had heard one of them ask his buddy for a cigarette, during the long drive from Cardiff. The accent had been unremarkable and was difficult to place. Maybe they were soldiers from one of the southern infantry battalions, tasked to chase him, with the promise of excitement, along with free beer if they caught him. He hoped they weren't from the Paras, his old unit, because they were sure to give him a hard time. If they captured him, they would 'soften him up' in interrogation parlance, before handing him over to the Directing Staff.

The light was fast approaching now and he noticed a tractor amble through the village and out the other side, the farmer no doubt still rubbing sleep from his eyes.

It would warm up soon, he hoped, stifling a shiver down his back.

Crawling back from the edge, he loped into the wood, looking for places to lay his snares. He saw rabbit holes and droppings everywhere and settled on a few sites, where little feet had created runs in the soil. Looking around for somewhere to rest, he chose a dip in the ground, with a large bush shielding it on two sides. Pulling up the collar of his greatcoat as high as he could, and wrapping the garment around himself, he adopted a fetal position, to try to retain the little heat he had. His last thought, before drifting off to sleep, was of a cosy English pub, with a fire raging off to one side and a half-filled glass of beer in front of him.

....

He awoke with a start, some hours later, with a loud and strange whirling sound nearby. Shaking his head to gain his senses, he sat up slowly, listening hard. The unmistakable sound of a helicopter raced into his brain and lowering his body into the dip, he scanned the sky through the trees above him. Off to his right, a few hundred metres or so, he saw the aircraft hovering over a patch of open ground. He recognised it as a Lynx and saw the camouflage paint down its side and wondered if he had been spotted. Slumping lower into his hiding place, he ducked his head and prayed that he was fully concealed. After a few minutes, the helicopter moved off, flying over the village and arcing to the east, towards distant wooded hills.

Looking around him cautiously, he slowly stood up, scanning the wood for movement.

Satisfied that he was still on his own, he arched his back and stretched out his arms to their full extent, getting life back into his weary limbs. He touched his toes, several times and happy with his condition, walked around the wood, checking on his snares. They were all empty and placing the wire back in the tin, he wandered disconsolately back to his hiding place, looking for mushrooms and berries on the way.

Sitting down, he studied his map and aligned his tiny compass with it. The sketch map was basic, showing only roads, rivers, settlements and the odd feature, like a mountain top or dam. He found a point, some twenty five kilometres from where he sat, in the direction he was heading, as a possible location for his next resting up place. Studying every feature on the way, he tried to memorise them, as he would only use the torch during the night as sparingly as possible. Satisfied that he had done as much as he could, he closed his eyes and allowed sleep to overtake him.

Later, as darkness began to fall, David checked his feet and was happy to see no blisters, only red patches around his toes, where the socks had rubbed against his skin. He was really hungry now and allowed himself the simple pleasure of imagining what food he was going to eat, when he eventually returned to London. Would it be roast chicken, pizza, curry or a bacon buttie? He couldn't decide and parked the tantalising thoughts, whilst he decided on his next plan of action.

Reaching down into the dirt, he grabbed some loose soil and rubbed it into his face, followed by the tops of his hands.

He then ruffled the leaves around where he had slept, to disguise his visit and crept to the edge of the wood to observe the village. The streetlights slowly came on, as darkness descended and he broke cover, walking slowly towards a stone wall that ran down to a farm on the village edge. Following it down the hill, he eyed the settlement cautiously, stepping gently as he trod.

On reaching the farm, he stopped and listened, scanning left and right. Off to one side, he saw a cow shed with a light above the main door and headed for it. Inside, he saw cows in stalls, munching on feed from a tray running alongside. Creeping cautiously, he noticed an office at the end, with a single lightbulb glowing inside. Reaching it, he peered around the door.

A newspaper was laid out on a small desk and a radio, on a shelf nearby, was quietly playing easy listening tunes. Next to the paper, was a mug of something, it looked like tea, and next to that a sandwich, half eaten and sitting on cellophane. By the kettle, was half a packet of digestive biscuits, with fragments scattered messily on the desk. Reaching for the sandwich slowly, he forced it into his mouth, not dropping a crumb. He picked up the mug and took a quick swig of lukewarm tea, which had a little sugar.

Suddenly, he heard a toilet being flushed.

Pushing a handful of biscuits into his greatcoat pocket, he darted out of the office, ran to the door of the barn, peeked out and stepped into the darkness. Running quickly away from the building towards a woodline, he only stopped when he was well inside.

He chuckled to himself about the farmer wondering where his sandwich had gone. At least he could make another. He could have come away empty handed, but he had struck lucky.

During the night, he crossed two streams up to his waist, scaled a huge wooded ridgeline rising high over the valley floor, traipsed over miles and miles of boggy, open moorland and stumbled through a forestry block, the size of a small town. Finally, as it was getting light, he reached the point he was aiming for, a wooded hilltop, with river valleys either side. His map showed a settlement nearby and looking down from his vantage point, he was disappointed to see only a hamlet of just a few houses, perhaps a kilometre away.

Pushing the negative thought out of his mind, he quickly set up snares a few hundred metres away and returned to a spot out of the wind. Pulling his boots off, he peeled off the sodden socks and wrung them out several times, as best as he could. Inspecting the soles of his pasty white feet, he saw that he had blisters on both and taking a safety pin from his tin, he pierced them, squeezing out what fluid was there. Satisfied with his work, he replaced the socks, re-tied his boots and curled up, waiting for the sun's rays to revive him.

Just as he was closing his eyes, some movement spiked his attention. He swivelled his head slowly to identify the cause and saw a fox, in all its magnificent glory, trot along the wood's edge.

It paused once or twice to sniff the earth and then sleekly carried on, its senses on full alert.

When it drew level, some ten metres away, it stopped again and sniffed the air. Slowly, it turned its head towards him, continuing to sniff and looked him directly in the eyes. It studied him curiously for a few moments, until a noise down by the hamlet caused it to turn and scamper away.

'What the hell was that noise?' he asked himself quietly.

He was tired and his brain didn't want to offer a clue. Reluctantly, he got on to all fours and crawled to the edge of the wood, aiming for a thick bush to observe from. Initially, he didn't see anything untoward. The hamlet was coming to life after the cold night and he could see smoke rising languidly from one of the chimneys. Looking along the single track road to just where it disappeared behind a brow, he saw the cause of the disturbance.

It was an army truck, parked on the soft verge!

The noise, coming back to him now, was of a tailgate, slamming down. Looking closer, he saw soldiers, perhaps ten, organise themselves at the back of the vehicle and start to pull on webbing equipment.

'Shit!' he uttered quietly.

His plan had been to rest up for the day and now these soldiers were going to make him run for most of it. Groaning quietly, he looked closer. The vehicle was a few hundred metres away and he tried to ascertain what kind of soldiers they were. They looked a fit bunch, slim and hardy, as they gathered around their leader for a briefing, their weapons held across their chests. His heart began to sink, as he studied the soldiers further and his fears were confirmed when the morning light caught the group in a moment of sunshine.

The berets they were wearing were maroon.

'Christ!' he whispered. 'That's all I need.'

These men of the Parachute Regiment would chase him hard and hound him like dogs after a fox. He wondered if they had found him, or were just doing a sweep of the area, or if one of the helicopters had perhaps caught him on a thermal imager.

Leaving the personal recriminations till later, he crawled back from the edge and stooped back to his rest up point.

Scattering the leaves as he had the day before, he checked that he had left no sign and turning, jogged quickly away from the soldiers, back through the wood.

After a few minutes, he stopped and looked behind him, listening out for any noise. All seemed quiet. He continued for another few minutes until he reached a point with commanding views over the road below. Further along, he saw a stone wall running from the wood down to the road and headed for it, staying in cover. He reached it and peered out, looking for soldiers below. Satisfied that all was clear, he ducked in behind the wall and crouching, ran as fast as he could down the grassy slope, all the way down to the road. There was a cattle grid where the wall met the road and he stopped once more to listen. Hearing an engine some way off, he knew he had to make a move.

Keeping low, he looked around the edge of the wall and saw the truck heading towards him. Without a second thought, he raced across the road, sprinted towards the woodline and crashed through the undergrowth.

He heard the roar of the engine, as the driver selected a higher gear and accelerated towards the grid. Not looking behind him, he sprinted through the trees, until he came to a sharp incline and pushed forward on all fours, his lungs gasping for air. Desperately grabbing the rocks and grass in front of him, he clawed himself up the hill, as he heard a door clanging and shouts behind him. On reaching the top of the incline, he dropped to his belly and looked over the edge, from where he had come.

Soldiers were running across the field, and entering the wood below him, shouting for him to stop. Ignoring their pleas, he crawled back from the edge and sprinted across flatter ground, before hitting a steep section again, forcing him to climb. Although gasping for breath, he kept going through the pain, desperate to get away from his pursuers. This time, he didn't stop at the top, but just kept going, forcing his legs forward. Seeing another rise in front of him, he headed for it, crashing through the brush, brambles clawing at his face, hoping that it would be the summit.

The soldiers behind him were shouting to each other, their shrill cries echoing around the wood, making their numbers seem greater than they were. David reached the top and stopped to catch his breath and look back down the slope.

He had made some ground on the chasers and turned and ran down the other side, searching the terrain in front of him. He headed northwards, off his course, intending to confuse them. The slope was steep with rocks scattered around and he had to take care of his footing, for fear of tripping over or breaking an ankle.

He reached the bottom of the hill, staggered through a bog and ascended once more. Taking a breath behind an old oak tree, his chest heaving hard, he listened again for the soldiers. They were much further away now, still shouting to each other, but he was now more concerned about cutoff forces lurking ahead of him. Taking another deep breath, he forced himself up the hill, trying to make life for them more difficult.

Eventually, he came to the edge of the wood and looked out in front of him. Below was a grassy, open field a few hundred metres across, before it hit a forestry block that seemed to go on for miles. There was no way round it, he had to break cover and get across. Descending the slope and jumping a barbed wire fence, he raced across the open ground, expecting to hear shouts any moment. He kept running, his thighs pumping like pistons and made it to other side, crashing into the thick forest. Pausing briefly and gasping for air he looked back the way he had come and was pleased to see nobody there. Taking out his compass and map, he quickly plotted his route.

He crashed through the pine trees, protecting his eyes with one hand, whilst looking where he was going. He made slow progress, but after an hour, he reached a fire break running east/west, and sitting on the edge, listened and checked for movement. All was still, and he stepped out into the ride and headed east, jogging at a steady pace. He felt dead tired and very alone. After covering a few kilometres along the fire break, he stopped and checking that no one was around, stepped back into the forestry block. Walking for several paces into the darkness, he leant his back against a pine, closed his eyes and fell into a deep sleep.

He woke in the late afternoon, his neck stiff and body numb. Moving to the edge of the forestry block, he retrieved his map and compass and tried to work out where he was. After a few minutes of contemplation, he decided that he was about twenty kilometres from the final RV, the place where the escape and evasion period transitioned to the interrogation phase.

He wasn't looking forward to it. During SAS selection, it had seemed that time had stood still and the hours filled with severe discomfort and dread. Clearing the dark thoughts from his mind, he peered out of his hiding place and stepped on to the fire break and headed east.

Darkness was approaching, but there was still some light and he knew he had to take the risk and keep moving, if he was to get to the RV on time. Following the fire break for another kilometre, until the end of the forestry block, he looked out across bleak, desolate moorland. He was at the western edge of the Sennybridge training area, a piece of real estate he knew well from his Sandhurst and Para days. He was hoping that his pursuers were not on the ball and still some kilometres behind him, as he climbed the rusting wire fence and set out across the barren landscape.

The going was tough, wet and undulating and the rabbit holes and tussock grass were a constant hazard to his ankles. Once or twice, he fell over in the dark and had to remonstrate with himself to stay focused. At around midnight, he heard a helicopter way off to the south and wondered if it was after him, or just supporting an exercise on the area. It started raining soon after and pulling up the collar on his greatcoat, he continued to press on, suffering in silence.

He trudged on into the night, shivering with the cold, until he stumbled upon a small metalled road, denoting the eastern edge of the training area. Sitting down under a sodden bush, he smiled to himself and breathed out hard. Looking carefully at his watch, he saw that it was just gone three and he knew that he had broken the back of the march. The point he was heading for was an old, disused pub called the 'Shepherd's Hut', several kilometres south of where he sat. It was a solid, stone walled structure, still with its roof on, which had stopped being a pub years before, but was a well-known feature to soldiers on the area.

Moving cautiously and parallel with the road, he covered the ground steadily and saw the outline of the building a few hours later. Parked nearby, he noticed an army Land Rover and a white civilian 4x4. He crept up stealthily to one of the windows of the building that was emitting some light through a hessian sheet, and listened through the glassless covering. He heard the static of a radio and two men talking quietly. Moving back to a position of cover in some gorse, a few hundred metres away, he wrapped the greatcoat tightly around him and watched the building.

Just before six, and before first light, he scanned the area directly around him and walked purposefully towards the old pub. All manner of thoughts were going through his head. His tiredness, his hunger, his sore feet, his past, but everything had come to this moment, as he trudged through the wet ferns and grass.

On reaching the structure, he paused and took a deep breath.

'This is it!' he murmured to himself, as he pushed aside the blanket, serving as a door and stepped inside.

'Morning Gentlemen!' he said cheerily. 'I'm David Lord.'

'Christ!' exclaimed one of the Paras, jerking in his seat by the radio table. 'You nearly gave me a heart attack!'

He smiled, pleased to have caught them off guard.

'I thought the lads had caught you yesterday,' grinned a corporal. 'There have been ghost sightings of you all night, but I suppose you must have slipped through the patrols.'

'Looks like it,' he replied, poker faced.

'Good effort anyway. Rest your feet and make yourself at home,' the soldier invited, pointing to a canvas backed chair, 'and Taffy here will get you a brew.'

'Cheers' he said, slumping into the seat and wrapping his sodden coat around him. It was slightly warmer in the building, out of the wind and rain, and he was grateful for the respite, however short.

Looking around, he saw a typical command post that he had seen a hundred times before. He was sat next to a foldable wooden table, up against the wall, and there were large maps of mid Wales in a frame, resting on top. He noticed red pins stuck in the map, probably to represent positive sightings of him, as well as blue pins dotted around. Two small strip lights, hanging from nails in the wall above, provided enough light to work to. On top of the table, were two dark green VHF radios, with headsets and speakers attached. There were also some log books lying open, with scribblings on the pages.

'Here you go' said the Paratrooper, handing him a steaming mug.

'Thanks' he replied, accepting the gift and taking a sip.

It was tea, heavily sweetened and at that moment, the best he had ever tasted. He was grateful for the warmth, transmitting from his throat and stomach into his body.

'Here, have a biscuit,' said the NCO, offering him the packet.

'Very good of you,' he replied, taking a few.

'Better tell the patrols to come in,' instructed the corporal to the other soldier. 'No point in them staying out there in the cold, when he's already made it.'

The Para picked up the headset and began speaking into the radio.

David heard the responses from the patrols out on the windswept moors, their disappointment clearly evident in their resigned voices. Taking another sip of tea, he closed his eyes for a moment, grateful for the hospitality shown.

'Better tell control as well, Taffy,' said the NCO, looking at him. 'They'll be pleased that they have a new guest arriving,' he grinned.

'Control' were the people running the exercise, David knew, and they would be leading the interrogation phase, commencing shortly. He shivered, the cold of the last few days catching up with him, or was it the thought of what was to come?

He wasn't sure.

After an hour, he heard a truck pull up outside, its tailgate banging down ominously.

'Time to go, Mr Lord.'

Standing up, he shuffled towards the door like a condemned man heading for the gallows. As he reached it, he turned and smiled at the two Paratroopers.

'Much obliged,' he said and before they could respond, stepped outside.

It was light now and he noticed the wind ruffling the damp grass in front of him.

Suddenly, figures in a blur of green on either side of the door grabbed his arms and pushed him roughly to the ground. He managed to get one arm free and elbowed a soldier viciously in the face, who staggered back grunting.

He felt a kick in the ribs and cried out, trying to stand, before another pair of arms held him and pushed him back into the wet grass.

'Calm down sunshine!' one of the soldiers shouted and he felt his arms being pulled behind him, as his head was pushed into the mud. He felt liquid rush into his nostrils and desperately moved his head and snorted to clear the airway. Someone pulled plasticuffs onto his wrists and he was aware of several pairs of boots close to his face.

'Bastard!' shouted one of the men, and he felt a sharp kick in his side.

Then another one, followed by another.

'That'll teach you to hit my mate!' snarled a voice close to him.

A sandbag was produced and placed over his head, as a savage punch hit him in the side of the face. He tasted blood in his mouth and closed his eyes, fearing being hit again.

There was a pause and he tensed his body. A sharp blow to the kidneys, on his right side, made him grunt and then another blow struck him on the other side. Someone grabbed his head and pushed it into the ground and he felt his nose bend to the side and start to bleed.

'That's enough!' shouted the NCO. 'Get him on the truck.'

He was lifted up and dragged to the vehicle, with shouts from his perpetrators ringing in his ears. Hauled up, he was made to lie on the floor, whilst heavy boots were placed on top of him. He heard more shouting and the truck lurched forward, as it tried to gain purchase on the sodden grass. Soon after, it turned on to a firmer surface and accelerated away.

Chapter Twelve

David's head rested on the floor and the rhythmic movement of the truck helped to make him doze off. After about an hour and all too briefly, the vehicle slowed and made a turn, banging his head against the side. It pulled to a stop and after the tailgate had slammed down, he was dragged off, landing in a heap on the hard, stony ground.

'Pick him up!' someone shouted, and he was escorted into a building.

They walked along a corridor, made a left and came into a brightly lit room, the footsteps crunching on stones. White noise was playing and would be for the days to come. His face was pushed against a wall, causing his nose to bleed again and his feet were pulled back, wide apart. His hands, still tied, were sore from the cuffs and he wiggled them slowly to improve the circulation. Someone came up behind him and punched him savagely in the kidneys, causing him to groan softly.

And then it went quiet.

Some time later, he wasn't sure how long, he was grabbed by the arms and forced out of the room, along a corridor and into another room. He could see some light through the sandbag, still on his head, as he was forced into a chair.

The bag was pulled roughly off and his eyes blinked rapidly, trying to deal with the harsh light. Sat behind a desk in front of him, was a man in civilian clothes of about forty, smiling broadly.

He had a balding head, weathered cheeks and a neatly trimmed beard. His jumper, a heavy affair, with rows of reindeer and snowflakes on it, looked cosy and warm and he felt envious.

'Welcome' said the man softly. 'I thought we'd have a little chat.'

He looked at him impassively.

'You see, you've now been captured and I have some questions for you,' he said in a calm, measured tone.

The man paused.

'So, a good place to start, is for you to give me your name, rank, date of birth and number?' he asked, reaching for a pad and pencil.

'David Lord, Mr, 2/6/79,' he replied, unable to give a number, as he was no longer serving.

'Very good!' replied the questioner, slowly. 'And your unit?'

'I'm sorry, I can't answer that question, sir,' he replied, giving the response he had been trained to give when he was at Hereford.

'Oh, come now,' said the questioner. 'Surely you can give me your unit? It's only a little question.'

The same response was uttered.

'Very well' smiled the man. 'Let's start with something easy then, shall we?'

David looked back at him, eyes unblinking.

'Show me the route you took, to get to the final RV' he asked, pulling a map towards him.

Not receiving the response he wanted, the man tilted his head.

'It's no great secret. We've been tracking you for days and pretty much know the route already'. He paused and stood up, bringing the map towards him. 'So, if you could fill in the blanks, I'd much appreciate it.'

He gave the same response as before.

The man grunted and returned to his seat, shaking his head.

'This is very unfortunate, particularly as I'm being nice to you. Let's just clear up these questions and you can have some food and rest a while. How does that sound?'

The questioner tried a few more times to get him to answer some questions, but knew that he was wasting his time. It was early days and they had heaps of time to pull back the veneer that was David Lord. He told the guard, standing behind, to take him back to the 'holding area' and sat down and began scribbling on his pad.

He was yanked out of the chair, the sand bag replaced and was dragged along the corridor, back to his cell.

This time, they cut his ties, made him adopt a stress position against the wall and kicked apart his legs until they were satisfied. It was good to get out of the cuffs, but the posture caused his arms and legs to ache.

Closing his eyes, he endured.

The clock in his brain ticked on. Later, he heard footsteps on the stones behind him and tensed his body in anticipation, his face in a grimace under the blindfold.

Nothing happened.

The steps retreated and he breathed out in relief. It happened again a little later. This time, when he relaxed, he felt a sharp punch in the side and he let out a gasp in surprise. He relaxed his position against the wall and received another punch, this time in the other side.

In the early afternoon, he was marched to another room by his thumbs and forced to sit. The blindfold was removed and he saw some bread and a plastic cup on the desk.

'Eat!' shouted a voice behind him.

He lunged at the bread and forced it into his mouth as fast as he could. Next, he picked up the cup and swallowed the water, not wasting a drop.

....

A few hours later, he was dragged into a different room and made to sit. The blindfold was removed and sitting in front of him was a woman of about thirty, staring hard at him. She was plain looking, with chestnut brown hair, cut to shoulder length with a harsh, unsmiling face. Her flat chest was hidden behind a plain navy sweatshirt and she wore no makeup.

She stood up and walked behind him, taking her time.

'Enjoy your food?' she asked, walking back in front of him.

'I'm sorry, I can't answer that question, sir,' he replied, looking at her.

She peered at him, as a Doctor would, when confronted with a difficult diagnosis.

'I said, did you enjoy your food?' she repeated, louder this time.

David gave the same response.

'Why won't you fucking answer me?' she shouted.

He looked at her, without blinking.

'OK, let's try another one' she snarled. 'What's your unit?'

He paused, looked at the floor and gave her the eight words she didn't want to hear.

'What's your fucking unit?' she screamed.

'I'm sorry, I can't answer that question, sir.'

'Where were you born?' she asked, before he could finish.

He gave the same response.

This went on for a while longer. She had kept asking questions, before he could finish his stock response, as if she was trying to catch him out in some way. She had asked about his route, who had helped him, how he had survived, how he had navigated, whether he had served in the military and so on. She had also asked him about his sexuality, his first kiss, his first sexual encounter and a range of other personal questions. Each time, he had responded in the same way, which had infuriated her more. He had seen her face redden and eyes harden, as the session continued.

Eventually, she took a deep breath, stared at him and spoke plainly.

'You're not going to answer my questions are you?'

Standing up, she had shouted 'Strip him!' to the two men standing behind.

They had pulled him out of the chair, kicking it away and unbuttoned his shirt, throwing it to the floor. Next, they had removed the rest of his clothes, throwing them aside. He stood before her, naked, staring straight ahead. The woman looked him up and down for a minute or so, smirked and pointed down at his groin.

'What are you going to do with that?' she laughed. 'No wonder you look unhappy. I've seen bigger dicks on a hamster!'

David looked straight ahead, unmoved.

'Your girlfriends must be really disappointed, when they see that!' she joked.

He stared at the wall behind her, wondering what she would be like in bed.

Would she be all aggressive as she was now, or would she turn into a pussy cat, wanting to be dominated? he thought.

Seeing his attention wander, she shouted at him, her spittle hitting his face.

'Well? Are they disappointed?'

She glared at him, but noticing the scar on his arm, ran her finger lightly over it.

'Ouch! Where did you get that?'

After receiving the same reply, she shouted at the guards.

'Agh, this idiot needs more time in the cells to get his thinking straight' she said in frustration. 'Take him away!'

....

Time moved on and despite leaning against a wall, he nodded off into a shallow sleep. He desperately tried to stay awake, but his exhaustion from running over hills and moors and not eating enough, overtook him. Occasionally, he would jerk awake and wonder where he was, before submitting to the embrace of sleep again. A few times, the guards came over to him and roughly shook him awake, but if his head was upright, they left him alone.

In the early hours, they came for him again and dragged him to a room, where he smelt recently cooked food as he entered. Forced into a chair, the bag was taken off his head. Sitting at the desk, was the man from the previous day, smiling the same smile. In front of him, was a plate piled high with food, the steam rising temptingly from it. To the right, was a white mug, with what looked like tea inside.

'Hello David' said the man cheerily. 'I thought we might have another chat.'

He looked at him, as he had the time before. Impassive, unconcerned and unflinching.

'Yes, I know that you weren't very talkative the last time, but now that you've rested, I thought we could try again. I've arranged some food for you. Steak and kidney pie, roast potatoes, carrots, cabbage and thick gravy. There's also a nice cup of piping hot tea' he said, pointing to his left.

He could almost taste the food from where he sat and although he wanted to, he didn't look at it again.

'Of course', continued the man, 'in return for my generosity, I would hope that you can give me some small pieces of information. Now, how does that sound?'

'I'm sorry, I can't answer that question, sir.'

'So, let's start' the man began gently. 'What is your unit?'

He received the same response.

'OK, where did you go to school then?'

He looked ahead, smelling the food, but wishing to be back in the cell.

The man asked a few more questions, receiving the same reply each time. Bending over the food, he inhaled deeply.

'Mm, that smells good. C'mon, enough is enough. You know you want it, so just answer these few questions and you can tuck in!'

He looked at the man and remained silent.

'So you're not going to answer me?'

The man nodded to the guards and they grabbed his arms, pulled him out of the chair and marched him back to the cell. He could still smell the pie in his nostrils and he closed his eyes with the thought.

....

Seven thousand kilometres away, in a small settlement just outside the district centre of Musa Qala in Afghanistan, a more severe interrogation was taking place.

A young British soldier, from the Yorkshire Regiment, had been separated from his section, whilst patrolling near the Kajaki dam at night.

Lost, disoriented and dehydrated, he had stumbled into an isolated compound, in the early hours, some miles from the dam. He was hoping to find sanctuary and the surprised farmer there had given him water, some unleavened bread and shown him a carpet to rest on in one of the outbuildings.

Hours later, when he was still dozing in the midday heat, an old pickup had pulled up and three Taliban fighters had stepped into the compound. They overwhelmed the dazed soldier and hauled him into their vehicle.

Driving across the rocky plain, towards the district centre, they had stopped in the isolated settlement, where he was now, to deal with their prize. The Yorkshireman had been bundled into a room at the dwelling and been searched, stripped and beaten severely.

'What do you want from me?' he had screamed, in between the blows.

The men had merely shouted at him, in a language he didn't understand and continued to hit him with their rifles. After the beating, the soldier's weapon and equipment were taken from him and his uniform returned, but his boots and socks had disappeared. Nursing his wounds in the dark cramped room, as best he could, he found bruising around his stomach, cuts on his legs, a swelling to his eye and counted two broken ribs.

For some reason, he thought that he might be let go, but his wishes were short-lived, when the fighters returned later to beat him again.

After they had hit him with their weapons and stripped him to his shorts, they had dragged him into the courtyard and pegged him out in the sun, using coarse rope and metal stakes. The heat was unbearable on his body and he could feel his skin redden and begin to blister.

After an hour, the men had untied him and forced him back to his room, shouting angrily as they did so. The soldier was forced on to his front and the breath knocked out of him, when a fighter sat heavily on his back, pinning him to the floor. Next, his legs were pulled ramrod straight and he heard the men talking quietly behind him.

Suddenly, the soldier felt intense pain, as an Achilles tendon was cut, followed shortly afterwards by the other. The pain was unbearable and the man sobbed in agony, as blood pooled around his feet.

After a time, the Afghan sitting on him got up and spat on the prostrate figure. The three had left shortly afterwards, chatting to each other, as they bolted the door and went outside.

When it was quiet, the soldier tried to stand up and move forward, but fell to the floor, as his tendons refused to take the load.

Sometime later, as he sobbed on the ground, his ears picked up the unmistakable sound of a helicopter, way off in the distance.

'At last!' he had muttered, thinking that he was saved.

Pushing himself off the floor and crawling to the door, he hoped to get outside and attract the pilot's attention.

The soldier put all his weight against the wooden obstacle, but couldn't shift it, only causing himself more pain, by aggravating the tendons. The chopper, on reconnaissance around the area, flew on towards the hills, oblivious to the anguish below. The soldier had sobbed, stronger than ever before and knew that the sand, slipping through his personal hourglass, had little left to fall.

Later, the men had returned to his room and roughly dragged him, out into the sunlight. They beat him with their rifles and the soldier had pleaded for them to stop, asking what they wanted. Not understanding the Englishman, they merely sneered and kicked him repeatedly. They undressed him, leaving only shorts and pegged him out, face down once more. It was later in the day now, but the intensity of the sun was still strong and the soldier cried quietly in pain, as his skin slowly burned.

His mouth was parched and tongue swollen from the lack of moisture and he began to feel delirious. Mumbling for help, he heard only the wind, blowing gently across the sand. Eventually, the sun dipped below the compound wall and the soldier began to cry again. He had never been in so much pain, or seen such darkness and he longed for it to be over.

During the night, while his head rested on the ground, he thought back to Otley, his home town and the girl waiting for him. He cursed himself, not for joining the army, which had been the best years of his life, but in coming to Afghanistan, a land that seemed stuck in the Middle Ages.

He had sniggered with the rest of his platoon, when they had seen their first faded blue burka in Lashkar Gah, all those months ago.

At the time, it felt like they had stumbled on to a film set, for some biblical 'B' movie. Those days were ancient history now, as he suffered in the muggy heat.

Suddenly, despite his weariness, he felt something moving on his back. Not sure what it was, he convulsed his body as best he could, trying to rid the creature. Without warning, he felt tremendous pain and shrieked, as whatever it was had bitten him and slid to the floor. The man, too exhausted to cry out, merely sobbed, his eyes desiccated from the lack of water.

The young soldier would not see dawn.

....

David sensed the arrival of morning and wondered what the day would hold. During the early hours, when he had drifted off, he had been pulled from the wall, forced to the ground and punched in the face, near to his eye. A few hours later, as he was thinking back to his time in Zambia, he heard footsteps crunching on the stones behind him and braced himself for a punch.

None came.

Instead, he gasped in shock as cold water was thrown at him with force, hitting him in the shoulders. Then, another bucketful was thrown, this time at his head, soaking the sand bag, which clung to his face. Then more water hit him, this time in the lower back, drenching his buttocks. He started to shiver and tried to control it, but after a few minutes, knew it was pointless. His clothes were soaked and there was a damp patch around his feet.

He stayed in that position for another hour, before being hauled along the corridors and into one of the rooms. This time, two men were sat behind a desk, eyeing him with interest. The man on the left was in his forties, he guessed, with black hair and a kind face. His colleague on the other hand, was younger, in his thirties with a shaven head and cruel smile.

The older man spoke first in a calm, deliberate voice.

'How are you feeling?'

He looked at him, unblinking and spoke.

'I'm sorry, I can't answer that question, sir.'

'Fair enough. I was only asking how you were, as I'm worried about you. All those days on the run and now being stuck in here. I want to help you and all this can stop, if you answer a few questions, that's all.'

He looked at him, still wet and cold, his face set in stone.

'So, we have a few questions for you, if that's OK?' the older man asked.

He gave the response that he could say in his sleep.

'Come now. All this can be over, if you just answer some simple questions. We can give you some hot food, warm clothes and let you sleep a while. All of that, for just giving us some simple information.'

He let the words hang in the air, allowing his captive to think about each of the offered items. Craving all, he knew he had to resist.

He gave the same reply.

On hearing his response, the man looked at him sadly and slowly shook his head.

Meanwhile, the younger of the two had stood up and walked to his side.

'What the fuck do you mean, you can't answer the question?' he shouted, spitting in his face. 'Things are going to get a lot tougher, if you don't start cooperating' he sneered.

He looked straight ahead, arms by his side.

'Come on, David. I'm trying to help you' said the older man. 'Tell us where you were born, eh?'

As he was giving his standard answer, the younger man moved closer, next to his ear, almost touching.

'Get a grip of yourself!' he shouted. 'You're a ridiculous piece of shit. How dare you refuse our questions!'

He could smell the man's stale breath and resisted the urge to knock him out. Instead, he looked at the plain wall in front.

'Tell me what you need and I'll get it for you,' offered the older man gently.

His stock answer provoked the younger man into a rage and he started shouting into David's face, covering him in more spittle, and asking questions, one after the other in quick succession.

This went on for another hour. The older man remaining calm and reasonable, whilst his colleague flew into rage after rage, every time he refused to answer.

Finally, the younger man screamed at the guards to take him away and he was marched out of the room by his thumbs.

His clothes were still damp and he began to shiver again. Tensing his muscles continuously, he tried to get some heat back into his body and it worked for a while, before he became cold again and began to shake. He tried to keep his mind away from his discomfort, with thoughts of happier times.

Whilst he was thinking of Sandra and the smell of her skin, he was pulled from the wall, forced to sit in a chair and cuffs were put on his wrists.

'We've brought you some company!' a voice said quietly behind him.

He felt his collar being pulled back and then the sensation of something, lots of things, being dropped down his back.

Christ! What now? he thought to himself, as what felt like worms, hundreds of them, began moving around, inside his shirt.

After a while, they seemed to settle, although the weight of the creatures pressed against his skin. Strangely, after more time had passed, they began to warm him.

'Take any plusses you can from negative situations,' his Platoon Sergeant in the Paras, and ex SAS, had told him before he had attempted selection years before.

Later, when the worms had been removed, and he was sat in front of the plain looking female interrogator from before, he thought back to his time on the moors, getting soaked and buffeted by the wind. At least now he was indoors.

'So, let's start again! Now that you've rested, we can go over the route you took over the hills. We know you were dropped off somewhere near here' she said, pointing to a place on the map, 'and we know you were spotted here' she said, indicating the hamlet from a few days before. 'You do confirm those locations, don't you?'

'I'm sorry, I can't answer that question, sir,' he replied.

'It wasn't a request, you idiot. I'm asking you to confirm places that you know!' she screamed.

He answered.

'What do you mean, you can't answer the question!' she shouted. 'You were at those locations, so you must bloody well remember!'

She walked around the table and brought her mouth to his ear.

'Tell me!' she shouted.

He could smell the coffee on her breath and wondered if she was SIS or army.

'Definitely army,' he decided.

Her manner was too rough for a spook and her language and demeanour hinted of stunted education.

'Military Intelligence,' he guessed.

'What route did you take over the hills?' she pressed, hurriedly.

Same response.

'I asked what route you took?' she screamed.

Knowing that his answer wasn't going to please her, he delayed his reply and looked straight at her.

'Well?' she asked.

'I'm sorry, I can't answer that question, sir.'

'Fucking tell me!' she shouted. 'Or you're going to suffer.'

He looked blankly at her again and kept his nerve.

She spent the next hour, shouting and screaming at him. As he would start to deliver the same response, she would interrupt and ask another question, not related to the first. Eventually, she tired of him and told the guards to take him away. As he was leaving, he heard her breathe out heavily and imagined her shaking her head in despair.

....

On the final morning, he was bustled to one of the rooms and after his hood was removed, saw the man who had questioned him on the first day, sitting with some papers in front of him.

'How are you feeling?' he asked gently.

David gave the only words he had used in two days and the man smiled at him, nodding his head, seemingly unoffended.

'Now, we have some papers here, that I'd like you to sign. They detail the personal effects we took off you, when you came here and also allow access to the Red Cross.'

Without looking at the papers, he remained silent.

'I'm just asking you to confirm what we have taken from you, for safe keeping. More importantly, signing the Red Cross form will make life better for you' he said.

He gave his standard response once more.

'So be it. Another twenty four hours in the cells and you may regret not signing.'

The questioner asked a few more general questions, but realised that he wasn't going to break and so he told the guards to remove him. He was desperately tired now, not having slept for a few days. His face still ached from the punch, his limbs sore from covering miles over unrelenting ground and his belly growled with hunger. He was at his lowest ebb, but he knew he had to remain strong.

For the next few hours, he leant against the wall, barely awake but his mind still active. Eventually, he heard the stones crunch behind him and felt his arms being pinned behind his back, as he was marched to one of the rooms. Forced to sit, his blindfold was pulled from his face. Standing there was an older man, with hair the colour of snow, wearing a white armband.

'Hello David' he said. 'Do you recognise me?'

He focused his gaze on the man and said nothing.

'Do you remember, when we briefed you on the exercise and told you that it had ended, when I stood before you with a white armband on? Well, that time has come. The exercise is over!' he smiled benignly.

He looked at the man in disbelief. His captors had beaten him, starved him and tried to trick him over the last few days and now it was over!

'Thank God!' he murmured.

'What time do you think it is?' asked the man.

He gathered his thoughts and tried to concentrate. His mind was full of incidents from his days in captivity and because his watch had been taken and hadn't been outside, it had been difficult to work out how long he had been there. He made some quick calculations.

'Midday.'

'Very good!' said the man. 'It's actually two in the afternoon, but you're close enough.'

Smiling openly for the first time in days, his facade finally allowed to come down, he slumped in the chair, closing his eyes.

'Now, go and get yourself a shower and put on some clean clothes and afterwards, we've got some piping hot food for you. After that, we'll do a debrief. The guards will show you where to go.'

....

That evening, as he lay in the bath back in London, David closed his eyes and went through in his mind the experiences of the previous week. Holding a bag of frozen peas against his sore eye, he wondered how long the mark would last. He felt weak physically, but his mind was strong and he knew from that moment on, that he was a tougher person. As he was reaching for the beer bottle by the side of the bath, his phone rang on the chair.

Stepping out, he picked it up and answered.

'Hello James.'

'David, how are you?'

'Oh, a little tired and beat up, but nothing a few days in a cushy office won't solve!'

'Good! I just wanted to check you were alright that's all.'

'Yeah, I'm fine.'

'By the way, I've just received the initial report on your performance over the week.'

'How did I do?'

'Very well. It says here that 'David Lord remained secure during interrogation'. I knew that you'd be strong.'

'Nice to know I've still got it.'

'Exactly. Rest up and I'll see you in the office.'

'Thanks for calling' he replied, disconnecting the call and stepping back into the warm embrace of the tub.

....

David got to his desk early on the Monday and spent the first hour going through emails from the week he had been away. He was pleased to see that his assignments were on track and clients seemed to be happy. Taking a sip of his piping hot coffee, he smiled at the week he had just had.

He heard footsteps in the corridor.

'Christ! Looks like you've gone a few rounds with Mike Tyson' said James, peering at his face.

'It feels like it!'

'You'll recover. Anyway, got to dash, as I've got a client coming in, but how about lunch today? You can tell me all about it!'

'That's very good of you.'

He returned to his emails and began to review the CVs that Suzie had prepared for a client in Madrid.

'Not bad' he said to himself and nodding his head, as he read through the pages.

Later, he heard colleagues coming in to the office, laughing and joking, as they prepared for the day. There was a tap on his door and looking up, he saw his favourite colleague standing there smiling.

'Hello Penny' he said coyly.

'Hello stranger' she replied. 'How's the relative?'

'Oh, not so bad' he said, remembering his cover story.

She walked in, up to his desk and looked at his black eye.

'Ouch, that looks painful' she noted, touching it gently.

'You should see the other guy! I got it during boxing training.'

'You men' she smiled. 'Always fighting!'

He nodded, knowing she was right.

'I could be your nurse?' she said cheekily, placing her hands on hips.

'Now there's a thought!' he chuckled, as an image of her in a nurse outfit appeared in his mind.

She play slapped him on the chin, in mock offence.

'Fancy a drink later?' he asked.

'That would be lovely.' She brought her lips close to his ear and whispered, 'I've missed you' before sashaying slowly out of his office.

Chapter Thirteen

Qatar

Walking down the access stairs from the plane, David could feel the heat pressing in on him. It was a July evening in Doha, 9pm, and the temperature was still well over thirty degrees. During the BA flight, he had managed to watch two films, make a dent in the history book he was reading, grab a quick nap and polish off a passable meal of chicken and rice. Never drinking alcohol on planes, he always wanted a clear head if anything ever went wrong.

Leaving the customs hall, he headed for a currency exchange booth and changed some sterling into Qatari riyals. The taxi queue was short and he was glad he had just brought a small grip bag, allowing him to make a speedy exit from the airport. A dark skinned Indian driver, standing by his light blue cab, beckoned him over and placed his bag in the boot.

'Where to, sir?' he asked politely.

'Hotel Oasis please.'

They headed off north towards the city and after a short journey, arrived in front of a modern hotel. Formalities completed, he headed up to his room on the fourth floor, which turned out to be adequate for his needs, clean, comfortable and quiet.

He smiled as he glanced up at the ceiling and noticed the luminous arrow pointing towards Mecca.

Even in your hotel room, you can't get away from religion in this part of the world, he thought.

As he started to unpack, his phone began to ring. It was an assistor making contact.

'I'll be in front of the hotel, fifty metres to the right. 10.30pm OK for you?' the man asked.

'Fine. See you then.'

'I'm in a white Land Cruiser, plate ending 33. 10.30pm, then.'

He had a quick shower and changed into chinos and a polo shirt. Whilst he was waiting, he turned on the TV to watch CNN.

Apart from the usual death and destruction around the world, a bombing in Mogadishu, a stabbing in Jerusalem, and an honour killing in Pakistan, he was interested to see a piece on whale sharks in the Arabian Sea. Apparently, once a year, there was a gathering of the mighty fish out in the middle of the Gulf and scientists were trying to work out why they were there. An overhead shot showed the magnificence of the scene, as there must have been thirty to forty sharks congregating.

Checking his watch, he realised it was time to go and, turning out the lights, headed downstairs. He spotted the car immediately, with its engine running. Tapping on the window, he saw the assistor gesture for him to get in.

'Good to meet you, Pete,' he said, shaking the man's hand.

'You too. Good flight?'

'Yep, good thanks,'

'We're just going to a place round the corner, five minutes max.'

They pulled away from the kerb and joined the other cars.

Once they had their drinks and were sitting in a quiet corner of the bar, David turned to the man.

'What's this place then?'

The bar, called the 'Crazy Horse!' was on the seventh floor of a hotel, similar in look to his own. On entering, there was a small dance floor to the right, a large bar in front, and seating and tables along the wall to the left. It was about half full he guessed, with a mixture of Western and Asian men and what he assumed to be hookers from a range of countries wandering around, judging by their tight fitting dresses and heavily made up faces. Stale smoke hung in the air like dead clouds and pop music played out from speakers dotted around the room.

'Ah, I've brought you to one of the best bars in Doha,' Pete explained. 'The Qataris and Saudis use the place at the weekends. They like it because there's no CCTV, so they can bring their girlfriends, boyfriends, whatever here and no one's the wiser. Good for us as well, as it's very discreet.'

He nodded, surveying the scene further.

Even though this was just a recce, it was good that they would not be seen together on camera. If he came back to carry out the sanction, they would have to be careful when moving around the city.

'So, what's the plan?' he asked, after they had both taken a few sips.

'Up to you mate, I'm here to help you out. I can take you around the city, show you some possible kill sites for the future and talk you through an exit plan, just in case you ever need it,' he replied, smiling.

'Thanks. It'll be useful to get a feel for the place, so that I know my whereabouts if I come back.'

'Oh, you'll be back, I can guarantee it!' replied Pete, grinning. 'They don't send guys out on recces for no reason. No, we'll be seeing each other again, I'm sure of it.'

Checking he was out of earshot, David leaned over.

'I probably shouldn't ask, but do you know who the sanction could be?'

'No, you shouldn't ask. In this game, you'll get the information you need, when you need it. But since you did ask, the answer is 'No'. I don't know who it is, but I've a fair idea. In this country, there are a lot of people with too much money and too much time on their hands. There's cash, millions of dollars' worth, flowing out of this country every year, to jihadist groups around the globe. This is a strange country. There's even talk of them allowing the Taliban to set up an office here for fuck's sake, so there could be a slack handful of targets!'

'Interesting' said David thoughtfully. 'Anyway, I have a few meetings tomorrow morning, so let's drive around in the afternoon and use the day after to discuss what's needed?'

'Sounds good. I'll be giving you quite a bit of information in the car, so by the time you leave, you should have the measure of this place.'

'Appreciate it.'

After he had bought another round, the conversation switched to lighter matters and from their conversation, he made the assumption that Pete was ex Royal Marines and had lived in the region for several years.

'Can't tell you where, but let's just say I've got a flat that overlooks the sea and where I can pursue my passions of scuba diving and distance running.'

David imagined Dubai, but it could have been any one of the countries that bordered the Arabian Sea.

'And you must be from some fancy unit, Pathfinders, SAS?' he asked, but then stopped himself. 'Sorry, I shouldn't have asked you that.'

'No worries. I did my time,' he replied, looking into his half empty glass.

....

Five thousand kilometres away in Frankfurt, the three men prepared themselves. The small flat they were renting on Kochstrasse, in the Muslim dominated Oberrad district of the city, had been transformed into a munitions factory. Over months, posing as engineering students in the famous university, they had accumulated bomb-making materials from unwitting suppliers in the city and surrounding areas of Hesse State.

Lying in the corner of the main room were the weapons that they would use, three AK-47s with magazines for each. On the table lay suicide vests for each man, heavy with the amount of ball bearings inside, painstakingly put together the week before.

Mohamed, the oldest of the group, stopped what he was doing and addressed his friends.

'Make sure that you're both ready to leave by midnight. I want to hit the club when it is at its fullest.'

The disco, right on the river and called H2O, was a popular evening hangout for the youth of the city and stayed open until dawn. The three had carried out a recce there a few weeks before and knew the layout of the interior by heart. It had been chosen because it was not only one of the most popular clubs in the city, but it also attracted a large number of Jewish kids, wanting to paint the town red.

'Sure,' replied Abdullah. 'Yasin and I will be ready, don't worry.'

Mohamed checked once more that the magazines were full.

A few nights before, they had all enjoyed an evening of blatant debauchery, which was permitted for 'shahid', or suicide bombers, prior to an attack. They had spent the night in the Bahnhofsviertel district, near to the city's main train station. It was a well-known red light area and perfect for their requirements. After visiting a number of bars, they had stumbled in to one of the brothels and sampled the services on offer. Mohamed knew that his friends were virgins, but after that night they were finally men. They had all slept through until lunchtime the following day, waking up with sore heads and realising from that moment on, there would be no more enjoyment in their lives.

A few hours later, they washed themselves and shaved off their body hair, making them ready for the afterlife.

Sitting quietly, they began reciting passages from the Koran to each other.

'....*And kill them wherever you find them, and turn them out from where they have turned you out....*' Mohamed uttered, recalling by heart his favourite passage from the holy book.

The younger men looked at him in adoration and began to chant, quieter at first and then louder.

'Allahu Akbar, Allahu Akbar, Allahu Akbar.......'

Mohamed smiled at them, knowing that his work was almost done.

'We leave in thirty minutes,' he instructed, glancing at his watch. 'Remember your training from Libya and make your final preparations. Let us make our brothers in Qatar, who have funded us for so long, proud of what we are about to do. Yasin, bring the van round to the front.'

The man nodded, stood up and walked out of the room.

Shortly before midnight the men, wearing their suicide vests, hugged each other for a final time and left the flat, Abdullah carrying a holdall with the weapons.

They drove the short distance to the club and parked in a side street nearby, the noise and thump from the venue clearly heard. Once the weapons were distributed, loaded and cocked, the leader set the timer on the car bomb.

He turned to his friends and smiled.

'We will meet again in Jannah, in paradise,' he whispered.

The two grinned back.

'For Allah,' were his final words.

The three checked their vests for the last time, took hold of their weapons and signalled to each other that they were ready. Stepping out of the vehicle, the men walked purposefully towards the club.

....

David slept well, apart from being woken in the early hours by the call to prayer from a nearby mosque. Once awake, he made himself some coffee and turned on the international news. He stood in horror, as grainy images of the Frankfurt attack were shown on the TV. The devastation to the club was clear to see.

A weary looking policeman appeared on screen with microphones waving in his face and he began to speak in German.

'…..so far, there are twenty seven confirmed deaths and over sixty injured, some seriously. We believe there were three attackers, who blew themselves up after firing their weapons. Most of the victims were inside the club, but a car bomb parked nearby also caused casualties to emergency workers treating the injured. No group has claimed responsibility so far, but we are working on a number of leads….'

'Animals!' he shouted at the screen. 'Fucking animals!'

He sat down and breathed out hard, not believing what he was seeing. Switching to another channel, he saw medics bringing out bodies, the green sheets pulled over the heads of the victims.

'This is why I'm here,' he snarled to himself. 'To make a difference.'

He watched further scenes, trying to gauge the scale of the attack, until he was sick of the images. Shaking his head, he knew he had to prepare for the day. Showering quickly and pulling on his suit, he tried to put the awful events out of his mind and spent the morning in a nearby hotel meeting candidates.

When he got back to his room, he changed into casual clothes and watched the news again.

The police in Frankfurt had raided a flat, the newsreader was saying and had arrested some people in the Oberrad district. A commentator was suggesting that the attack had been carried out by Islamic extremists and began to set out his thesis.

Keeping the TV on, he fired up his laptop and began searching articles on Qataris supporting jihadist groups. One or two names kept popping up and he wondered if one of them had financed the atrocity.

'Which one of you bastards will be in my sights in the coming months?' he whispered, studying the faces on screen.

Later, he met up with Pete.

'Did you see the attack in Frankfurt?' he asked, pulling on his seat belt.

'Yeah. Fucking horrendous.'

'Let's hope they catch the vermin behind it. Germany used to be a nice place.'

'You're right. I went to a stag night there once. Hell of a place.'

They drove on, Pete pointing out the main sights as they went. They had a good look at the West Bay district, the diplomatic area and a number of key neighbourhoods in the capital. Pete was particularly keen to show him some large houses north of West Bay.

'These are of interest,' he said.

'Where the financiers hang out?'

'Some of them,' he replied.

The next day, they drove an hour south of the capital, stopping at a resort on the coast. Whilst they were taking cold drinks by one of the pools, he turned to his companion.

'What's this then? Is this where I come to chill out after the hit?' he smirked.

'No, this is your exit route,' replied Pete. 'If things go bad, you have to make your way down here, about a mile south of this resort. Myself or another contact will collect you from the beach at night and take you by jet boat to Dubai. Once there, you'll get the first flight back to London.'

'I guess the airports and border crossing into Saudi would be closed once the shooting has taken place?'

'They would close the border for sure, and as you wouldn't have a Saudi visa, it's not a tenable route for you anyway. With regards to the airport, we believe that they would halt all departing flights for at least twelve hours, so you could be caught there, if you tried to leave too soon. There is one other possible route out and that's on the western side of the country.'

'Same drill, we would pick you up by boat and take you to Bahrain, where you would catch a plane out. The problem with that side is the Qataris have border posts and fast boats there, so you may not get away cleanly.'

'So after our drinks, you can show me the pickup point down the coast.'

'Sure, we'll do that and then skittle back to Doha, to show you a few more sites,' offered his friend.

Later, whilst nursing cappuccinos in a cafe, Pete spoke quietly as he started to discuss logistics.

'On the weapons front, I'll provide you with the gun. After the job, we'll meet at a prearranged spot, somewhere quiet, and I'll get rid of it for you. Probably into the sea,' he explained. 'If you're caught and they find it, you'll be done for murder. Forget any help from the British Embassy, they'll run a mile. Oh, and don't forget, Qatar still has the death penalty, so make it a clean kill, give me the gun and disappear!'

Pete emphasised his point by poking him in the chest.

'Ammunition. Whatever you specify, will come with the gun. Vehicles – I'll rent you something for the hit, which will be boring but will do the job. Just hand it back to me after the hit and I'll give it back to the agency. I'll clean it of prints, so don't worry about that.'

'Thanks.'

'You'll be wearing surgical gloves when you handle the weapon, so have a practice with them in the UK, before you come back out here. They give a different feel than flesh, so get used to them.'

'Got it.'

'The hotel you're staying in is fine I guess, but I would always recommend going somewhere else for your next visit. Not leaving tracks and all that.' Pete gave him a few names of other hotels near to his own. 'You'll need some dark, unassuming clothes to take the shot in. I suggest black jeans, a dark hooded sweatshirt and dark trainers. You'll be getting rid of them after the hit as well.'

They ran through other issues, with him asking many questions.

'So you leave tomorrow night?' Pete asked, as they were getting up. 'Give me a call if you want to meet up in the afternoon to discuss anything, otherwise I'll see you when you return.'

'Thanks, mate. Appreciate all your help,' he replied, shaking the man's hand.

The two left the cafe, with Pete heading back to his car and David to the hotel, his mind spinning.

Chapter Fourteen

England

It was early morning when David arrived back at Heathrow and London was yet to stir. He took a taxi home, not wanting to endure the tube and when he got to his flat, he dumped his bag and flopped onto bed for some much needed sleep.

He awoke five hours later when cars outside blared their horns, and reluctantly made his way to the bathroom to shower and change. Suitably refreshed, he ventured into the kitchen to see if there was anything in the fridge to eat, but found only a few cans of beer, some butter and a jar of gherkins. Instead, he made himself a black coffee and wandered into the living room, to catch up on the morning news.

Glancing at his watch, he thought it best to head into work. He could have spent the rest of the day at home working on his laptop, but he wanted to go into the office and see his colleagues and above all, James. The rush hour had passed and the tube to Piccadilly was fairly empty, apart from a few tourists and some business people heading across town.

Walking down the corridor, he passed Penny's office and saw that she was tapping away at her keyboard. He knocked on the door and she looked up in surprise.

'Hi David!' she called out. 'How was your trip?'

'Productive. Met some interesting candidates, which will hopefully be useful to James. Oh, and I got you these,' he said, handing her some dates in a fancy box.

'Err, thank you,' she responded unsurely.

'Good for the digestion,' he smiled.

'I'm sure my body will be grateful!'

'That's just a fun present. Here's the main one' he said, passing her a small shopping bag.

'Oh, wonderful,' she uttered gratefully this time, holding up a perfume box.

'The girl at the airport told me that this is what the rich Arab ladies wear, so I thought it would be perfect for someone of your financial status!'

She smiled at him, her look lingering for a while.

'Well, that's very kind. I shall enjoy trying it out,' she said. 'Now, one good turn deserves another.'

He raised his eyebrows.

'I have a client, who is looking for a CEO in France. You speak French don't you?'

'Ah oui, bien sûr.'

'Excellent! I'll brief you later, when you've had a chance to settle.'

Walking up to Suzie's desk, he placed a carrier bag in front of her.

'Wow! What's this?' she asked excitedly.

'Just a small gift from the desert!'

She opened the bag carefully and withdrew a box of chocolates and a small stuffed camel.

'That's to remind you of me, when I'm away!' he grinned. 'He's better behaved than I am.'

She began to blush and delicately tucked some hair behind her ear.

'Err, that's very kind, thank you. It shall have pride of place on my desk, just here,' she said, placing it on some books to her side.

'Pleasure, Suzie!'

He walked towards his office, thinking what the rest of the day would bring. Checking his emails to see if there was anything pressing, he saw that it was mainly routine stuff about assignments and candidate offers. He was copied in to an email exchange between Penny and Suzie, discussing an offer that a candidate, recently interviewed at one of the major banks, had received.

Pretty good offer, he thought to himself.

If the candidate accepted, Penny would be in line for a massive fee, which would take a nice bite out of her target. She deserved it. His musings were interrupted by the phone ringing.

James wanted to see him.

'Welcome back!' he said, getting up from behind his desk, shaking his hand and closing the door. 'So how was it?'

'Really good' he replied, settling into a chair. 'Had some useful sessions with the contact out there and had a great look around.'

'Good, good. Terrible business in Frankfurt,' he said. 'Funny that you were in Qatar when it happened. Early reports suggest that the operation was funded by someone there, so I think it highly likely you'll be going back. The target we particularly have in mind has been very busy with his money.'

He nodded slowly, some of the faces from his research flashing through his mind.

'Now, let's discuss the development of your skills. You've completed RTI, which is good, but you also need to complete the basic tradecraft modules. Lock picking, cryptography, surveillance and counter surveillance, that kind of stuff. You'll have covered some of this in the SAS, but we'll update and in some cases enhance, what you've previously learnt.'

'Sounds interesting.'

'There's quite a lot of ground to cover, so you'll need to give up every other weekend for the next few months, at least. Also, you'll need to spend a week covering some of the modules at our site on the south coast. You'll do a fair bit of weapons training down there as well.'

Just as well I don't have a social life, he thought.

'We'll need to come up with a reason why you're away again, but you might have to come up with an illness that takes you out of action. With the modules, we'll bring you up to a decent level before your first sanction, but for the next year or so, you'll be honing your skills, until you become one of our 'premium assets,' he explained. 'One final thing. I want you to join 'L' Detachment.'

His heart skipped a beat.

L Detachment was a reserve unit within 22 SAS, made up of ex regular soldiers from the Regiment.

'Now, I know that you had a bad time in Afghanistan and probably want to distance yourself from your old unit, but it makes sense to join. You'll be able to keep your military skills up to speed, particularly with weapons, but more importantly, you'll be able to go on operations for short periods, which will truly add to your value as an operator.'

'I had thought about it, but felt I needed to focus on carving out my two lives first, rather than adding complexity so soon,' he said defensively. 'And besides, with all the tradecraft training I'll be doing over the next few months, when would I fit it in?'

'Fair point. I understand that you're pretty busy at the moment, but I do want you to join them. Why don't you go and meet the OC down there, nice chap called Ben Caruthers and see what they get up to and discuss a joining date?'

'OK, I'll contact him,' he agreed.

'What, with service with 22 SAS as a Troop Commander and operational experience in Afghanistan and Iraq, they'll want you starting this week! That's all for now. I'll give you details of the training later in the week, but you should now concentrate back on to your headhunting duties,' he said with a smile.

He left James's office feeling enthused about the months to come, and spent the next hour reviewing some CVs that Suzie had given him for a CIO role in Madrid.

The client was SIB, the Spanish International Bank, who the firm had worked with for a few years, mostly on senior roles.

They paid good fees and were usually quick to make decisions on shortlists, candidates and offers, always good from a headhunter's point of view.

On top of the documents, she had placed a pink post-it note.

'Hope you like these David, they were a bugger to find!' and she had drawn a smiling face at the bottom, along with a few kisses.

The CVs were good, very good. He glanced through the job description, written by the company, just to check his familiarity with the role again and decided that the profiles were very much on target. He wasn't sure about one of the candidates though, as he was ten years older than the rest and his tenure in most jobs was typically no more than three years each time. He called her into his office, to discuss him and the other candidates.

'Great shortlist,' he began.

'Thanks David, we sweated blood to get some of those guys!'

'I'm sure,' he replied, glancing down at the first CV in his hand. 'The one that I don't quite get is Javier Lopez, though. The client is very ageist as you know and I'm wondering if they would take someone well over the age of his peer group?'

'Ah, I thought you might not like him! I know this candidate from a previous position we worked on and he was offered the role, but turned it down at the last minute. The client even offered him ten percent more salary, but he wouldn't budge. Talking to the client afterwards, Javier is an IT superstar by all accounts. What he doesn't know about technology and running a large IT Department, isn't worth knowing apparently.'

'So you think he'll move this time?'

'Yes, for the kind of salary that SIB is offering, I think he'll move' she said confidently.

'Fine, let's send all four candidates and your notes on each to the client later today, and hopefully we can start the interviews next week.'

'Thanks, I'll do that,' she replied, smiling at him.

As she was walking towards the door, she turned.

'Oh, some of us are going out for a drink after work, to the Lamb and Hare. I was wondering if you'd like to come?'

He considered the offer for a moment and grinned up at her.

'Sure, what time?'

'Err, 6.30?' she asked.

'Great, look forward to it!' he replied, turning back towards his laptop.

Her footsteps echoed down the corridor.

Christ! he suddenly thought.

The last thing he needed right now was for Suzie to get a crush on him. For a few weeks, he had noticed that her hemlines had been rising and she had been turning up for work with more makeup on than before. She was a nice girl, but just not his type. Concentrating back on his computer, he hoped that she was just being friendly.

Deep in this thoughts, he didn't hear the tap on his door. He was reading a recent online story by a *Telegraph* reporter about the funding of terrorism from Middle East donors.

The article claimed that hundreds of millions of dollars were flowing from rich Arabs in the Gulf to extreme jihadist groups across the world every year. The prime donors were from Saudi Arabia, Kuwait and Qatar and the recipients were those groups who subscribed to the hardline Salafist ideology of their paymasters. Bahrain had also been a centre for terrorist funding in the past, but that had wilted over recent years when the GDP of the small country had shrunk.

The tap on his door was louder this time and looking up sharply, he saw Penny standing there.

'You are focused today!' she joked, walking towards him.

He quickly changed his screen from the article to a CV he had been looking at earlier and tried not to look guilty.

'Ah, Penny! Is it time already?'

'Yes it is and we've got work to do!' she chided. 'That CEO role I was going to brief you about?'

He caught a whiff of her scent as she sat down close to him.

'You smell good!' he remarked, looking into her eyes.

'It's the perfume you bought me from Qatar. I like it,' and she held out her wrist for him to sniff.

He brought his head down to smell the scent, his nose just touching her skin.

'Not bad!' he agreed, raising his head.

'Good choice. You can go on other foreign trips, if you bring me such nice things back.'

He smiled.

'Now, this client, Sante Progressive, who I'm sure you have heard of, is a big multinational pharma company, with offices around the world. Their headquarters are in Paris, where they have over five thousand staff, but they also have quite a presence here. They develop and manufacture all kinds of drugs and they have made a name for themselves in recent years for developing those drugs faster than their competitors. They have done this by hiring the smartest people in the business and pushing them hard to deliver.'

She paused.

'You seem a little distracted?'

'No, no,' he protested. 'I've just got quite a lot going on in my head at the moment. Apologies, please continue.'

Looking at him seriously, she resumed.

'Now, we have worked with them for just over a year and they push us hard on every assignment. The candidates have to be perfect, we have to respond to them quickly and they demand that offers we make to candidates are accepted.'

'And on the plus side?' he asked, jokingly.

'Ah, the plus side,' she pondered, looking up at the ceiling. 'Oh, they pay great fees, thirty percent, and pay their bills quickly, so the money is always good. It's just…..'

'…a bloody nightmare every time,' he suggested.

'Something like that'. She paused thoughtfully. 'Anyway, I'm swamped at the moment and this assignment will do you good. You'll learn a lot and if you do well for them, they'll love you forever! I've placed a few people there in the last year, so I think they're happy with us. It's also good for them to see another face and not just work with me.'

'Makes sense.'

'They're looking for a new CEO. Apparently, the previous one, who left a few weeks ago, did so under a bit of a cloud. My guess is that he wasn't making the kind of profit they were expecting. He had only been there eighteen months, poor chap,' she reflected sadly. 'I heard he upset some of the senior folk there, which is a shame as he seemed to be navigating the company in the right direction. The problem with that industry, is that it takes so long to develop the drugs, ten years plus in most cases, that unless a CEO stays in place for some time, he or she is unlikely to see the fruits of their labours.'

'So,' he summarised, 'they're going to want a superstar, with a strong pharma background, a record of bringing in good profits, excellent leadership skills, to get the ship back on course and oh, be able to start in fairly quick time.'

'Yep, that's pretty much it', she confirmed. 'He or she, it's likely to be a 'he', as not many females make it to that level, will probably be in their early forties, have a scientific background, plus a strong sales mentality and have an MBA from one of the good schools.'

She paused, making sure he was taking it all in.

'They'll also be working for one of the main competitors. Sante Progressive won't be interested in candidates from smaller companies. They want to see people who have operated on the big stage and successfully.' Seeing his expression, she added, 'Don't worry. I'll hold your hand all of the way and vet the candidates before you send the shortlist. I'll be the figurehead for the assignment, but for all intents and purposes, you'll be running it.'

She then spent a further half hour talking about Sante Progressive and how it was structured. She explained the finances of the company and talked through some of the drugs it had developed in recent years.

'I know that the Chairman is coming to London in the next few days, so we'll go and meet him when he's here. Their office is on the South Bank.'

As she walked out, she patted him on the shoulder.

Chapter Fifteen

A few days later, early in the morning, David was standing outside the Sante Progressive offices, grasping a cup of steaming coffee and trying not to shiver from the cold. He looked up at the red brick structure, and for a moment his mind transported him back to the heat and dust of Zambia. He pictured himself lying in bed, early in the morning, Sandra's head resting gently on his chest.

All too soon, a beeping taxi snapped him back to the present.

He thought back to the evening spent with Suzie and some colleagues, and grinned.

They had gone straight from work to a quiet pub in Piccadilly, still fairly empty before the regulars arrived. They had selected a table set back from the bar and had chatted about work, their backgrounds and their plans for the future. To him, it was just a gentle little talk with colleagues after work, or so he thought. After several hours, when a few rounds had been drunk and the rest of the group had melted away, the mood changed as Suzie asked him if he had a girlfriend.

He had responded that he was too busy for anyone else in his life, as he was concentrating on his new career and trying to make that work. She had smiled and said that a good looking man like him could have the pick of the girls in London. He had smiled awkwardly and changed the subject, but he could tell by her look that she wanted to put herself forward for the role.

They had left the pub shortly afterwards, David saying that he had to prepare for the meeting, but not before she had kissed him on the lips and bid him goodnight.

His phone rang, snapping him out of his thoughts.

'Hi Penny. Are you nearly here?'

'Morning David. Apologies, but I'm on my way to the office. The Chairman just phoned me and postponed the meeting. Seems like they have a bit of a crisis in France, so he's staying there to deal with it. We'll have to meet him when he's next over.'

'Oh well, can't be helped,' he replied, disappointment in his voice.

'But as you're there, you might as well meet the HR Director, who is in town. Your journey wouldn't be wasted.'

'Sure, why not?'

'Her name is Jenny Pascoe and she's helped us a lot in the past. I'm sure you can use your charm to get some roles off her!'

'I'll do my best. Can you let her know I've arrived?'

'Will do and I'll call you back to confirm.'

'Thanks.'

'Oh, there is one thing that you should know. Jenny has a bit of a reputation for polished young men, so be on your guard!'

'I'll keep it in mind,' he replied, hanging up and smiling.

He wandered into the reception area and found himself a seat by the window, picked up a copy of *The Times* and scanned the headlines. An air crash in Colombia, a bombing in Baghdad, the oil price dropping again and a British politician caught having an affair with his secretary.

'Things never change' he murmured to himself.

His phone rang, and he answered it quickly.

'You're on. She's on floor twenty three and is looking forward to meeting you! You can tell me all about it, when you get back.'

He reached the level and was met by a pretty blonde girl in a tight fitting skirt. She introduced herself as Amie, informing him that she was Jenny's PA, as she smiled sweetly. They made their way through an open plan area and he grinned when he saw a sign written in large letters on one of the walls: 'An organisation's most important asset are its people'.

'Who writes this stuff?' he thought to himself, as he watched Amie's behind sway rhythmically from side to side.

As they neared a door in the corner marked 'Director of Human Resources', the girl leant over her desk, reached for something and handed him a business card.

'Just in case you need to reach me…..' she smiled suggestively, walking towards the door.

He grinned and pocketed the gift.

On entering the office, he saw a woman of about forty, with grey streaks in her shoulder length brown hair, look up from her laptop and smile broadly.

Jenny Pascoe was a good-looking woman, with an oval, slightly bronzed face. She carried a lot of makeup, but it was applied well, accentuating her features. She had on a cream blouse, buttoned just above her cleavage, a well cut blue skirt and light stockings. Standing in front of him, he was surprised how tall she was, not missing her slim figure.

After they had shaken hands and he had detected a whiff of expensive perfume, they took their seats.

'So, David' she asked, as he was sitting down. 'What do you know of Sante Progressive?'

He gave her some facts and figures that he had learnt the previous day. Turnover, profit margin, number of global offices, number of employees and some of their best selling products.

'I am impressed!' she said, clapping her hands quietly.

He smiled humbly and looked back at her.

'It's always nice to meet new Consultants' she confessed.

He shuffled slightly in his chair.

'So how is business?' he asked.

'Couldn't be better!' she beamed. 'We're leaders in many fields, our profit margins are strong and we have some of the best people around.'

'Excellent! So, as you know, we were due to meet the Chairman today, to discuss the new CEO position, but sadly he had to postpone.'

'Yes, it's unfortunate,' she smiled. 'But let's make your trip worthwhile.'

'That would be kind.'

'The CEO role is obviously the most important one right now, but I have three other positions that are giving me headaches.'

'Oh?'

'Yes, Regional Director for South America, Head of Finance for Sante Progressive Associates or 'SPA' for short and CMO for South East Asia region.'

'Senior roles,' he acknowledged. 'Why the problems?'

'Oh, it's a long story. What I want to know, is can your firm help me and do you have expertise in all those areas? Penny has found us some excellent people in the past, but they were mainly for Europe.'

'Yes, we can. The expertise in the firm is truly global. I can send over some examples of similar roles we have worked on, if you like?'

'That would be useful.'

She paused and glanced across at him.

'I have an idea.'

'Oh?'

'Why don't we meet up this evening for a drink? You can bring along your case studies and we can get to know each other a little better. See if we can work together.' She gave him an inscrutable look.

He realised the position he was in, but without giving it much thought, readily agreed.

'How about the American Bar at the Savoy, say seven o'clock?'

He knew it well. He had taken numerous girlfriends there, when he was trying to impress. It was discreet, away from London's limelight and often frequented by A-Listers, seeking privacy.

'I'll be there!' he replied, wondering what he had let himself in for.

'See you then.' Her tone hardened slightly as she said, 'My PA will see you out.'

....

'How did it go?' asked Penny, tapping on his door a little later.

He straightened in his chair and looked at her standing in the doorway, the sunlight shining through her hair.

'Oh, pretty good!' he replied. 'Looks like they'll give us some assignments to work on. Big roles too!'

'Very good, David,' she said slowly, studying him with interest. 'Must have been your charm and knowledge of the market.'

'Something like that,' he grinned.

She looked at him and when it was clear he was giving her no more information, turned and walked back to her office.

He considered his appointment with Jenny and wondered if he should cancel. But she would be disappointed and likely not give him the assignments she had promised. And then he'd be disappointing Penny.

He smiled to himself. Sod it. If the risk is little, the reward is little, he thought to himself.

Just after seven, David found Jenny sitting at a corner table in the American Bar. As he walked towards her, he noticed that she had changed into a low cut cocktail dress and her hair seemed wavier than earlier. As he pecked her on the cheek, she smelt as if she had just stepped out of the shower, his nostrils bombarded with scent.

'Hello,' he said casually, taking a seat opposite her.

She eyed him cautiously, before replying.

'Hello David. How was the rest of your day?'

'Been busy pulling together the case studies for you,' he replied, holding up a thin, buff folder.

'We can deal with that later,' she said, taking the file and smiling at him seductively. 'Now, I'm having a gin and tonic. Care to join me, or would you like something else?' she asked, raising her arm to get the barman's attention.

'I'll have the same. Thanks.'

She nodded and gave the barman the order.

'So,' she began, settling in to her seat. 'We had such little time today and it would be nice to get to know you. Penny tells me you were in the army?'

'Yeah, that's right. I served as an officer for six years, mainly with the Parachute Regiment.'

'Impressive! You must have seen some interesting things and been to exotic places?'

'Yes, I saw a few things,' he replied 'and travelled around a bit. Afghanistan, Kosovo, Iraq, Kuwait. You know, the sort of places that tourists don't tend to visit!'

'Mm, you're right. None of those are on my holiday list.'

'Where would you go?'

'Oh, south of France, Greece, Maldives, Goa. You know, five star luxury, with a chilled glass of wine no more than a reach away!'

'Sounds good! I don't mind a bit of luxury, but I would always like to spend my leave climbing mountains, trekking over deserts or diving with sharks.'

He suddenly realised that she might think he was showing off, so finished speaking by talking of the reality.

'But often, a friend would be moving house, so I'd end up humping boxes or emulsioning the walls.'

She laughed and tilted her head back, so that her gaze lifted to the ceiling. He noticed a string of small pearls for the first time.

'Beautiful necklace,' he offered.

'Oh, thank you,' she replied, demurely. 'They were a gift from my husband on our tenth wedding anniversary.'

'Very nice.'

He had noticed her wedding ring earlier in the day and wondered if she was still married and if so, what her husband was like.

'He's away at the moment, in New York.'

'So, is it common for you to meet strange men in London bars when your husband is away?' he asked, looking into her eyes and smirking.

'Only those I fancy!' she replied unashamedly.

He nearly choked on his drink, which was at his lips, but he quelled the urge and placed the glass back on the table.

Fetching some more drinks to give him time to think, he returned to the table with her looking up at him.

They talked more about their lives for another hour, the pros and cons of working in London and trips of a lifetime they each wanted to take.

The bar had filled up a little and there was a greater hum in the room from the many conversations. Jenny seemed to want to find the perfect beach as her aspiration and seemed impressed when he talked about wanting to spend time with remote tribes in Africa, as his.

After a pause, she reached over and gently ran her finger down his chiselled jaw.

'There's something I want to show you,' she said, finishing her drink and looking across the table.

'Oh?'

'Yes, it's in my room. I'm staying in town tonight.'

'Err, OK,' he mumbled, feeling like a fly caught in a spider's web.

Part of him felt concerned where this was headed and the other part was exhilarated, excited and alive.

She stood up and told him to follow her. They moved through the lobby and towards the lifts, comfortable in each other's stride. When they got to her door on the third floor, she swiped the key card and walked in, her hips swaying from side to side.

'Fancy a drink?' she asked.

'Sure' he replied. 'What do you have?'

She leant down to the minibar and peered inside.

'Scotch, wine, beer….'

'I'll take a scotch.'

Handing him the miniature and a glass, she invited him to take a seat. The woman then moved towards the bathroom, closing the door with a loud click.

He poured the spirit and closed his eyes. What the hell am I doing here? he wondered to himself, in a hotel room with a married woman, a client no less!

After a few minutes, the door opened and she walked out, towards where he was sitting, wearing devil red underwear, stockings, suspenders, an intricate bra and a broad smile.

'What do you think?' she enquired, placing her hands on her hips and looking straight at him.

He thought for a moment about telling a joke, but thought better of it. Instead, he smiled and looked at her from head to foot.

'You look a picture' he replied. 'Things are moving a little quick here though, aren't they?'

He had known many women in his lifetime and was no amateur, but in all his experience, he had rarely seen things move so fast.

She looked down at him, took a pace forward and smiled again.

'Why waste time, when we want the same thing?'

She leant down and kissed him on the mouth. He could taste the gin on her warm breath and felt a surge of passion for her. Reaching up and wrapping his arms around her, he pulled her body towards him, making her sit across his lap. They kissed passionately for several minutes, both enjoying the intimacy of the moment, until she stood up and led him to the bed next to them.

'Time to get acquainted,' she whispered in his ear, forcing him down on the bed.

....

When David woke, it was dark and he could hear Jenny's breathing next to him. He fluttered his eyelids and stared at the ceiling.

'Christ, what have I done?' he murmured to himself, looking around the room.

He felt drained and knew that it was going to be tough to stay awake all day. He smiled though, running through the events of the night in his mind and realised that he had barely slept. Every time he was about to drop off, she would snuggle up to him and kiss him lightly on the cheek, before insisting on making him perform again.

He felt her shift in the bed and her hand began exploring his nipples.

'Time for an encore,' she whispered in his ear, before her hand moved over his stomach, ever downwards, caressing him gently.

They made love once more, frantic, desperate love.

After their breathing had subsided and they had untangled themselves, he rested his head on the pillow and closed his eyes for a moment.

'Got to go,' he said, stroking her hair and kissing her on the lips.

Swinging his legs off the bed, he walked over to where his clothes were scattered.

'Will I see you again?' she asked, sitting up and pulling her knees to her chest.

'I don't know if I can keep up with you!' he replied, as he dressed quickly.

Chapter Sixteen

Early the following Saturday, David was driving south along the A24 in Surrey to begin some of his tradecraft training. It was a misty, late summer morning and he was glad that he had set off early. He was looking forward to starting the modules he had heard about, as he knew himself that his skills were primarily military in nature.

Passing through Dorking, he headed further south, until he saw the turning on the left, next to an old red phone booth. Making the turn, he continued for another mile, before spotting what looked like a small industrial complex.

The sign on the fence read, 'Prime Logistics'.

Turning in, there was a small guard post and a barrier across the road. On seeing his car, a man dressed in a blue security uniform and holding a clipboard, left the post and approached him.

'Good morning, sir!' said the guard, studying the visitor's face.

'Morning!' he responded cheerfully. 'I'm here for some training.'

'Can I see some ID please?'

He produced his documents, which were checked carefully.

'Right you are Mr Lord. They're expecting you. Pass through the gates and park in front of the far, grey building if you would,' the guard directed.

He handed back the documents and pointed towards one of the two story blocks.

Parking up next to two other cars, he turned off the engine. For a moment, he looked straight ahead and began to breathe deeply. He wasn't sure why, but he just needed time to gather his thoughts. Suitably composed, he grabbed his things and walked towards the main entrance. It was 8.30am.

On entering the building, he saw a woman of about fifty, with straight greying hair, standing in the foyer. Reading glasses, attached to a thin beaded chain, were hanging from her neck.

'Hello David, I'm Katherine,' she said, shaking his hand warmly.

He greeted her and looked around.

'You're well off the beaten track here!'

'That's how we like it. Please come this way.'

He followed her down the bare corridor, her heels clicking loudly on the stone floor, and into what looked like a classroom at the end. Standing at the front by a desk was a man with white hair and beard, shuffling some papers.

'Ah, you must be David!' he said in a broad Scottish accent, as he saw them enter. 'Good to meet you. I'm Donald,' he said, shaking his hand and looking at the face of his guest closely.

He was asked to show his ID again and invited to take a seat.

'Welcome,' the man said. 'I'll take you through the facilities we have and what Katherine and I will be doing with you. We've been asked to bring you up to a basic level quickly, but you'll be returning to this place quite often. You'll also be going to our setup on the south coast now and again.'

He nodded and glanced around the room.

The trainer then went through security procedures and highlighted the importance of keeping any notes that he took safe and secure.

Outside again an hour later, at the back of the building, he breathed in and out deeply, savouring the air. He knew that he was going to enjoy this. It was peaceful down here in Surrey and nice to get away from the noise and dirt of the city.

'How was the air?' asked Katherine, when he returned.

'Clean!' he grinned.

'Yes, we're lucky down here. We have all this space and beautiful countryside and yet we're only an hour from London.'

'Maybe I should go into training one day!'

'You could do worse,' interrupted Donald. 'I mean, when you're tired of operational work and want a more settled life. Katherine and I both spent time overseas on operations.'

He wanted to ask them both about their experiences but he knew that protocol didn't allow it.

James had been very specific about it and had warned him that his SIS trainers would never discuss what they had done in their careers. He understood all of that, having served with the SAS, where even in the officers' mess it was frowned upon to discuss previous operations.

'Alright, let's resume,' the man said, breaking his thoughts.

For the rest of the morning and afternoon, he was taken through the topic of surveillance and learnt various techniques, from basic through to advanced. By the end of the day, his head was spinning a little and he realised that although he was covering a raft of information, he was probably only scratching the surface. He knew that to become a 'primary asset', he was going to have to work hard and spend many hours at Prime Logistics.

As it approached 5.30pm, Donald looked up at the clock on the wall.

'That's enough for your first day. We don't want to overload you! Get yourself home, get some rest and we'll see you back here tomorrow.'

'Sounds good,' he replied. 'Thanks for an interesting day!'

'No, thank you for coming and for being a good student.'

He smiled at the compliment and began to collect his things.

'Before you go,' Katherine said, walking towards him. 'Here is some bedtime reading for you!' and she handed him three books. 'These are the main texts that cover the material you will be taught over the coming months, so read well and keep them secure.'

'Thanks Katherine. There was me thinking I had some time off!'

'No such luck!' she smiled. 'Have a good drive back and we'll see you tomorrow.'

All too soon the next morning, Sunday, his alarm was ringing and, rubbing the sleep out of his eyes, he headed to the bathroom. He was out of the flat and on the road before seven, listening to one of the local pop stations on the radio. The morning was clear and the sun was beginning to show itself.

Stopping for a bacon sandwich and a coffee at a snack van on the A3, he made steady progress towards Dorking. He hadn't slept that well and couldn't work out why. Maybe because he was so busy at work and now with the tradecraft training, he hardly seemed to have a moment to himself anymore.

'Things will get better,' he said to himself. They always did. He thought back to selection into the SAS. It never seemed to end. The endurance phase, the jungle phase, the combat survival course, officers week, the patrol skills course and continuation training. But it did end and it was worth it. Time seemed to drag for much of selection and he had felt so tired for most of it, but he remembered gritting his teeth and urging himself on, whenever he felt down. And finally it was all over and he was standing in front of the CO of 22 SAS, shaking his hand and receiving his sand coloured beret.

What a moment that was. It wasn't actually over, he had still to complete further training and prove himself to his new squadron, but he had broken the back of it.

What he was learning with Donald and Katherine that weekend was theory, but the Scotsman had explained that on some of the weekends they'd be out in the field, putting that theory into practice in the local countryside and towns. He was glad that he would have a chance to put his new found skills into practice outside the classroom, but he also knew that in reality it could take years to become a master in any of the techniques he was being taught. That afternoon, they would focus on surveillance operations, particularly the planning, conduct and withdrawal phases. David felt confident about much of the information, as he had spent months learning about surveillance at Hereford.

....

The following Friday was just another normal day in the office, or so David thought, but he could sense a change in the air.

Towards the end of the afternoon, he heard titters along the corridor and when colleagues walked past his door, he could feel them lingering a little longer than normal. He had been busy all day, talking to clients and interviewing candidates and was looking forward to getting home and collapsing in front of the TV for a few hours.

He wondered what was going on, but couldn't put his finger on it. Hearing footsteps in the corridor, his colleagues seemed to be moving down towards the meeting rooms. Then his phone rang and Margaret asked him to join her.

'Sure, what's up?' he asked unsurely.

'Oh, I just want you to check something.'

Walking down the corridor, he turned the corner and stopped himself. Standing in front of him were all of his colleagues, grinning at him. In the middle of the group was James, with a smile from ear to ear.

'Ah, David. Welcome!' his voice boomed.

'Err, hello James' he replied, looking from colleague to colleague for any clue.

'To put you out of your misery, I'm delighted to inform you that you have been promoted to Senior Consultant. Well done!' he said, striding over and shaking his hand firmly.

Everyone in the room began clapping and he broke into a huge grin.

'Oh, thanks. This is a surprise.'

'Well, the seniors in the firm had an easy decision to make in promoting you. We all believe that you've earnt it and have made an excellent start with us.'

The clapping continued and he bowed his head in jest, as his colleagues walked towards him, patting him on the back and shaking his hand.

'Congratulations, David. Very well done,' said Penny, winking at him as she shook his hand.

'I owe this to you and I'm grateful.'

She smiled at him, as another colleague stepped in. The noise level had risen significantly and there was an excited, celebratory air in the room. It took a while for James to get his voice heard.

'Excellent, excellent' he said, clapping his hands. As the room quietened, he turned to David and asked casually, 'I hope you haven't got any plans for this evening?'

'Well, err, I suppose not.'

'Good, because we're all going out to celebrate! First, to the pub around the corner and then to a French restaurant across town. One of my favourites. Get your coats everyone, we're leaving!'

The party was superb. After a few drinks in the Bulldog pub, James had organised some minibuses to take everyone to Brasserie Sete, just off Covent Garden. It was a smart but unassuming place and the group had virtually taken over the restaurant. They had dined on the finest delicacies from southern France, and tasted some of the best wines he had ever had. It had been a raucous affair and he couldn't remember a time when he had enjoyed the company of friends so much.

After eleven, people had started to drift home until only himself, James and Penny were left. After a final cognac, his boss had paid the bill and, rather unsteadily, had made his way home.

David and Penny left shortly afterwards, with David thanking the maître d' and escorting Penny outside to a waiting taxi.

'There's something that I've been meaning to do for a while,' said Penny, as she and David sat in a black cab.

'Oh, what's that?' he replied, glancing over at her, the bright lights of Piccadilly flashing across her face.

She leant over and kissed him, the two staying in the embrace for several moments.

'What took you so long?' he asked, as she slid back to her seat.

Turning to face him, she smiled. 'Oh, I wasn't sure you felt the same way!'

'Maybe I don't!'

'I didn't see you resisting just now.'

'Fair point,' he grinned.

Shortly after, they pulled up outside her flat in Chelsea and made their way inside.

'Nice pad,' he remarked, as he looked around the home.

'Thanks. I've had it for a few years now and it's served me well. Now, make yourself useful and open this would you?' she asked, handing him a bottle of white wine and an opener.

When he was done, he poured into the two glasses and handed her one.

'Congratulations Mr Lord,' she said, putting on a posh voice and tapping his glass, giggling.

'Thank you, my Lady,' he replied, bowing his head in mock formality.

They drank, savouring the taste and looked into each other's eyes.

'You really are something, aren't you?' she whispered into his ear.

'How do you mean?'

'Well, you've only been with the firm a short while and you're already rising fast. I've also noticed the way women look at you, as if they want to be with you.'

'Not noticed that,' he pleaded modestly.

'Oh yes, it's true.'

He smiled at the inference.

'I'm going to have to keep my eyes on you!' she said, swaying slightly.

'Keep them there as long as you like.'

She leant over and kissed him gently on his scarred cheek.

'You should stay the night,' she offered.

'Sure?'

She replied by taking his hand and leading him into the bedroom.

....

A few weeks after his promotion party, David was sitting at his desk one Friday morning, preparing for some interviews later in the day, when he heard James talking in the corridor talking. As he reached his office, he peered in and invited him to his office.

Taking the seat offered while James was closing the door, he took a moment to look out of the window.

It was a beautiful day. The sun was shining and there wasn't a cloud in the sky. It was the kind of day he loved to be out climbing in the mountains.

Out there, in the stillness, he could forget all his troubles, just worry about the here and now and soak in the scenery.

James began to speak, asking him how he was, shaking him out of his reflections.

'Fine thanks. I've been very busy. I've got a number of new assignments to work on and am trying to finish off another three, which are dragging due to client indecision. I'm also looking for my own researcher now, as Suzie is snowed under with Penny's work.'

'Good to see it's all going well for you.'

'On my other life, it's been hectic as well. I've completed the basic tradecraft modules and I'll be going down there quite a bit for the foreseeable future, for further training. I've been on the ranges a few times as well, honing my skills further on the sniper rifle. Thanks for putting me in touch with the Range Warden down there by the way.'

'Don't mention it. It can be tough for the first year, while you balance your working life with your new responsibilities, but it gets easier once you've done the training and have mastered your day job,' James reflected. 'Your performance on the tradecraft modules was good by the way.'

'Oh, great.'

'Yes, they were very pleased with you and have signed you off as 'operationally ready', albeit with further training to come, of course.'

'Of course. I put a lot into it.'

James nodded in agreement.

'Anyway, I wanted to talk to you about something else' he said, turning serious.

'Oh, what's that?'

'You're going back to Doha.'

....

He hadn't slept. In the early hours, around four, he swung out of bed and begun to do press ups. He always found it comforting for some reason. After a hundred, he took a shower and walking into his living room, turned on the news, towel around his waist. There had been an attack on an American base in Kunar province in Afghanistan. Early reports said that three Americans had been killed and seven Taliban.

There was another story about North Korea, test firing some long range rockets, and an American senator was saying that sanctions had to be tighter, to teach them a lesson.

'What is it with North Korea?' he muttered. 'Maybe I should go there?' Its leader seemed determined to rattle the international community and spend billions on the latest weapons technology, while his people starved in the fields.

He made himself some breakfast, dressed and pulled on a Gore-Tex jacket and stepped out of his flat. Arriving at the office, which he was glad was empty, he turned on his computer and began to look through the email traffic that had come in overnight.

Then he was ready for his meeting with James to discuss the man his boss called 'candidate 32'.

Mohamed Al Obedi.

James explained. 'The target is a nasty piece of work and been on and off our list for some time. For political reasons, perhaps when HM Government were discussing an arms deal with the Qataris, or something, he would drop off the list for a few months, because it was deemed too sensitive. But he has upset too many people now to get a reprieve.'

The former colonel leaned over the desk and handed him a colour photograph. The man was wearing a plain white keffiyeh, secured on his head by traditional black cord. He looked to be around fifty years old and his eyes stared at the camera with indifference. His beard was full and greying at the edges and apart from some lines near his eyes and small wrinkles around his mouth, his face was unmarked. He had a traditional Arabic hooked nose.

'That one was taken for some journal a few years ago, when he used to give interviews in business magazines, but he doesn't do that anymore. He keeps a lower profile these days, ever since the Emir there told him to cut his funding to jihadist groups. It didn't stop him though, he's just a bit more discreet about it these days,' James explained.

He handed over another photo, this one in black and white.

'The colour photo I gave you is the best for showing his full face. This one is side on, taken this year and you can see that his face has filled out a bit. Here is another one from the other angle,' he said, handing him a third photo. 'I want you to burn his image on to your brain, so that you can see it even in your sleep. When you get to make the shot, you won't have long.'

'Tell me about him,' he asked.

'Aged fifty four. Qatari citizen. He's a businessman, with interests in construction, facilities and retail. He owns a number of smart and not so smart apartment blocks in the city that are rented out to expats. He has two wives and seven children, three girls and four boys. He has a large house, in a place called Sumaysimah, about forty kilometres north of Doha. It's a small, discreet place on the east coast, very quiet and very conservative. Apparently, he moved there some years ago because he grew tired of what he saw as 'immoral behaviour' in the capital. Alcohol, bars, girls in short skirts, things like that upset him.'

'He is ultra conservative, but that in itself is not the problem. Heck, we don't mind if he follows a strict Salafist form of Islam, forces his wives and daughters to wear the niqab and decries the West at any opportunity. No, that's not the problem. The issue is that he has been and continues to be, one of the biggest donors to extreme Islamic groups in the region. SIS has evidence over the years that he has sent large sums of money to groups such as the Taliban, Al Qaeda and Hamas. Recently, we've also tracked some of his money to suspected Islamists in Birmingham, albeit small amounts. Most years he would send millions, in total, to these groups in the region, but over the last year or so, he has become more generous and we estimate that he is sending tens of millions overseas. Each year.'

'Estimate?'

'In the past, he would wire transfer the cash and we could track it fairly easily. Now, he still uses that method occasionally, but often his private jet will land in some dust bowl somewhere and throw out duffel bags full of cash. Occasionally, his jet gets caught, as it did in Lahore last year and the money impounded, so we have a pretty good idea of the amounts he is spending to fund terrorism.'

'And we need to hit those groups were it hurts.'

'Certainly. He was educated in Qatar, in one of the state schools, up until the age of eighteen and then sent to university in Paris for four years, to study engineering. He was not a bad student by all accounts, quite smart in fact and he ended up with a decent degree. He speaks French fluently and English quite well. He enjoyed life in the capital and had a French girlfriend there. Like many of his classmates, he drank alcohol and smoked pot. After he finished his degree, he wanted to stay in France to work and be with the girl, but his father, who was ultra-religious, dragged him back to Qatar to work in his own construction company.'

'He was rebellious for a few years, drinking in the hotel bars and chasing western women, but he seemed to settle down after a while and worked hard for his father. He was given more responsibility as he progressed and he began to earn big money. But then something happened and he became very religious. We're not sure why, but we think he met a friend who had fought against the Soviets in Afghanistan in the early 1980s. Anyway, he started going to the local mosque more frequently, growing a full beard and even went on Haj during this time.'

'Interesting,' he pondered. 'Something must have tipped him over the edge. Maybe it was this friend coming back from Afghan?'

'Maybe, but a year or so later, Mohamed disappeared for a few years. We think he went to Afghanistan in the mid-eighties to fight. Wherever he went, he was quite badly injured and walks with a limp now, although it's pretty indiscernible.'

'So he could have been mujahideen?' He knew the harshness of the Afghan terrain well and how these 'holy warriors' were tough and determined and had ultimately driven out the Soviet Army.

'I think it's very likely. So, he came back to Qatar to convalesce and rejoined his father's company. Thereafter, he began to fund these extremist groups around the world. He detests the West with a vengeance apparently and hates to see so-called 'infidels' in Muslim lands. And this brings us up to date. Do you recall the murder of the British aid workers in Gaza last year?'

'Yes, of course. There were five, or was it six workers killed, in the most brutal way in the Gaza strip?'

'It was seven aid workers, who were trying to set up a school for traumatised kids. They were tortured in the foulest way and then executed by Hamas. The group is the biggest show in town in Gaza and prior to the killings, had suffered at the hands of the Israelis due to leaks in their organisation. For some reason they blamed the leaks on the aid workers, who were living nearby, and executed them.'

'Very nasty,' said David bitterly.

'Yes,' acknowledged the former colonel. 'So, this brings us back to Mohamed Al Obedi. His dirty money, sent to Hamas, helps the group grow like a cancer and probably paid for the weapons that killed those innocents. Also, the money sent to the UK is a worry and HM Government wants him taken out.'

For the next few hours, they discussed the target and logistics around the operation.

....

The following week was a blur. David was busy but he found it difficult to concentrate. He even snapped at Suzie, when she was asking for the CVs she had given him to review and he couldn't find them. He apologised later, but for two days she avoided him. His cover story for the trip to Qatar was that he was meeting some new clients and candidates.

He had carried out more research on Al Obedi and found some interesting articles on groups he had probably funded. He found it amazing, that the man could send money to some of the most extreme terrorist organisations on the planet, and appear to get away with it.

James had told him about the time the British Ambassador in Doha provided information on Al Obedi's activities and was told by senior figures in the Qatari Government that they would look into it. Nothing happened.

When he got home every evening, the first thing he did was to study Al Obedi's pictures again. He would look at them from close, from distance and in between.

He would have the lights bright and down to dim. He repeated this each morning, so by the end of the week, he was confident that he could recognise the face anywhere.

He was sleeping better now, although he would occasionally wake up in a cold sweat, worrying about things going wrong. When he did wake early, he reverted to his normal routine, pushing out the press ups, watching the news and drinking strong coffee.

On the Thursday evening, James called him into his office and asked if he was ready.

'Yep, good to go,' he replied cheerily.

'Pleased to hear it!' he responded, looking at him directly and handing over a small box. 'I've got something for you.'

'A new phone?' he replied.

'Take it out of the box and see if you can find anything unusual.'

He did as instructed, examining the object closely. 'Ah!' he exclaimed. 'A recessed button, down here on the bottom right edge.'

'Well done. That is now your operational phone. That button is an emergency signal to tell us that you're in trouble. It is for our benefit, rather than yours. It also tells those assisting you to make a rapid exit and get away from you. Sadly, by pressing it, you won't get a rescue party coming over the hill. You'll be on your own. There's one more thing we need to agree on,' asked James. 'We need a codeword to signal that you've been successful. Any ideas?'

David thought about it for a moment before replying. 'Damocles.'

The man looked at him and nodded his head slowly. 'The sword of Damocles. An allusion to the imminent peril to those in power. I like it.'

Chapter Seventeen

Qatar

He queued at immigration, along with other business types and hundreds of Nepali workers, probably going to the construction sites, he guessed. He eventually made it to one of the desks, occupied by an attractive Qatari woman of about thirty wearing an abaya.

'As-salaam aleykum,' he said and offered her his passport.

'Wa aleykum salaam,' she replied, smiling, and studied his documents.

'What brings you to Qatar, Mr Lord?' she asked, in heavily accented but flawless English.

'I have business meetings here for a few days.'

She nodded her head and instructed him to place his credit card in the reader, to pay for the visit visa. Once payment had been cleared, she stamped the passport and handed it back to him.

'Enjoy your visit!' she enthused.

'Thank you, I'm sure I will!'

He took a taxi to the Palm Tree hotel, close to where he had stayed before, and after checking in, took the elevator up to his room on the fifth floor. Dropping his bag on to the floor, he stretched out on the bed, closed his eyes and took a moment for himself.

Could he pull this off, he wondered?

He recalled all the training he had done, all the preparation, all the hard work.

Walking over to the window, he opened the curtains and looked out over the city. Bright street lights shone back at him and cars, honking their horns, made their way along the still busy streets.

His phone rang, distracting him from his thoughts. Pleased to see that it was Pete, they agreed to meet up ten minutes later. He went into the bathroom to rid his face of the grime that had collected there during the day. Checking his pockets to make sure he had everything he needed, he stepped out of the room, towards the lifts.

'Good to see you, mate!' welcomed his friend, as he climbed into the car. 'Back for the real thing, eh?'

'Yeah, couldn't stay away,' he answered, a hint of irony in his voice.

'Let's go to a bar and we can catch up.'

He nodded and they drove away, joining the traffic on the other side of the road. After five minutes, they pulled up near a hotel and made their way inside.

'What delightful spot have you brought me to this time?' he enquired.

'Ah, one of my favourites! This is the 'Moonshine'. I like it, because it's quiet and a bit like a pub. Old pictures, stuff on the wall, that kind of thing.'

There were probably thirty people in the bar, a mixture of men and women.

'It's emptier now, because most of them will have gone to the disco upstairs, so it's perfect,' Pete was saying, leading him to a table in the corner.

A waitress came over to take their order and Pete punched his arm playfully.

'So this is it. Time to earn your pay!'

'Yes! Time to put all that training to good use.'

They made small talk, until the waitress returned with their drinks and once she had left, David turned to his friend.

'Have you got anything?'

Taking a sip of his lager, the assistor spoke quietly.

'This could be your lucky week!' he chortled, checking around him that no one was listening. 'I've got info that our friend is holding a meeting on Tuesday night in the Marriott, the one by the airport.'

'Go on,' he encouraged.

'Apparently, he's called together some of his senior business associates for a meal, followed by a meeting, to be held in one of the private rooms there.'

'How reliable is this info?'

'Very. Premium level,' confirmed his friend. 'I'm just waiting for some more details, which I should get on Monday or Tuesday morning, latest.'

He wondered how Pete had got the information. As long as it was accurate it didn't matter and besides, his friend wasn't going to tell him anyway. Taking a long drink from his glass, he spoke again.

'Got the gun?'

'Yep, she's here waiting for you,' he confirmed. We'll check zero out in the desert, early one morning and I'll hand her over a few hours before the hit.'

He smiled in appreciation.

He didn't know how the weapon had got into the country and he didn't care. What mattered was that it was in country and ready for his use.

....

The following morning, after a restful night, David met some candidates for a job that didn't exist. In the afternoon, he met a potential new client, an old contact of James. Doha Investment Group, DIG for short, was located in one of the skyscrapers in the West Bay part of the city, along with other investment companies, consultancies, law firms and government agencies.

Clearing reception and being taken to the CEO's office on the twenty first floor, he was struck by how quiet the place was. Apart from a few staff tapping away at laptops and the odd worker wandering the corridors, it felt quite empty, barely living almost.

'Hi David!' welcomed Doug Heindseck, the American CEO stretching out his hand.

He was a bear of a man, barrel chested and tall, with a neatly trimmed beard and deep Southern accent.

'Good to meet you at last,' he replied. 'Great view you have up here!'

'Yep, it's pretty cool. Better than some of the shitholes I've worked in elsewhere in the Gulf. You've come a long way for a meeting. I hope we're worth it.'

'Well, actually I do have a number of meetings whilst I'm here. So, you knew James years back, when you were working in Kuwait?'

'That's right, for KPP. He found us some good people there, finance guys, risk guys and even a CIO, if I recall.'

'Yes, he told me about it. We don't work with them much anymore, since the new CEO came, as he had his favourite headhunters to use. Good times though, I hear.'

'Yeah, great times. We did a lot of good there and made the shareholders a shitload of money. I was the COO then and had a great relationship with the MD, a nice guy called Jassem Al Othman. He was a smart man and he was going to go far. Unfortunately, his family fell out of favour with the royals and he was fired, for no reason. Can you believe it?'

'Yes, I can,' he replied. 'I've heard in this region, that your job is never safe, anything can happen, especially if you're a local.'

'True enough. Anyway, they threw out Jassem and brought in this shit for brains, who knew nothing about finance or investments. Must have had serious 'wasta'!'

He had heard about wasta, a system of influence that affected many aspects of daily life including recruitment, pay and other privileges. It operated throughout the Middle East and was far more powerful than merit.

'The guy was a total disaster! Within six months, our worth had gone down the toilet and the shareholders were asking questions. I knew that it was a good time to get the hell out of there and so came here,' the man sighed, shaking his head.

'How's it going here?'

'Yeah, not bad man. We had a good couple of years, attracting a lot of investment, but things have kinda slowed down over the last year or so.'

'I'm sure they'll pick up again.'

'Let's hope so,' replied the American, looking at the bay out of the window.

There was a tap on the door and a young Asian man walked in, carrying a tray. Placing the cups delicately in front of them, he left the room without speaking.

'So, thanks for inviting me here, Doug. You said you were looking for some key people.'

'Yes we are. We've had a lot of folk poached this last year and have struggled to replace them. Our HR Manager, Khalid, who you might meet, is totally useless in finding quality staff. He thinks putting an advert in the paper will get us all the talent we need. '

'*Really*?' he asked, frowning.

'The worst part is that we can't even get rid of him. Removing a Qatari is nigh on impossible, with the labour laws here. What we need right now is senior staff, and quite a few of them!'

'So, what are the roles that need to be filled?'

The man pulled some papers towards himself, mumbled something, and proceeded to list the requirements. There were four senior roles – COO, Chief Legal Officer, Senior Finance Manager and Head of Internal Audit, seven mid-level roles, mainly in investment management, and over twenty junior positions.

'Oh, and we'll need a new HR Manager long term, but that's between you and I,' winked the American, conspiratorially.

'Understood' he replied.

'What I was thinking, is that you take on the four senior roles and then work with Khalid on the mid-level roles. Find him some decent agencies to work with and then hold his hand through the process, that kind of thing.'

'Sure Doug, I can do that.'

For the next hour, the CEO went through the role profiles for the senior positions, discussing their key responsibilities and his preferences on candidates. David had a few questions, but on the whole he was happy with what he was looking for and confident he could find the people.

'For each candidate, we'll charge twenty five percent of the annual salary. Half of the fee will be paid as a retainer at the start and the remainder will be paid when the candidate starts work,' he explained.

'Sounds fine! Just what I was looking for. Send me your contract and terms when you can and we'll get the ball rolling.'

'Will do. I'll work on it over the next few days and send it over to you.'

'It'll be nice to get some pace around here!' joked the American.

David nodded and smiled, not believing that he was preparing for a sanction and bringing some large fees to the firm at the same time.

Doug paused, looking out of the window again and rubbed his chin.

'There is one more thing.'

'Oh?'

'You should probably meet Khalid. He's a pain in the ass but I suppose the sooner you meet him, the better. He'll probably try and reduce your fees or something, but don't worry. I've already agreed them and it will be me that signs off on your invoices, and gets them paid, not him.'

His PA appeared and Doug instructed her to introduce him to Khalid. The two men made their farewells and he was led out of the office and across the large open plan area, to the other side of the building. They came to a large door marked 'HR Manager' which the PA tapped. Hearing no response, she tapped harder and he heard a muffled voice inside, instructing them to enter.

Nodding to the girl, indicating that he didn't need any more help, he pushed open the door. In front of him was a large wooden desk and sat behind it, an overweight Qatari with a designer beard and small, beady eyes. He looked like he had been sleeping.

'Salam Aleykum,' he greeted, as the man reciprocated and struggled out of his chair.

'Mr David,' he said, shaking the Englishman's hand. 'Mr Doug asked me to meet you, but I'm not sure why, as our recruitment is working perfectly.'

He indicated a chair for his guest.

Taking a moment to look around the medium sized office, he noticed the TV on the wall, live streaming pilgrims at Mecca. There was a bookcase to his left, which housed what looked like religious texts, as well as company manuals and business books.

'I'm sure it is, Khalid. Your CEO thought it would be good to meet though, in case you need any help in the future, that is.'

The Qatari tutted and asked what fees he was proposing.

'Impossible!' snorted the man, on hearing the response. 'I would only give you half of what you are asking.'

David smiled and contemplated his host, who had probably never had to apply for a job in his life, was undoubtedly overpaid for his limited capabilities and seemed to view his role as hindering companies wanting to work with his own. He despised the man in front of him and those like him, who just took and never gave.

Concealing his distaste, he smiled broadly and confirmed the fee levels that would be charged, if he was ever to work with DIG.

'OK, maybe I give you a little more than half,' the Qatari sneered, as he began to reel off a series of ridiculous conditions that would be part of any agreement.

Biting his tongue, he continued to smile.

'Khalid, we wouldn't agree to those conditions,' he said, looking his host squarely in the eyes. 'We prefer to work in partnership with our clients, where both prosper.'

His host looked at him coldly.

'But anyway,' he said, standing up and signalling the end of the meeting. 'I can see that you're a busy man and wouldn't want to take any more of your precious time.'

'You are right. I am a busy man. Perhaps we will meet again in the future. Inshallah.'

'Inshallah,' he replied, relieved that the nonsense was over.

David left the offices of DIG and made his way back to the hotel by taxi.

Driving along the corniche, looking at all the glamorous buildings and construction going on, he marvelled at how the small desert nation had grown from virtually nothing seventy years previously to one of the richest countries in the region, all because of oil and gas.

Ordering a sandwich and Coke on room service back at his room, he opened his laptop to see if there were any emails of interest.

A note from Penny pricked his attention. She had won a new assignment with a client in Morocco and wanted them to work on it together. Suzie was chasing him for a response about some CVs and a few candidates were asking for feedback after interviews they had recently attended.

There were a few emails from clients who had questions about the contracts he had sent them and there was a note from James about the financial performance of the firm for the last quarter. It looked like they had made some good money in the period, he noted, as he looked at the headline figures.

Later on, as he was working on the draft contract for Doug, his phone rang and it was Pete. Thirty minutes later, the two were sat in an empty car park, near to a museum by the water.

'I don't want us overheard. I want to run through the plan and agree some of the comms procedures we might need. Bear with me, this'll all make sense and don't worry, you'll have glass in your hand in no time!'

He smiled.

'So, our man will be in the Marriott, having dinner with his friends. It'll start around seven and should be done by about ten, ten thirty. I'll be showing you the firing point tomorrow night, so don't worry about that.'

'When do you think I should be in position?'

'I would say eight, just so that you're all settled. It'll be nice and dark then as well. You may have some bugs flying around your head at that time of night, so make sure that you've got plenty of mozzie rep on.'

He made a mental note.

'I'll be at the hotel around six, wandering around the lobby, looking like a tourist. We went there remember, when you were last here?'

'Yeah, I remember.'

'So, I'll mainly be based in the large sitting area by reception, with my baseball cap on. Way at the back, away from people's attention. For this op, we'll be using a fictional birthday party as our theme for comms.'

He looked sideways at the assistor.

'OK' he said unsurely.

'Now, we'll refer to the target as 'Mike', so every time that name is used, we both know who we're talking about. When the target arrives at the hotel, I'll call you and say something like, 'I'm calling about Mike's birthday'. You'll be somewhere nearby in your car and you'll know that you can start to think about getting into position. No point in moving, if the prick doesn't turn up,' he smiled.

He nodded his head slowly, taking it all in.

'So, after the target, 'Mike', arrives, you won't hear from me for a few hours. Make sure that your phone is on vibrate only, by the way. I know that you've already blacked out any light on the handset, so you'll be completely hidden in the dark.'

He could feel his heart rate begin to quicken, but shrugged it off.

'The next thing you'll get, at around ten/ten thirty, is a vibrating phone, with me at the end of it. That means that I've seen the target, he's on his way out and we're in business. To repeat, I'll say something like, 'Hi mate, can we talk about Mike's birthday?' Just grunt back at me, to acknowledge, as I know you'll want to keep as quiet as possible.'

'OK, got it.'

'I'll then ramble on about the arrangements. What you've got to listen out for are numbers, as I'll be counting you down to his arrival at the front entrance, where you'll hit him.'

'Fine.'

'So, I'll be saying, 'maybe we should have it on the 30th?' That means that the target is 30 seconds out from the entrance. Then it will be 'No, maybe the 15th is better?' That means that he is 15 seconds from the door.'

He nodded, looking at the modern designed museum in the distance, bathed in bright spotlights.

'If for some reason the target stops to talk to someone, I'll just use the 'hold off' procedure and say 'maybe we should wait', and I'll waffle on about the arrangements again. When the target is moving back towards the entrance, I'll resume from before and say 'No, let's go for the 15th'. That's your cue again to prepare for firing. So, that's the comms process for the hit. Does that all make sense?'

'Perfect sense' he confirmed.

'I've used the same method on other operations and it works well. Nice and clear and nice and simple. Don't forget that there may be people around me in the lobby, so if I start to talk shit, don't worry about it!'

'I won't,' he said grinning.

'So, the drill after you've fired, is to stay still for a few moments, then back out slowly and make your way to the car. Then drive to the meet up point. I'll show you the location tomorrow night.'

'As for me, I'll wait to hear the screams and commotion and then make my way slowly out of the rear of the hotel, over a few walls and back to you.'

'Got it.'

'OK, let's just practice the comms procedures a few times, particularly the 'hold off' and then we can go for some refreshment!' said Pete, grinning.

....

He wasn't looking forward to the client meeting midmorning with Al Baadi Group, a large family company with interests in retail, construction, finance and real estate. Researching their website before his visit, David saw that they were a very wealthy organisation, with a strong presence in Qatar but subsidiaries in Kuwait, Bahrain, Saudi Arabia and Oman. They were worth billions.

His first attempts to contact the CEO, Rashid Al Baadi, had proved fruitless. The man was never in the office it seemed and his PA guarded his privacy well. He had been taught to always go after the CEO or other senior figures, when targeting new clients. Support players, like the HR Director, often didn't understand, or even know the strategic direction of the company and were often reluctant to take on new search firms.

On the fifth attempt to contact Rashid, the PA had relented though and pointed him in the direction of the HR Director, Abdullah Al Sada instead. Abdullah was almost as difficult to track down as the CEO, but phoning three or four times a day, over several days, he had eventually caught him at his desk.

Knowing that he had little time to impress the man, he spoke in Arabic about how he could support Abdullah's talent initiatives. Initially, the HR man was reluctant to hear about taking on a new search organisation, but gradually he persuaded him of the benefits and finally agreed to a meeting. If nothing came of it, at least it would be more cover for the trip to Doha, he had thought.

Al Baadi Group's main office was located in the Al Waab district of the city, a well-to-do area, with extravagant houses peppered around. Many were fronted with tall pillars, lavish gardens and fountains in abundance. Driving through an archway, he found himself in a large compound, about the size of two football fields side by side. There was a parking area in the middle full of Land Cruisers, top of the range sports cars and a few cheap saloons, surrounded on all sides by two-storey buildings. The driver dropped him off at the front of what looked like the main building, judging by the large fancy sign with the company logo on it. Below the sign, in Arabic and English it read, 'For a better tomorrow!' He wondered how long it had taken them to think that one up and headed inside, out of the blistering heat of the morning.

After a short wait he was met by a plain looking young girl dressed in an abaya, who took him up to the executive offices. They walked along the corridor, passing offices along the way, some with doors open, others closed. The titles of the occupants were written on white card in Arabic on each door. He saw 'Finance Manager', 'Investment Manager' and 'Chief Marketing Officer', occupied by a Qatari woman, chatting on her mobile.

Continuing down the corridor to where he assumed the more senior people worked, he saw a large Qatari man dressed in a thobe step out of the office at the end, about fifty feet from him. Glancing at him, his heart rate quickened. He would recognise that face anywhere. He looked away and then back towards the man, who was now only twenty feet away.

David realised with horror that he was looking at the face of Mohamed Al Obedi.

Chapter Eighteen

His mind raced.

In a city of over a million people, what were the chances? Gathering his thoughts quickly, he offered a greeting to the Arab, who was now only feet away.

'Salam Aleykum,' he said in a strong voice, studying the man's face.

The Qatari looked him in the eyes, face still, and walked past without responding, his thobe swishing as he went. David felt cold, as if he had seen death.

He turned to the girl.

'Who was that man?' he asked.

'Oh, that's Mohamed Al Obedi. He doesn't like foreigners I'm afraid!' she replied, looking embarrassed. 'I'm sorry for his rudeness.'

'Don't worry,' he replied, as they walked on. 'Tell me, is he a client of the Group?'

'Oh, yes sir, he is a big investor with us!'

Interesting, he thought, as they reached a door.

She knocked and after a brief pause, it opened to reveal a stooped figure in traditional dress, with a friendly face and a lazy eye.

'Mr Lord!' he said in welcome.

'Salam Aleykum,' David greeted.

'Wa Aleykum Salam,' replied the Qatari, nodding his head.

He offered his hand and Abdullah took it, shaking it slowly.

'Thank you for agreeing to see me.'

'You are most welcome Mr Lord. Always a pleasure to meet an Englishman! Come and sit down here,' he said, gesturing to a chair opposite his own.

He spent the next thirty minutes trying to convince the man to try Coldridge Partners for their senior positions, but deep down, knew that he was probably wasting his time. Not a total waste though. He had seen the face of the man he was to kill! That was a stroke of luck and he had noted every line and wrinkle on the man's face, storing it in his brain for the right moment.

Abdullah spoke about the talent war in the Gulf and how annoying it was that expats often stayed somewhere for two to three years and then moved on to a better paid job, somewhere else in the region.

They talked on about selecting candidates and expat salaries for the region and David brought the meeting to an end by saying he would like to keep in touch, so that they could discuss any senior roles that came up in the future. The HR Director seemed happy with the approach and took his business card gratefully. The Arab handed one of his own over, retrieved from a small, carved wooden box on his desk.

Leaving the office and making his way downstairs, the adrenaline still flowed through his veins.

....

When David reached his hotel, he took a light lunch in the restaurant and returned to his room. He settled down to watch the international news. His mind was soon distracted though, as he couldn't believe that he had seen Al Obedi.

He replayed in his mind the image of the man walking down the corridor again, the thobe swishing as he moved. He saw every footstep and movement of the Arab, as if he was watching from a new angle. Hearing someone, himself, offer the traditional greeting, he recalled the rebuke he had suffered when the Qatari had just walked past. There was something new this time, in his mind. It was the look in the Arab's eyes as he drew level with him.

A look of hatred, a look of loathing.

Checking his watch, he realised that his first candidate meeting was due to take place shortly, down in the lobby. He turned off the TV, took a long drink of water from a bottle in the fridge and collected his jacket. Gathering up his daybook and the candidate's CV, he headed downstairs.

These interviews with candidates about jobs that didn't exist were purely to provide extra cover for him being in Qatar, nothing more. He would speak to them about a great job in a neighbouring country and pretend to show interest in their CVs and backgrounds. Headhunters did it all the time.

He recalled, when he was starting out with the firm, Penny sending him to meet candidates in London about a job she had made up, just so that he gained experience in interviewing people.

Initially, he had sat with her, watching how she conducted the meeting. Over time, he led the interviews, with her watching and giving him feedback afterwards. It worked well. There were always plenty of candidates willing to be interviewed, so there was never any shortage of practice.

One thing always mystified him though. He was always surprised how people in supposedly great jobs, with big salaries, were always on the lookout for a better role. He thought it might be because folk these days never seemed happy with what they had. He had seen a report a few days earlier about the divorce rate in the UK going up and it was often the same story. A successful man, with a beautiful, doting wife and lovely kids, goes off and has an affair with a female acquaintance, a colleague, an old school friend. All of a sudden, his life changes. The man loses his family and is divorced, all because he wasn't happy with what he had.

Shaking his head and stepping into the lobby, he saw his first candidate straight away, sitting in one of the comfortable chairs by the window. He recognised him from his LinkedIn photo: Amit Patel, an Indian accountant from Goa, was of medium build and height and had a ready smile. He stood up when he saw him approach and the two men shook hands.

'Good to meet you, Amit!' he said.

'Likewise!' replied the Indian. 'Sorry I'm a little early, but I have to dash off in half an hour for a management meeting. I could have postponed, but I wanted to meet you, as the job you discussed sounds interesting!'

'Ah, that's OK. We'll just have to be quick then and we can discuss things further on the phone at another time. How about I spend fifteen minutes telling you about the opportunity and then you tell me about yourself and what you're looking for in your next role, and we can take it from there?'

He then talked about the fictitious role, the responsibilities, the organisation and the likely package. The man's eyes lit up when he heard the figures and was clearly keen to hear more. Glancing at the clock on the wall, he realised that they were running out of time and, assuring the candidate that they could discuss the role further on the phone, he encouraged him to speak about himself. Taking notes in his daybook, he captured information that he was never going to use, but it seemed to impress the candidate. He drew the meeting to a close, knowing that he would never see the man again.

Back upstairs, he took his jacket off and sat down on the bed. Taking the remote control, he switched on the news, but there wasn't anything on of interest. He reached for his book, about explorers in Africa, and read a few chapters before his mind wandered. He didn't seem able to settle and his mind kept overturning the events of the morning. With relief, the clock ticked on and before he knew it, the time had come for his second candidate meeting of the day.

This time, in the hotel lobby as before, he met a French accountant, Pierre Dubois, to discuss the same fictitious job. The candidate was clearly unhappy with living in the desert state and his wife was threatening to divorce him if they didn't move soon.

After an hour had passed and the two had exchanged a lot of information, he wrapped up the meeting, saying he had another appointment in West Bay.

....

At eight that evening, Pete picked him up near to his hotel to visit the kill site near the Marriott. The evening was hot, but a gentle sea breeze helped to make the temperature less oppressive. Once they had reached the Corniche road, David turned to his friend with a grin.

'You'll never guess who I saw today?'

'Don't tell me' answered his friend. 'The Pope?'

'No. Mohamed Al Obedi!'

'What!' answered his friend. 'Where the hell did you see him?'

He recounted the story while his friend listened in silence.

'What a coincidence! Good news for you though,' the assistor said, as they joined the airport road, 'you've had a good look at his ugly mug and you'll know you've got the right target.'

They drove on for a further ten minutes, until Pete found a place to park, off the main highway, down a service road and under some trees. The lights from the car showed that they were in a scrubland area and there were no houses visible.

'There's a two storey building, about three hundred metres over there' the man explained, pointing into the darkness. 'It must be an old facilities building or something, that never got finished, but it's perfect for you. It has a good elevation and there's a date palm that arches over it, providing excellent concealment. The entrance of the Marriott is seven hundred and twenty metres, give or take, from the firing point.'

He'd practiced on the ranges back in the UK in most conditions, at some targets well over a thousand metres away and was confident in his ability.

'The stairs of the building are on the south side and go all the way to the roof, from where you'll be taking the shot. There's all sorts of shit up there, wooden planks, a boiler and tins of paint, so be careful with your footing.'

'Roger,' he said in confirmation.

'The way that we're going to go in now will be different to the one you use, to avoid putting tracks everywhere. I suggest that that you drive further down this road and park by some mounds of rubble. I'll show you before we leave tonight.'

'Got it.'

'Now, put these on would you?' asked the assistor, handing him some surgical shoes with elastic around the tops. 'They'll help to mask your tracks. The second pair is for tomorrow night. You'll also need these,' he said, handing him some surgical gloves. 'We don't want to be leaving any prints up there, do we?'

'Nope,' he replied quietly.

'When we get to the building, I'll go straight up the stairs to the roof and show you where the firing point is. You'll see the lights of the Marriott through the trees quite easily, so there shouldn't be any dramas. All clear?'

'Crystal,' he replied, face like granite.

'Follow me across the scrubland.' The two men exited the vehicle and headed towards the building in the darkness.

They walked stealthily northwards, across sandy and stony ground, pausing only once to listen for anything unusual. Reaching the building, they went up the stairway cautiously, taking care where to place their feet. Once on the roof, the assistor tapped his shoulder to get his attention and pointed out the debris. He then led the way along the side of the roof to the firing point at the end. Once there, he got down on his belly. David noticed the big palm tree to his right and the foliage arching over his head.

He smiled to himself. Even in daylight, he knew that it would be a well-hidden spot. Adopting the same position as his friend, he looked to his front and immediately could see, through the trees, the entrance and drop off point of the hotel. It was a well-lit area and he could see a car pulling up and people being directed inside. Glancing left and right and looking at his immediate surroundings, he noticed there was a small rim of about six inches high, running around the edge of the roof.

No problem, he thought. The bipod on the rifle would push the muzzle well above that.

Pete handed him the laser range finder and pointing it at the stonework above the entrance, he pressed the button and saw a reading of '718' metres. He took further readings around the entrance and satisfied with the range, handed the laser back to his friend.

Then he just watched.

He wasn't looking for anything in particular, he was just getting used to his environment. Taking out his binoculars from a pouch on his belt, he studied the entrance again in more detail this time. To the right of the wide entranceway was a hair salon, with dimmed lights inside, indicating that it was closed. To the left was an ATM of one of the local banks, its lights beaming into the darkness.

He looked at the entrance one more time. In twenty four hours, he would be in this same spot, waiting to kill a man. He was more concerned about failing and being caught than anything else. There was another feeling.

It was exhilaration.

He was excited about going on an operation again and using the skills he had developed over so many years. He was looking forward to putting a terrorist fundraiser out of action. Savouring the moment of calm, he knew that tomorrow would be a different story. Tomorrow, he would be lying here on his own, listening and waiting to deliver death out of the shadows.

Tapping Pete on the shoulder, he indicated that he was done and the two men walked back along the edge of the roof and quietly down the stairs. They took a different route back to the car, heading off further to the right and then cutting left through the scrub.

....

David rose early after a good night's sleep and watched the international news. There had been an attack on an Indian base in Kashmir and two soldiers had died and six insurgents. The conflict never seemed to end. So much violence. He wondered if the politicians would ever be able to resolve it.

There was another story about a bus crash in Germany, which had resulted in the deaths of thirteen school kids. They had been on their way to Paris for a school trip and the driver had hit a lorry on the motorway, which had caused a fire. The pictures were horrible. The bus was gutted by fire and ambulance crews were treating those that had survived, on the grass verge. He felt for the parents.

Trying to lift his spirits, he turned on his laptop to see what was going on in his other life. There were emails from clients and candidates, but nothing urgent. Of more interest was a message from Penny, who had sent out a note about her birthday party in a few weeks. She always liked a party and never failed to gather an interesting group together. She had a lot of very attractive friends from the City, which was always a bonus.

Satisfied that he wasn't missing anything, he called Pete and arranged to meet for a coffee that morning. He was due to see a few candidates in the afternoon, but planned to push through them quickly, so that he had plenty of time to prepare for the night's work.

'Thanks for coming' he said, as the two sat down at a table. 'I just wanted to run through things again. You know, just to be clear.'

A waitress approached the table and after taking their order, the assistor spoke.

'There would be no shame if there are nerves about tonight and that's understandable. You're about to take a life, in a civilian setting. This isn't a battlefield. Everyone has doubts on their first hit, but it gets easier over time.'

'Thanks mate. My mechanism for dealing with nerves and doubt, is to study the plan hard, look at all the options, all the angles.'

'Good method,' replied his friend, handing over the keys to the car he would be using that night. 'OK, let's run through how the night will pan out.'

An hour and two coffees later, they were done. Every aspect had been discussed. Every potential problem dealt with. Every contingency agreed.

That afternoon, David met the two candidates he had arranged to see: one an accountant from Finland wanting to move to Saudi Arabia in the long term and the other an Englishman wanting to go to Dubai. Both were interesting individuals, with good backgrounds. As before, he talked about his 'interesting opportunity' and both men assured him of their interest. He cut both sessions short, saying he had to go to other meetings and assured them he would be in touch.

Back in his room, taking his shoes off, he settled on the bed and closed his eyes. He wasn't sleeping, he was thinking. He prepared himself mentally for the night ahead. After an hour of quiet reflection, he walked to the window and again watched the bustle down on the street.

Maybe there would be a quiet funeral and the Arab would be buried out in the desert somewhere.

Or perhaps there would be a bigger response and senior members of the establishment in Qatar would offer shared, false grief. Thinking about it, he wasn't bothered what the response would be. He was there to get a job done and leave.

At half past four he began to prepare.

He laid out on his bed all the clothing and gear that he was going to need. His clothing was simple and inconspicuous. Dark running shoes, blue socks, black jeans, grey T-shirt and black hooded sweatshirt.

For his gear, the needs were small. Half foam mat to lie on, insect repellent, buff, surgical gloves, pull-on shoe covers, bottle of water, binoculars and a lighter. He ran through the items a few times, making sure he hadn't forgotten anything. Packing the items away in a green daysack, he threw it over his shoulder, making sure it was comfortable. Once satisfied, he left it on the bed and went into the bathroom. Washing his face with cold water, he smiled at himself for a moment in the mirror.

Grabbing the pack and turning off the light, he made his way downstairs and out to his car, parked around the corner. He threw in the pack, started the engine and drove down to the meeting point, twenty minutes away. Once there, he changed from his suit into the jeans and sweatshirt and liberally applied insect repellent around his head, hands and ankles. Shortly after, he heard a car approach and turning round, saw Pete at the wheel, smiling.

'Nice evening for it!' he said cheerily, drawing up alongside.

Pete walked to the back of his car and looked around, checking that no one was about. Satisfied, he opened the rear door, as David joined him. There was a black gun case lying on the floor, next to a small grip bag.

'Here's your beauty!' said his friend, tapping the case. 'We've gone to a lot of trouble to get this to you, so make sure it counts.'

'Don't worry, I won't miss,' he replied assuredly.

The assistor pulled on his gloves and unzipped the bag, lifting the L118A1 rifle out and placing it gently back on top, as if he was cradling a baby.

'The suppressor is in a sleeve inside and I've given it a light oil, so it's good to go.' He opened the grip bag and pulled out the magazine, tapping the side. 'It's half full, five rounds inside.'

He smiled. 'Hopefully I won't need all of them.'

'You'd better not, otherwise it'll be left to me to kill the bugger with my cocktail stick!'

'Any more intel on the target and his plans for this evening?'

'No, nothing new. We can safely assume that he's coming to the hotel as planned. Don't forget, when I see him in the hotel, I'll let you know. Don't go to the firing point until then, OK?'

'I'll park up a mile or so away, wait for your call and then prepare to get to the site. After the hit, I'll meet you at the car park, as agreed.'

'Regarding the conditions, well, you can see for yourself,' explained Pete, glancing around and looking skyward. 'The conditions are perfect, with no breeze to speak of, so what you aim at, you'll hit. No need for any additional corrections.'

He nodded in agreement.

'Anything else to discuss, anything else you want to talk about?'

'No, time to kill,' he answered plainly.

'You're more than ready and although it might not seem routine, it should be.'

'You're right.'

'You'll be fine,' said his friend, patting him on the shoulder.

He reached into the car and replaced the rifle back into the case and tucked the magazine into a pouch on the side. He handed it to David, who transferred it to his own car.

'Oh, you'll need this' said the assistor, handing him a plain rug, 'to throw over the rifle.'

'I'll see you after the shoot.'

For a moment, he felt very alone. 'Time to step up!' he said aloud, clenching his fist, as he stepped into the car and drove to the holding area.

He parked up and turned off the engine, then stepped out of the car, taking in the sights and smells of the evening. In the distance, he could see a plane taking off, climbing quickly and then heading eastwards.

He took in a lungful of air and exhaled slowly. He did this several times, enjoying the sensation. Sniffing the air, he smelt only dryness and parched undergrowth. In a region that didn't see rain for six months during the summer, everything had to cling on to life, make the best of it and survive.

Looking at his watch, he saw that it was approaching seven. His friend would be in the hotel by now, trying to remain unobtrusive, whilst monitoring the entrance like a hawk.

He wondered again whether something would happen and Al Obedi not turn up. But this was quite a big event for the Arab and it would cause offence if he didn't show, particularly as he was meeting some of his most senior business associates.

His thoughts were interrupted by his phone vibrating.

Pete's voice sounded tense.

'I was just phoning about Mike's party.'

His heart skipped a beat.

'Oh, right.'

'Yeah, we need to discuss it and organise things.'

'Yes, we do,' he replied firmly. 'Listen mate, I'm in the middle of something right now, so could we talk about this later?'

'Sure, no problem. I'll call you in a few hours, OK?'

'Yeah, perfect.'

He breathed deeply again, savoured this time alone, the calm before the storm.

Darkness was falling and he felt comforted by the blanket of secrecy that it would provide. Another plane was taking off, this time heading west.

A dog was barking, way off behind him, its sound carrying some distance in the still night.

He looked at his watch again, saw that it was approaching eight and decided to ready himself. Reaching into the top pocket of his daysack, he retrieved the insect spray and squirted it liberally around his face and hands. He started the engine and moved to the parking spot. Facing back towards the highway, he turned off the engine and cut the lights. He took out the gloves and shoe covers and put them on. Stepping out of the car, he closed the door gently and listened. Happy that all was well, he opened the rear door and retrieved the rifle case.

Shouldering the pack and rifle and orienting himself towards the derelict building, he set off at a slow and deliberate pace. He stopped once, dropped to his haunches and listened. Moving his head from side to side, radar like, he tried to pick up any sound out of place. But there was none, only the traffic in the distance.

He arrived at the building and crept up the stairs slowly, taking care where to place his feet. Reaching the roof and crouching, he made his way stealthily to the firing point. Placing the rifle case to his right, he reached into his daysack for the piece of foam mat and lay it on the floor. It was better than lying on a hard concrete surface for hours. Unzipping the case, he pulled the rifle out, stock first.

'Hello, old friend,' he whispered, as he ran his hand along the rifle, caressing it as if it were a female form.

Pointing the weapon towards the hotel, he dropped the bipod legs, which took the weight of the rifle, and checked that the safety catch was on. He slid the suppressor out of the case, fitting it to the front of the weapon until it was tight. Next, taking the magazine out of the pouch, he fitted it to the rifle with a reassuring clunk. He then fitted a cartridge bag to catch the empty case when the weapon fired. Finally, he cocked the weapon and smiled to himself at the smoothness of the operation. The rifle was lifted to the right, so that it was parallel with his body.

He was ready.

He made himself as comfortable as possible on the mat, frequently moving the joints that were touching the ground to release the pressure. He stretched out his arms to their full extent and rotated his head a few times to prevent stiffness. Taking the binos, he peered at the hotel in the distance, wondering what was going on inside. He studied the entrance and the people coming and going. It was mainly expats going to one of the restaurants or bars, but there was an Arab or two, the men dressed in thobes and the women in abayas.

The time ticked by and he noticed that it had turned nine o'clock. It was still warm and his sweatshirt was a little damp from perspiration. Stretching again, he forced the blood to pump effectively around his muscles.

He heard the traffic in the distance, on the main road to his left, thinking that it should die down soon. Listening again, he heard a dog bark, no more than a few hundred metres away.

I wonder what's upset you, he whispered to himself.

Chapter Nineteen

Inside the private room, Mohamed Al Obedi cleared his throat, signalling his intention to speak and slowly looked around him. Gathered here was his oldest son Rashed and his six best friends, some of whom he had known since childhood. They were business acquaintances as well of course, but their friendship was deeper. They were all dressed in traditional Qatari dress, immaculate white thobes and white keffiyehs secured with black cord and all had full, dark beards.

They had enjoyed a sumptuous meal of basmati rice, succulent lamb and goat with herbs, along with freshly baked pita bread, washed down with cool pomegranate drink. There was no alcohol to be seen, as this was a gathering of true believers.

Once the table had been cleared, Rashed checked with the bodyguards standing outside that they would not be disturbed. On his return, Al Obedi stood and raising his right finger high, offered a Koranic verse and all bowed their head.

'Our Lord, forgive us our sins, and our transgressions, strengthen our foothold, and grant us victory over the disbelievers.'

Once over, he looked around the table again, to check that he was the centre of attention and began to speak.

'My friends, thank you for coming tonight. I know that we are not able to meet very often these days, but I am grateful that you are here.'

Murmurs went around the room, as the guests nodded their heads and smiled.

'We have accomplished many great things together over the years, both in business and in supporting our brothers overseas, waging jihad. We have all become wealthy, with riches beyond our wildest dreams and have lived pure lives, which Allah would be proud of.'

Those around the table nodded once more, agreeing with the sentiments of their host.

'But it is the fight against the infidel that I have brought you together for, tonight. Yes, we have all given much of our wealth to our brothers on jihad and they have achieved many victories in Allah's name. In Somalia, Afghanistan, Gaza, Pakistan, Yemen and Iraq, our brave fighters have carried the true word of Islam and their foes have cowered in terror. But have we done enough?'

The room went silent, as Al Obedi cast his eyes mockingly around the group.

'No!' he screamed, banging his fist on the table and overturning some glasses. 'We have not! Every day, the apostates in those countries laugh at us and the infidels from the West send more and more troops to our lands. Our so-called governments bow down to these unbelievers and do not contribute to this global fight.'

Seven pairs of eyes studied him nervously.

'My friends, the time has come for all of us here to truly back our brothers waging this war on our behalf. We need to give them the tools they need to complete the task in hand, so that when we enter heaven, we know that we could have done no more.'

'My friends, I am asking you to dig deeper into your coffers, so that we as a group can send our beloved fighters ten million dollars a month.'

Gasps were uttered from those present and some shook their heads.

'Mohamed. These sums of which you speak are far higher than in the past,' exclaimed Abdulaziz, one of the oldest at the table, his eyes wide in astonishment.

'Indeed my friend, they are. But to spread the true word of Islam, I believe that we all have to make further sacrifices and I am sure we can achieve this goal, if we will it.'

'It seems very high,' pleaded Ahmed, sitting to the right and shaking his head forlornly. 'Profits have been falling for most of us this year. Can we at least discuss these amounts and how they might be paid in more detail?'

'We can, but would you have our brothers go into battle without the ammunition to win the fight?'

He let his words sink in, as the men looked at one another unsurely, trying to gauge each other's feelings.

'My friends. Think about what I have said and I am sure, when you think about it, what I propose is the right path. It can be discussed again, when next we meet.'

Heads nodded ponderously around the room.

'There is one more issue that I wish to discuss with you, before we leave' he said, clasping his hands.

The eyes of the room fell upon him in expectation.

'My beloved friends. I am dying.'

There was a brief silence, followed by gasps.

'Mohamed. What are you saying? You look like you could live to a hundred!' offered Ahmed, staring at his host in disbelief.

'Alas my friend, it is so. I have been receiving cancer treatment in Pakistan for the last year and my doctor has told me that I have months to live.'

'I am sorry to hear that Mohamed. May Allah grant you every happiness in your remaining days.'

'Thank you my friend,' uttered Al Obedi, smiling benignly.

He paused and gathered his thoughts.

'So, my task is more urgent now than before and I seek your support on what we have discussed. Rashed, my oldest son…' he said, sweeping his hand towards his first born, '…was invited here to listen to my views and to carry on my wishes, when I am gone. I ask you to support him.'

Al Obedi coughed into his fist and wiped his mouth shakily with a napkin.

'We will support him Mohamed, according to Allah's will,' said a strong voice at the table.

He could hear words of encouragement from those around him, but he was looking at his son, sitting opposite him.

'Allahu Akbar, Allahu Akbar, Allahu Akbar!' he was shouting, almost desperately, whilst staring at his father, tears streaming down his face.

....

Ten o'clock came and went.

David took some deep breaths and looked through his binos towards the hotel. The footfall going in and out had dropped to a trickle and the doorman looked bored.

What a job, he thought. He spends his life opening doors for ungrateful people and wearing that ridiculous uniform.

He was thankful for the life he had led so far, which had been interesting and rewarding, challenging and unique.

He picked up the rifle and brought it close to him. Putting the weapon into his shoulder, he got his body position comfortable and looked through the sights. The cross hairs were resting on the doorman's chest, the worker unaware how close to death he was. He looked through the scope for a few minutes more, studying every inch of the entranceway. Laying the butt of the rifle back on the floor, he rested his eyes.

The dog was barking again, somewhere off to his right.

Strange, he thought, wondering what had upset it.

What if the operation had been compromised and the special police were about to sneak up and arrest him? He thought he heard a scraping sound behind him and instantly froze. Slowly, he turned his head back towards the stairway and stared into the darkness. He could easily make out the edge of the building behind him.

Nothing was there.

Shaking his head and breathing out, he castigated himself. He settled back into position and waited.

Half an hour passed.

Feeling thirsty, he reached into his pack for the water bottle and took a long swig, grateful for the relief. Placing the bottle back in the pack, he settled down again. He was just getting comfortable again on the mat, when he thought he heard a car on the road behind him.

Slowly, he reached for his binos and began crawling back towards the corner of the rooftop. On reaching it, he listened again and heard the unmistakable purr of an engine as it moved slowly along the service road. Raising himself cautiously on his elbows and pulling the hood over his head, he pointed the glasses into the darkness at the threat.

His heart skipped a beat.

In the gloom, he could just make out that the car, a four wheel drive Toyota, had stopped in front of his own, its headlights menacing and intrusive. He imagined the blue and yellow markings along the side, but it was the distinctive light rack on the roof that instantly gave it away as a police vehicle.

'Bollocks!' he whispered, studying the scene.

After a few moments, a uniformed officer stepped out of the car and walked deliberately around the parked car, flashing a torch through the windows and peering inside. Turning, the man strolled to the edge of the road and shone his torch into the darkness, sweeping it from side to side and towards the unfinished building. He took a few steps towards the structure, but then stopped and swept his torch again.

As the beam of light approached him, David ducked his head, his senses on full alert.

Scenarios of what could happen raced through his mind as adrenalin coursed through his veins. From his cover, he listened again, hearing only palms nearby fluttering in the breeze. After what seemed an age, he raised his head towards the car.

The policeman had moved along the road and was shining his torch into some undergrowth at the side.

'OK plod, time to disappear,' he mouthed. 'I've got work to do.'

After a few more paces, the man turned and walked back to the police car, shutting the door loudly. After a pause it moved off slowly, back towards the highway and the darkness returned.

He exhaled and closed his eyes, wondering what might have been.

He waited for a few minutes, watching the road and checking that all was calm again. Once satisfied, he crawled back to the firing point and waited.

Shielding the luminous dials on his watch, he saw that it was 22:47 hours.

'C'mon Al Obedi. Time to meet your maker,' he murmured.

Bringing the binos to his eyes, he saw a large, white Lexus pull up at the entrance. A Qatari of middle age got out of the car and stepped towards a rear wall. Taking out a packet of cigarettes, the man lit one and inhaled deeply.

A few minutes passed.

Suddenly, he felt the phone vibrate in his pocket and knew the moment had come.

'I wouldn't stand there if I were you,' he muttered quietly, hoping the man would move, 'or it really will be bad for your health.'

Placing the binos back in the pouch, he answered the call.

'Just wanted to talk about Mike's party?' Pete began.

'OK,' he replied at a whisper.

'Yeah, how about the 30th?'

'Sounds good,' quieter still.

He pulled the rifle into his shoulder and began breathing deeply, forcing oxygen into his lungs. Gently, he took the safety catch off and stretched his index finger along the trigger guard.

'Actually, the 15th may be better?'

He didn't respond. He was watching the entranceway, as if nothing else in the world mattered. Slowly, he took a firmer hold of the pistol grip and moved his finger lightly to the trigger. A passing mosquito buzzed annoyingly around his ear and settled on his skin. He felt the stab of the proboscis of the thirsty insect, but ignored it completely.

His breathing was shallower now, as he concentrated fully on the entrance

He held his breath and was perfectly still, like stone.

From the right, coming out of the hotel, he saw a Qatari of about thirty, in traditional garb and another Arab in a suit walk towards the Lexus. Several steps behind them was Al Obedi, limping slightly. David tracked his progress as he moved towards the car.

Suddenly, a car backfired on the highway, sounding like a shot.

Stopping, Al Obedi's head turned and for a moment he seemed to be looking directly towards his assassin. He saw the face he had seen so recently and for a split second, actually felt sorry for him.

He squeezed the trigger gently and the bullet found its mark, dead centre in the Qatari's forehead.

He watched and waited, staying dead still.

A woman began screaming from somewhere and men were shouting.

He continued to watch impassively.

He saw Al Obedi's body lying on the ground, his once white thobe gradually turning red. Looking beyond, he saw another body lying on the floor and realised that it was the Arab he had seen seconds before, smoking a cigarette. The bullet had clearly gone through the target and hit the unfortunate soul behind.

Wrong time, wrong place.

Peering through the scope once more, he saw a scene of confusion, utter confusion. Men were running around and a group had gathered around the body, looking at it in shock.

Satisfied that his work was done, he crawled backwards, cradling the rifle. Removing the magazine, he pulled the cocking lever backwards, allowing the unfired round to eject into the case catcher. He then placed the bullet back into the magazine and settled the spent case in the dirt next to him.

Firing off the action, he grinned when he heard the working parts race forward with a dull clunk. Working deliberately, he removed the other rifle attachments and slid the rifle back into its case, placing the magazine into the pouch.

He rolled up his mat, pushing it into the pack. He then checked the area, making sure that nothing was left behind. Shouldering his gear, he made his way along the roof, down the stairs and out of the building. Stopping to listen for anything unusual and once satisfied that all was well, he headed back towards the car, taking a different route to the one he had taken a few hours before. He moved swiftly and reached the car in a few minutes. Placing the rifle case and pack on the back seat and covering them with a rug, he jumped in the front, started the engine and drove away.

It was time to get rid of the gun and start to cover his tracks.

....

David awoke the next morning fully refreshed and ready to start the day. Looking outside his door, he found the newspaper that had been ordered. Shuffling through the pages, he saw no mention of the shooting, just stories about the climate change conference in Cape Town, famine in Sudan and more killings in Nigeria. Turning on the TV, he switched to CNN and immediately noticed a banner running along the bottom of the screen.

'Shooting in Doha. More details to follow,' it read.

He checked his diary. He deliberately had set up meetings throughout the day, both to take his mind off the killing and to give him plausible cover should he need it. His first meetings in the morning were with candidates for a senior marketing role in Oman he had invented and in the afternoon, he was due to meet a potential client in the oil and gas sector. Afterwards, he had scheduled two more meetings with candidates about a banking role in Kuwait.

He showered, shaved and changed and went downstairs to the restaurant. Settling for cereals, fruit cuts, fresh coffee and orange juice, he sat down in a corner where he had a view of the TV. The killings in Nigeria were the main story, but the banner along the bottom remained unchanged.

'Shooting in Doha. More details to follow.'

The Qataris are trying to suppress the story, he thought. Finishing his breakfast, he went back upstairs. There was some time before his first meeting, so he prepared himself by reading CVs and doing some research on the client that he was due to meet in the afternoon.

The day passed quickly and he was pleased to be back in his room and able to relax by five o'clock. Something was missing, though. He felt that he should be celebrating or something, but instead he was on his own, sober and he had to admit it, a bit lonely. Getting rid of the thoughts, he turned on the TV to watch the news.

The female newsreader had the usual straw-coloured hair and orange skin that he detested. She was talking about the Nigeria killings again, as if she were describing a village fair.

Horrific images were shown on screen, in what looked like a suicide bombing at a bus station. On finishing the story, she began talking about 'the shooting in Doha yesterday'. She explained that the police were reporting it as a feud between families.

'Two men have been killed and the police have a suspect,' she said.

Interesting, he thought.

The police were obviously trying to cover things up under instruction from the senior leaders, who no doubt wanted to remove the glare of international publicity as quickly as possible and go back to making money.

He watched the news for a while longer, but grew tired of the death and destruction on screen and, trying to lift his mood, decided to go out and get a drink. The place he found was one that he had been to with Pete before, The Crazy Horse. Settling into a corner seat, he ordered a beer and looked around the half empty bar. It had the usual crowd of white middle-aged oil workers, young Indian subcontinent professionals and Filipino service workers.

He missed speaking to his friend and craved his sense of humour and irreverent view on life. They had agreed, though, that it would be safer to keep their distance and not meet up after the hit. Pete was a good guy to have around and he wondered if he would work with him again.

Next morning there was nothing on the news of the killing of Al Obedi.

Checking the local newspaper that had been left outside his door and flicking through the pages, he saw that there wasn't a single mention of the story.

He wasn't seeking any fame or glory for the sanction, far from it. The fewer people knowing of his involvement, the better. He just found it strange that in a country trying to modernise, it still couldn't bring itself to tell the truth and allow the police and media to do their jobs.

It was as if the event had never happened.

After taking a quick breakfast and checking out, he caught one of the many turquoise taxis cruising the city and headed for the airport.

As soon as reached there, he felt the tension in the air. Armed police and soldiers were positioned in small groups around the departures hall, looking around furtively. He also noticed numerous plain clothes police officers hanging around, trying to look inconspicuous, but failing.

Adopting a poker face, he walked towards the immigration counter and presented his passport to the young Qatari on duty. The Arab took the document and studied it carefully.

He leafed through every page and reaching the personal details section, spent what seemed like minutes, reading the content. His heart began to beat more rapidly and he could feel the drop of sweat on his temple start to slide down the side of his face.

'What brought you to Qatar, Mr Lord?' the official asked.

'Business,' he replied amiably.

'What business?'

'Executive recruitment. I was meeting candidates and clients.'

The Arab began tapping on his computer keyboard, occasionally looking up at the Englishman, who returned the blank stare.

Minutes passed.

This is just a game, he told himself. They're just picking out the odd westerner, hoping to get lucky.

The Arab picked up the phone and called someone, presumably his manager.

'I've got someone you should see,' he said in Arabic.

He couldn't hear the response, but the young Qatari went on. 'I've got an English here. Lean man, no glasses, looks like a soldier. He arrived on Saturday, lots of stamps in his passport.'

The Qatari put the phone down and a few minutes later, an older national, immaculately dressed in a thobe, walked up to the counter and took the passport from the younger official.

'Please follow me,' the older man instructed.

He followed him to some offices to the side of the immigration counters. As he walked, he could feel his heart beating stronger and he took the opportunity to wipe away the sweat at his temples with the back of his hand. He was confident that he had got away with the killing, but there was still a nagging doubt that they had something.

'Please sit,' instructed the Qatari, pointing to a chair.

There was a knock on the door and a policeman entered and stood behind David, who noticed the pistol on his hip.

The Qatari, occasionally glancing up, leafed through the passport at length.

'You are well travelled' the man observed.

'I suppose I am.'

'So, Mr Lord, why are you in my country?' he enquired.

He explained, again.

'Where were you on Tuesday night?'

'I was in my hotel room after a busy day.'

'On your own?'

'Yes,' he said flatly.

'There was a shooting that night. Did you hear about it?'

'I saw something on CNN, yes.'

The Qatari nodded his head, slowly.

'What did you hear?'

'They said there was a family feud I think, but there weren't many details.'

'What do you think?' asked the official, leaning towards him.

'Sounds like a family feud.'

'Yes, a family feud,' agreed the Arab, nodding his head.

Looking up at the policemen, the official asked in Arabic, 'What do you think?'

'We don't have anything on this man, Abdullah. Let him go.'

The official looked through the passport again, paying close attention to the visa stamps he had received over the years. Still studying the document, he spoke again.

'Were you ever in the army, Mr Lord?'

The question took him by surprise and he felt a thump in his chest.

'Yes, for a few years,' he answered casually.

The Qatari nodded his head.

'Did you ever use sniper rifles?' he asked.

'No, just ordinary weapons.'

The official nodded his head slowly.

'OK, that is all. You can go. Enjoy your flight,' said the man, reaching for a stamp, pressing it into an inkpad and banging the passport hard, before handing it back.

'Thank you,' he answered and getting up, was shown out by the policeman.

He walked through departures, towards one of the cafes, his heart still beating fast, but his mood elated.

Chapter Twenty

England

Exhausted, David stepped over piles of letters and junk mail on his doormat. He dropped his bag, walked into the kitchen and opened the fridge. Selecting a bottle of Stella Artois, he flipped the top off and made his way into the living room.

Nothing could beat coming home, having your favourite beer cooling in the fridge and the comfort of your own bed.

Simple pleasures, he thought.

He noticed the red light on his answerphone flashing in the corner and walking over to it, pushed the 'play' button.

'Hello David, James here. Give me a call when you get a moment. Thanks.'

'Well, succinct as ever.'

He retraced his steps back to his armchair and took another swig of beer, relishing the taste as the cool liquid went south. He took another, then another and in quick time, the bottle was empty.

Strolling back to his phone, he dialled the number.

'How was the trip?' his boss asked cheerily.

'Excellent!' he replied. 'I achieved everything that I went out there for.'

'Splendid! Listen, I don't know if you are around tomorrow night, but do you fancy meeting up for a pint?'

'Sure. It would be good to meet up,' and he was given the name of a pub in Piccadilly.

....

David found the pub, the Rum and Riddle, easily enough and strolled in just after six. He had often walked past it, when shopping around Piccadilly and Oxford Circus, but had never gone in.

It was off the beaten track and very much a 'locals' pub, but he liked it. It had a dark wooden interior and there was a large fireplace at one end, perfect for those long winter evenings. Old prints of times gone by hung on the walls, along with farming implements from a bygone age, hanging from rusty nails. He was pleased that pop music wasn't blaring out and smiling, knew why his boss had chosen the place.

The pub was fairly empty, apart from what looked like a few regulars and he made his way up to the bar. An older woman, with dyed blonde hair, greeted him in a northern accent and asked him what he would like. Opting for a pint of Carlsberg, he paid and found a quiet spot by the window, facing the door.

Minutes later, James walked in wearing a green tweed jacket, camel coloured corduroys and brown brogues.

The look of an English gent, he thought to himself. He felt a little underdressed in his cotton shirt, fleece jacket and jeans.

David asked him what he was having.

'Oh, a pint of bitter please,' the man answered, pulling out a chair.

'Nice pub, this,' he noted, when returning with the drinks.

'Yes, it's a good place for a quiet pint,' agreed James, who was studying him, a look of quiet contentment on his face.

'You really did it! Of course, I was never in any doubt.'

'Yeah, it went well. It was good to have an assistor at the top of his game,' he answered.

'It's the team that gets the result.'

He smiled, wondering where Pete was at that precise moment. Probably chatting up bimbos in some sleazy Dubai bar.

'Now, tell me all about it,' instructed the former colonel, taking a large swig from his glass.

The two men chatted for over two hours, James pausing half way through to recharge their glasses. David did most of the talking and was interrupted regularly to clarify a point. The pub had filled up a little and conscious that they might be overheard, his boss raised his hand.

'We'd better call it a day.'

He paused and looked straight at the younger man.

'Would you go back?'

He considered his response for a moment.

'Sure, why not? Do you have someone else out there on the list?'

'We may have. We can talk about it in the future. No rush.'

He thought for a moment. He had enjoyed the trip and was confident he could return, sometime in the future.

'Anyway, this is for you,' James announced, taking out a buff envelope from inside his jacket and sliding it across the table. 'For services rendered.'

Taking the package quickly, he placed it into his fleece pocket, zipping it up securely.

'Thanks,' he said.

'No problem, you've earnt it! That's the going rate for a third lister.'

James finished his drink and stood up.

'Thanks for coming out to meet me.' Changing the subject, and leaning closer, he said, 'What I want you to do now, is to settle back into your other life and develop your business experience. We'll talk about another operation in a few months.'

....

He settled back into routine, completing some of his more testing assignments and starting to win lucrative work for the firm. A business trip to Angola had been particularly fruitful, where he had persuaded one of the major mining conglomerates to use him for some of their senior positions. He had come back from Luanda with three executive roles to work on, netting him a small fortune in potential fees. He had enjoyed using his Portuguese again and was relieved that it hadn't let him down during the tough negotiations there.

Then one morning, he woke suddenly in a cold sweat, despite the warmth of his flat. Glancing over at his alarm clock, he saw that it was just after three in the morning.

'Shit!' he cursed, as he swung his legs out of the bed and padded to the bathroom.

Pouring water into his cupped hands, he washed his face and stared at himself in the mirror. He looked older, he could tell. Something in the eyes frightened him. They seemed colder and darker than before.

Walking into his lounge, he slumped onto the couch and brought his hands up to his face. The vision from the nightmare that he had woken from had him kneeling in a sandy, open air courtyard, somewhere in Qatar. He was blindfolded and somehow knew it was the hour before dawn.

Something had gone wrong with the operation, which his brain would not reveal. Al Obedi had been killed – the image of his blood soaked corpse, lying on the ground, was very real in his mind – but something had happened after the hit and he had been captured.

He had been found guilty of the killing and sentenced to death, held in a stinking, eight by eight foot tomb, never seeing anyone, just the hands of the jailer, pushing food once a day through a flap at the bottom of his cell door. His body had wilted and his mind was beginning to weaken.

On this day, guards had dragged him from the bare floor, where he had been sleeping and forced him along quiet corridors into the courtyard, where he was kneeling now. A blindfold had been placed over his eyes.

He could hear Arabic voices in hushed tones behind him and wondered if they were prison guards, keeping an eye on him, or others who wanted to watch the spectacle.

He heard footsteps to his right.

Deliberate footsteps of someone with purpose. The unknown man stopped in front of him and there was silence. For what seemed an age, nothing happened and there was no sound, save for a dog barking somewhere, off in the distance. He had loved dogs all his life. In the flyblown patrol bases of darkest Iraq and Afghanistan, it had always been him who had given scraps and unwanted rations to the strays, much to the annoyance of his fellow soldiers. He didn't care. He wanted to let the poor creatures, many with wounds and open sores, know in some small way that they were loved, if only by him.

Maybe the dog in his nightmare was telling him that he was not alone now.

'Kafir!' the man in front shouted in Arabic.

He raised his head a little and his heart rate doubled.

'Kafir! You have come here to die and I am your executioner!'

He had taken a deep breath and exhaled slowly, knowing he had seconds on earth to live. His mind raced with everything he had done in his life and visions of friends and family flashed past his eyes. He had lived a good life and had no regrets, save for being captured this time, of course.

He took another deep breath of the early morning air and exhaled through his mouth this time, savouring the moment.

'Make sure the blade is sharp,' he uttered quietly in Arabic, lowering his head, as the executioner moved to his side.

The last image in his mind was that of Penny, sitting on a bench by the river Thames, her hair fluttering gently in the wind. Her smile told him, without words, how proud she was of him.

A tear formed in the corner of his eye and began to slide down his face.

He heard the rustle of the man's thobe, as the heavy sword was lifted high above his head and the world went black.

David shook the vivid nightmare from his mind and curled up on the couch, drifting back into a fitful sleep until dawn. When he woke, he stretched like a cat and headed for the bathroom to complete his morning rituals. Changing quickly, he was out of the flat before seven and after a ride on the tube, at his desk by eight.

Checking his diary, he saw that he had a full morning of candidate interviews, but was pleased to see that the afternoon had gaps. He wanted time to plan some more overseas trips and eyed his new mouse mat, showing a map of the world, with interest. The Far East would be good; it was a region he didn't know well and one that he craved to explore.

Later that day, as he was briefing his researcher about a new position, Margaret called and asked him to drop in to see James before he left for the evening.

As the nearby church bell chimed seven, he walked along the corridor, wondering what was up.

'Hello James,' he said, after he had knocked on the door and peered inside. 'Margaret asked me to come down.'

James had been away in the States, he said, having meetings in the booming technology sector, which it turned out was screaming out for software developers. David smiled. The man had an uncanny knack in disappearing for a week or so and returning with deals that helped to keep his consultants busy for months. He wondered if he would be as good, when he was older.

'Anyway, that's for another day. There's a potential job coming up, if you're interested?'

'Sure, what is it?' he asked eagerly.

'Ever been to Pakistan?'

He looked across at the older man with wide eyes.

'Err, no. Never been. Got close to the border a few times, but never needed to cross.'

'Mm,' muttered James, glancing at some papers in front of him. 'It looks like our friends at SIS need some help out there. Something to do with a local trying to sell nuclear material. A chap called Khan. He's been on our list for a while, designated as 'candidate 44' and previously not a high priority. But it seems that events out there are hotting up, excuse the pun, and there is a danger that some of the material could end up in the UK. So, VX have asked me to provide someone to work with their agent out there. They want it low key, as you can imagine and don't have anyone available at short notice.'

'What's the plan?'

'Should be fairly straight forward actually. This is a 'non kill' operation.'

He looked at the man for a hint of humour, but there was none.

'You'll be protecting the agent, when he talks to Khan. No doubt he'll tell him he's been rumbled, slap his wrist and you can come home.'

'OK, I'll take it.'

'Splendid! You'll be briefed by the agent when you get out there. You'll be leaving in a few days, if that's alright with you?'

'Fine,' he replied, as he stood up. 'I'll get prepared.'

'You'll be armed. Obviously. Dangerous place Pakistan.'

....

Leaving work a little early the following evening, David found the Barracks where L Detachment were based, just off the Kings Road. He remembered the time he had stayed there briefly, when he was on the SAS counter-terrorism team. His troop had bunked down there, whilst spending their days driving around London, getting acquainted with the layout of foreign embassies and other structures that might need to be assaulted.

As he crossed a rain soaked square within the camp, he heard a shout off to his right.

'Bloody hell, I don't believe it!'

Turning his head, he recognised a familiar figure bearing down on him.

'Christ, Nobby Clarke!' he exclaimed. 'What the hell are you doing here?'

The soldier had served as an NCO in the same squadron as him, but had left the army to pursue the security circuit in the Middle East.

The two men reached each other and shook hands enthusiastically.

'I'm part of L Detachment,' explained the soldier. 'The work out in Iraq was getting a bit spicy, so I've taken a job in London that looks after celebrities and provides muscle for some of the pubs. Also, I've two daughters to look after now, so I need to be home more. The wife was killing me, being away all the time!'

'Good for you!' he beamed, slapping the soldier on the back. 'How is it, L Detachment?'

'Fantastic! It's good to keep your hand in. Anyway, what are you doing here?'

'Oh, I was thinking of joining and have dropped in to see the OC.'

'Excellent! C'mon, I'll take you to him,' said the soldier, smiling and pointing to a red brick building in the distance.

He guessed that the OC, Ben Caruthers, was in his forties as they were introduced.

He was of a similar height, but was thicker set and his shoulders were broader. His greying hair was longer than regulation standards and his darkened skin gave away a life spent outdoors. He invited his guest to take a seat and took his own, behind a large metal desk.

'Glad that you could make it,' the OC began. 'James mentioned your name to me some months back, but I guess you've been busy?'

He moved in his seat uncomfortably and shrugged.

'Yes, you could say that. What, with starting a new job and going overseas on business, it's been a busy time.' He didn't mention that the memories of Afghanistan had also made him hesitant.

The major nodded, looking at his guest and David noticed his grey and piercing eyes.

'So, do you have time for us now?' he asked, matter of factly. 'We're going to need a month off you every year, if it's going to work.'

'Yes, I do. The firm has agreed that if I join, then I'll take the time as unpaid leave.'

'Fair enough. Now, let me tell you a little about us. We basically support the regular SAS with manpower, to cover any gaps that they have for their operations. Although we're reserves, when we operate with sabre squadrons, we operate as regular troops. Right now, we have soldiers in Afghanistan, Iraq and one or two other interesting places....'

The man then went on to explain at length how the unit operated, what training they did and what he could expect if he joined.

David nodded thoughtfully.

'You would resume your previous rank, Captain, and be paid and rewarded at that level. Typically, you would cover any Troop Commander gaps, if one was out of action for some reason. Occasionally, you may go in as an individual, or to beef up an operation, if a squadron is short of men. Typically, you would join us for a week or two on operations overseas and then come back to the UK, to resume your civilian life.'

'Sounds interesting.'

'Yes, I think you would find it so. The beauty of course, is that you can plug in and plug out. You would get all the excitement of working with the best Special Forces unit in the world again, without being in the army full time.'

'Yes, that appeals' he muttered.

The major reached for some papers on his desk and looked up at his guest.

'When I knew you were coming here today, I took the liberty of phoning your old boss, Peter Shelton.'

'Oh, right. How is he?'

'He's fine. Actually working at the MOD now. Enjoying a period of calm.'

'That's good. He's earnt some quiet time.'

'Yes, he has. He lost some good men out in Afghanistan, but the squadron had many successes.'

He let his mind wander back to the harshness of that country and the faces of those who were lost flashed through his brain.

'Anyway, he sends his regards. Says you were one of the best Troop Commanders he ever had. He also says that you would have got your own squadron, if you'd stayed in.'

'I wanted to do something else, develop in different ways. Earn some decent money, too!'

The OC chuckled.

'Yeah. I know what you mean. He said that I should take you like a shot and that you'd be a star within the unit.'

Smiling modestly, he looked at the floor.

'So, I guess I should take his advice. I'd like you to come and join us. There's no shortage of interesting jobs coming up, in this dangerous world we live in. Anyway, have a think about what I've said and let me know if you want to proceed. We can have you kitted up and ready to go in short order.'

'Thanks Ben, it's been interesting,' he said, standing and offering his hand to the man.

As he reached the door, he turned to the major and smiled.

'I'm in!'

Chapter Twenty-one

Pakistan

David landed at Benazir Bhutto International Airport in Islamabad a little after midday. Picking up his bag and clearing customs, he walked into the arrivals hall looking for the agent. All he saw was a sea of dark faces, some impassive, some questioning and a few openly hostile. Some were wearing cheap suits, but the bulk were in shalwar kameez, the traditional dress of most men in Pakistan.

After a few minutes, unable to spot the SIS man, he made his way over to an ancient tea stand, ordered himself a drink and sat down on one of the hard wooden benches.

The airport had seen better days, he thought. It was distinctly 1970s in design, with everything functional but not attractive, the sort of place one wanted to pass through as quickly as possible. There were armed police and soldiers everywhere, reminding him of the underlying threat in the country.

A young man, probably in his twenties, dressed in jeans and check shirt, shuffled up to him.

'Taxi, sir?' he asked.

'Err, no thank you. I'm waiting for a friend.'

The man nodded and moved on to another traveller, sat a few seats away.

His phone rang and he answered it quickly.

'Tariq here. Sorry, but I'm running a bit late. I'll be with you shortly.'

'No problem' he replied, lying. 'I'm having a tea in the arrivals hall. See you in a bit.'

He sipped his tepid, oversweet tea and looked around once more. The airport had an undercurrent of danger. Shifty looking characters with furtive glances walked the halls, looking around as if they were casing the joint.

Thirty minutes later, a man who looked like a local, but dressed in an expensive suit, walked up and spoke in a plummy English accent.

'You must be David?'

'Yes! Tariq is it?'

The two men exchanged pleasantries and walked out of the airport, the dry heat hitting David unexpectedly. He could feel sweat forming on his skin and dampness under his shirt.

'Wow, it's baking.'

'Yes, it's always hot this time of year,' replied the agent, looking over his shoulder. 'You'll get used to it!'

'I'm sure,' he replied, following his contact into the car park and looking up at the building clouds. It was March and oppressively hot, but he was glad he wasn't arriving in torrential downpours, due a few months off. They came to a grey Toyota saloon and seeing them arrive, a local man quickly stepped out of the driver's side.

'This is Bilal,' announced Tariq. 'Our driver and bodyguard.'

He shook his hand, noticing the bulge under the man's jacket as he did so. Probably a Browning, he thought. Standard issue for protection teams.

The driver made his way out of the airport complex and headed towards the city. David watched people sitting by the side of the road in the sweltering heat. Some were selling fruit and wilting vegetables from rickety old carts, whilst others had laid out their wares on plastic sheets on the ground. Nobody seemed to be smiling.

Eventually, after passing through several police checkpoints, they reached the embassy in the diplomatic quarter and once their car was searched at the main gate, were dropped off at the entrance.

'Welcome to the British Embassy!' grinned Tariq. 'We'll need to go through the metal detectors and sign in and we can get started.'

Once they were cleared, Tariq led him up a staircase, through some doors and into an open plan area, where embassy staff were busily working.

'We're over there,' he said, pointing to a door.

One or two of the workers looked up at the pair, momentarily curious to see who the visitors were, but soon lost interest and returned to their laptops.

Approaching the door, he saw the word 'Int' for 'Intelligence' written above and stepped inside. It was quite a large room, with desks along three sides and an electric fan whirling above. The five people in the room didn't look up but continued to stare at their laptops, tapping away at the keys.

On the walls, he could see maps of Pakistan showing physical geography, ethnic groups and transportation links. There were also maps of the major cities: Islamabad, Lahore, Karachi, Rawalpindi, Faisalabad, Peshawar and Multan. On one of the walls, there were four white clocks, showing local time as well as that for London, New York and Dubai.

'Hello everyone,' said Tariq loudly, once he had closed the door. 'This is David from London, who has come out here to help us for a week or so.'

'Afternoon!' he said smiling and looking at each person in turn.

There were nods of welcome as the analysts acknowledged him, but they soon resumed their work, as their eyes focused once again on their screens.

'This way,' said the SIS man, gesturing to another door in the corner.

He followed him into what looked like some sort of secret communications room. There were blinds on the windows and the artificial light from above provided a strange peachy glow. There were three phones on the far desk, in white, red and black and two high tech radio transmitters further along in the corner. A dinner sized table dominated the middle of the room, with chairs neatly tucked in. On the wall opposite the window, a screen was set up.

'Grab a seat and make yourself comfortable,' he invited. 'We're going to be in here for most of the day.'

Taking off his jacket, he hung it on the back of his chair and sat down.

Tariq turned on the projector and connected his laptop to it, glancing at him as he did so.

'I appreciate your help in coming out here,' he began, with a big smile on his face, 'and I'll brief you today on what we have and what your role will be.'

'Happy to help,' he replied.

The face of a man appeared on screen.

'Hamza Khan,' the SIS man imparted simply.

Studying the face closely, he saw a dark skinned man of about forty. His hair was jet black, but greying at the temples and his neatly trimmed moustache was drooping slightly at the edges. The Pakistani had one or two moles on his right cheek and was clearly forcing a smile for the camera, his eyes cold and clear.

'That was taken about five years ago. For one of the government websites. As you can probably tell, he doesn't like his picture taken! To get recent photos, we had to get him as he travelled around Islamabad.'

The agent flashed up a few more photos of Khan, walking up steps, looking over his shoulder and getting out of vehicles.

'Looks like he's put a bit of weight on,' David commented, peering at the screen.

'Yes, he has. Apparently, he likes to exercise, but in this country that could mean anything. We've tracked him going to the gym once or twice a month on average.'

He grinned, thinking of his own rigorous fitness regime.

'He's a family man and has a wife and two daughters. He studied nuclear physics at Karachi University and received his doctorate there. He was a brilliant student and was destined for a life in academia. After his PhD, he lectured for a few years, but we think he got bored of that, because he moved to Kahuta, the centre of Pakistan's nuclear weapons programme. It's about thirty kilometres from here, towards Kashmir. Have you heard of it?'

'No,' he admitted, 'although I know that Pakistan has had nuclear weapons for a few decades now. Didn't want India to have an upper hand?'

'Yes, you're right,' said Tariq, flashing up satellite images of the Kahuta complex on screen. 'Pakistan has had them for a while now and thankfully, haven't had to use them, although it's been touch and go on some occasions. Their weapons and delivery systems aren't as sophisticated as other countries, like the US and Britain, but they're dangerous enough and could wipe out major conurbations within a few thousand kilometres, if they chose to do so.'

David shook his head.

'Khan did well at Kahuta, working on the uranium enrichment programme for several years with some of the brightest minds in the country. He was regularly promoted and well regarded by his seniors and peers. But something happened a few years ago, because he stopped rising and became disgruntled by all accounts. We know this, because one of his colleagues at the plant defected and went to the US to help on its own nuclear programme.'

'What happened then, fall out with his superior?'

'Something like that, yes. At about this time, he also started getting into debt. We know because the CIA had someone working in one of the large banks here and for some reason, Khan was haemorrhaging money every month. It started small, but began to increase and a little digging showed that he had developed a bit of a gambling habit. On top of that, he was funding a decent house near to Kahuta, private education for his girls and his wife's expensive taste in fancy western clothes.'

'Ah,' he said. 'So his problems at work made him turn to gambling and money problems quickly followed.'

'Yes! And this brings us to why you're here. A few months ago, GCHQ picked up a phone call Khan made to someone called Bahram Noorzai in Peshawar. On that call, he talked about the possibility of selling nuclear material. The UK's concern is that this material, in the form of a 'dirty' bomb, could ultimately find its way there.'

'So, how far as he got?'

'Well, after that initial call, it went quiet for a bit. We think that Khan was asking for millions and so the group had to rob a few banks and get their Gulf sponsors to replenish the coffers.'

'Millions, you say?'

'Yes, it would have to be. If he managed to get the material and sell it to the undesirables, he would be finished in Pakistan and would have to try to make a life somewhere else, probably one of the Gulf states. Since that first call, we've been monitoring him closely and even managed to get a tracker on to his car. Five weeks ago, over a weekend, we tracked his car to Peshawar. We think he met Noorzai there.'

'Think? Didn't you have eyes on?'

'No, unfortunately. We didn't have the resources at the time, as our people were heavily involved in watching a high value British Islamist in Quetta,' conceded Tariq. 'But since the meeting in Pesh, things have picked up. Two weeks ago, when I requested VX for support, which resulted in you being here, GCHQ picked up another call between Khan and Noorzai. On that call, Khan confirmed that he could get the material and Noorzai told him he had the money.'

He breathed out audibly, looking at the picture of Khan staring blankly down at him.

'So, Khan has got to be working with someone else at Kahuta, to get the material out? That's going to need transportation, protective containers and God knows what else.'

'Almost certainly. He'll be bribing people up there for sure.'

'So it's only a matter of time before the trade is done?'

'Yes, we think in the next few weeks. There's a religious holiday coming up and my guess is that Khan will use it, to get the material up to Pesh and collect the money.'

'OK, so what's the plan?'

'Before I go into that, why don't we take a short break and grab a coffee?' said Tariq, turning off the projector.

'Great idea,' he replied, arching his back and stretching his arms.

....

When they resumed, with steaming coffee mugs on the table, the agent laid out his plan.

'I've been working on this a while,' he began. 'A few weeks after the first call between Khan and Noorzai was picked up, I approached Khan through another contact and pretended to be representing an extreme group in Europe, wanting nuclear material. He was extremely hesitant at first, but once we started to talk about the amount of money available, he became more interested.'

'How much were you offering?'

'Three million US, for two hundred pounds of enriched uranium.'

'That's a pretty good retirement fund,' he said, 'especially in some third world Islamic country that he would end up in.'

'Yes, absolutely. So, we then had regular dialogue about the arrangements for delivery and so on and I told him we had to meet. It's due to take place on Friday night, three days from now.'

'Alright. Where shall we meet him?'

Tariq brought a picture up on the projector of a plain looking hotel entrance.

'The Almond House Hotel. Out of the central district, but lively enough. I've been there a few times before.'

He scrolled through other photos of the hotel, showing the lobby, restaurant, and reception.

'I've booked a meeting room there, so we'll be undisturbed. '

'Will he have bodyguards, do you think?'

'Unlikely. What I've learnt is that he's a very private man and not some hoodlum who surrounds himself with muscle and guns. I think he'll come alone, but if he does have company, we'll have to deal with it then. Anyway, that's why you're here.' He smiled. 'If Khan has company and they come with us, they'll hear the discussion. So I'll start the conversation in Urdu, which will get him comfortable, but then I'll ask to switch to English, as you're the buyer. Khan speaks good English by the way, we've checked. You'll need to put on a fake foreign accent and stumble on some of the words, to really convince him.'

'What do you reckon, German, Spanish, French?'

'I would go with German. After the pleasantries are concluded, I'll explain why you're there. We'll come up with a story together, over the next day or so. Something realistic, but simple. Then, once the greetings are over, I tell him that we are British Intelligence and that we know about his plans to sell nuclear material.'

'He's not going to take that very well!'

'No, he won't, but I'll tell him that we will pay off his debts, estimated to be in the tens of thousands of dollars, and give him a generous allowance every month. We will also tell him that we won't inform the Pakistani authorities if he plays along. Who knows, we may even get him to tell us some secrets for our own benefit over time?'

'Sounds fair enough. He gets to remain in his own country too.'

The SIS man nodded.

'As long as he agrees to side with us at the meeting. We've lost if he stalls us and then sells the material anyway,' David warned.

'Agreed. He needs to accept before we leave the hotel, otherwise it's a non-starter.'

David nodded slowly, his mind calculating as he studied the image of the hotel on screen. 'Do you have the pistol and ammunition for me?' he enquired.

'Yes, we have it. I'll give it to you on the day.'

'OK, good. Let's run through the plan again and talk through contingencies and logistics. I'll want to have a look at the hotel tomorrow evening, to see the layout for myself.'

'Sure, no problem. Bilal can take you and drop you off afterwards.'

'Thanks. I'm guessing that using taxis around here could be a death sentence?'

'Could be. There are Islamist thugs and sympathisers everywhere, so it pays to take precautions.'

The two men discussed the upcoming operation until early evening, when he glanced at the clock on the wall and declared that he needed to check in to his hotel.

As he was standing up and gathering his things, he turned casually to the SIS man.

'Oh, by the way, which group is Noorzai representing?'

Tariq looked across at him with a fixed stare and spoke quietly, without emotion.

'Al-Qaeda.'

Chapter Twenty-two

When David arrived at his hotel, a modern three star place close to the embassy, he took some time to reflect on what he had heard during the day. He felt uneasy about the upcoming meeting, not because of the potential danger, but more about Khan's thinking. Why would he entertain a rival bidder, when he already knew the dangers he was running? Maybe he was desperate to sell the damn stuff and be out of Pakistan and live his remaining years in obscurity?

He wrestled with the thoughts for some time, before drifting into a long, deep sleep.

The next day, back in the embassy, the two men went over the plan again, discussing and debating what lay ahead, as the ceiling fan rotated sluggishly above them.

That evening, David travelled to the Almond House Hotel with Bilal. They drove through the diplomatic district and he saw the flags of Saudi Arabia, Indonesia, the Netherlands, Egypt and Turkey on the way. It was certainly a well-to-do area, judging by the buildings they passed, grand villas with manicured lawns and tight security.

They passed through more police checkpoints and transitioned into a less salubrious, busier district. There were more people on the streets, some looking suspiciously at the car. Stalls were set up by the side of the road and he could see meat being grilled on makeshift burners.

They arrived at the hotel a little after seven and parked in the street opposite. He took a moment to examine the front of the property, estimating that it was about twenty years old. Four stories high, it had a light brown facade and wide entrance staircase of three or four steps. He couldn't see any armed guards, but they could be out of sight, or in plain clothes somewhere. There wasn't much traffic going into or leaving the hotel, and those he did see looked like normal businessmen, carrying cheap briefcases or bundles of paper held together by string.

Exiting the car, he strode across the road, taking care to avoid a speeding old taxi, which had local music blaring out of the windows.

On entering the building, he headed for the seats in the empty lobby and sat down, picking up a tattered English language newspaper on the table next to him. He glanced at it, scanning the pages, but kept looking up to check his surroundings. To the right of the entrance was the reception area, a long marbled desk with a young man behind it, peering at something, probably a computer screen, out of view. The lobby area had groups of chairs and tables in random fashion, resting on a worn light blue carpet. On the walls were prints of almond trees, with white and pink petals radiating in the sunshine.

Satisfied, he approached reception and asked the man if he could view the meeting rooms. He was handed some keys and pointed towards a door that led to a corridor.

'There are four meeting rooms in that corridor, sir,' explained the receptionist. 'I've given you the keys for the first two rooms, as the others are exactly the same in layout.'

He thanked him and walked through the door and along the corridor. He reached the first meeting room, unlocked the door and walked in, turning on the light. Inside was a medium sized wooden table with four chairs on either side, notepads and pencils laid out neatly in front of each place. A picture of a tree on a hillside, laden with snow, was the only distraction. Walking to the window and, pulling the light curtains aside, he saw a bare brick wall, twenty feet away. He noticed that the windows could be opened and saw that the drop to the ground below was about six feet, into flower beds. Sitting in one of the chairs, he visualised the meeting that was going to take place in a few days, and ran through a few scenarios in his mind.

He did a similar exercise in the next meeting room, then walked back to reception and handed over the keys.

'All fine, sir?' asked Bilal, when he returned to the car.

'Yes, thanks. Take me back to the hotel would you?'

They drove back in silence, David deep in thought, wondering if he had considered everything. It was quicker now and the traffic seemed to have thinned out, he noticed. The food stalls were doing a roaring trade though, with small crowds gathered around each one, eyes, young and old, looking eagerly at the sizzling meat.

....

Friday dawned bright and early and, padding to the window and pulling back the curtains, David saw the mist hanging over the city. It would be burned off by the sun later, but for now there was a magic to the sight.

After a shower and shave, he headed down to the restaurant, to set himself up for the day. There were two other diners already there, a large, middle-aged western man in a business suit, with a younger, pretty Pakistani woman. He noticed them, from the corner of his eye, holding hands under the table and exchanging furtive and loving glances. He wondered if she was a secretary from the man's embassy, if that's where he worked, or just a co-worker he had met on his travels.

After he was served with fresh coffee by one of the waiters, he walked over to the breakfast buffet to see what was on offer. Bypassing the local selection of nashta dishes, consisting of minced meats, savoury pastries, eggs and fruits, he opted instead for some sachets of Alpen and adding milk to his bowl, headed back to his table. He often skipped breakfast back in the UK, preferring to snatch a coffee and watch the headline news, before racing off to work. When he was on overseas trips though, he liked to take his time with the first meal of the day, to allow him to think about what could be in store.

Breakfast over, he walked back up to his room, gathered his stuff and took the ride to the British Embassy. Once there, after going through security, he made his way into the inner sanctum. He found Tariq already staring despondently at his laptop screen.

'Hi Tariq, how are things?' he asked casually.

'Not great,' the agent replied, breathing out hard.

'What's happened?'

'I asked my contact at GCHQ to see if Khan had been in touch with anyone over the last few days.'

'And?' he asked impatiently.

'He called Noorzai, yesterday afternoon.'

'Oh Christ! He's playing dangerous games.'

'Yes, he is and that's not all. He's set up a meeting in Pesh, for the weekend after next. That's eight days from now!'

'Not good. Maybe we spooked him?'

'Possibly. Although he's made the stakes even higher. I think he's set up the AQA meeting so that he can hear both offers, then quickly decide who to go with and get the hell out of the country!'

'Does it change anything though?'

'I don't think it does. We still have to meet him and tell him he's been spotted. We have to push hard to convince him to side with us and take our offer. I've already been in touch with the Head of South Asia Operations at VX this morning, to increase the amounts we have to bribe him with, but I'm still waiting for approval.'

'OK, good move,' he said, looking hard at Tariq. 'We may need a lot of cash to outbid Al-Qaeda.'

'So let's continue as normal, meet Khan tonight and take it from there.'

He nodded.

'Can I take the pistol now?'

'Sure. Follow me and we'll go down to the armoury in the basement.'

The two men made their way downstairs and came to a door marked 'Stores'. The SIS man tapped on the door and walked in, greeting an older colleague sat behind a grand wooden desk.

'Hello Waqas, how's life?' he asked cheerily.

'Oh, not too bad,' the man replied with a resigned smile. 'Who's your friend?'

'This is David from London. He's come to assist me on something and he needs one of the Sig Sauers. Do you remember, I mentioned it the other day?'

'Yes, yes, come this way.' He led them over to a large metal door in the corner.

Opening it, he swung back the door, turned on the light and went inside. He emerged moments later with a pistol and two magazines in one hand, a suppressor in the other and a large blue hardback book under his arm.

The man laid everything down on a table and handed David the weapon, who took it carefully. He smiled when he saw that it was a Sig Sauer P226, as it was like meeting an old pal. He had carried one with the SAS in Afghanistan and had been forced to use it once, when his main weapon had failed. It was a powerful and accurate pistol and far better than the Browning he had used in the Paras. Checking it was safe, he inspected it for wear and tear, noticing that it was in very good condition, with few scratches.

'It's quite new,' said the storeman, studying the visitor. 'We've only had it for a few years and it hasn't been used much,' he smiled conspiratorially. 'Read off the serial number, would you?'

He did so and signed the notebook.

'How much ammunition do you want?'

'Oh, I would think thirty rounds would be enough,' he replied, after doing some quick calculations in his head.

The man shuffled over to a cabinet near his desk, opened it and pulled out a small, half- filled box of 9mm rounds, which he handed over. Closing the cabinet, the storeman walked over to some shelves with all manner of equipment, torches, batteries, holsters, pouches and handheld radios. Selecting a sturdy, green plastic pouch, he handed it to David.

'One cleaning kit,' he explained. 'Try to bring back all the items in the same state as you received them.'

'I'll look after them, don't worry,' he replied, grinning.

'Thank you,' said the Pakistani, looking up at his face. 'You look like someone who takes care of himself and his equipment. I wish you good luck!' and he walked back to his desk and sat heavily down.

The men walked back up to the communications room and placed the weapon and other items in the safe.

'Let's run through the op one more time,' he said.

The agent walked him through the plan once more, dealing with the questions that were fired at him. They paused for coffee half way through and after an hour they were finished.

'We'll go over it again later this afternoon and we need to make sure that Bilal is clear what his responsibilities are,' instructed David.

'Agreed. We'll brief him later. I've worked with him before and he's a steady hand, I assure you.'

'OK,' he replied. 'Now, tell me more about Noorzai.'

Tariq tapped away on his laptop and brought up the picture of Bahram Noorzai on screen.

'Well, what we know is fairly dated,' he began. 'He comes from a place called Kohat, about a hundred kilometres west of here. His family is middle class and his father was a lawyer, with a practice in the town. He had an ordinary childhood, studied hard and managed to get a place at the medical college there. After being there a few years, his father was tragically shot and killed by the army one night, at one of the checkpoints outside the town, and Bahram lost it.'

'Lost it?' he questioned.

'Yes. He dropped out of college, walked over the border to Jalalabad in Afghanistan, and joined Al-Qaeda. Many of the leaders were based there at the time, even Bin Laden passed through on occasion, and young Noorzai was noticed for his determination and religious zeal. We think, as a youngster, he took part in some operations when AQA joined up with the Taliban against the Soviets in the 1980s, but he was more of a strategy man. From informers at the time, we know that he planned a number of operations in eastern Afghanistan, in particular the attacks on the Soviet bases at Khost and Gardez, as well as a multitude of other, smaller attacks.'

'Quite a player then?' he commented, scrutinising the face on screen.

'Oh yes, he was well regarded in AQA and the Soviets had quite a price on his head apparently. Like many of the senior people, he moved around a lot, never staying in the same place for too long and they couldn't catch him.'

'A real survivor.'

'Yes, they couldn't get him and regarded him as something of a ghost. That is until the late eighties, when the Soviets' power in Afghanistan was starting to crumble. He was travelling by car one night with some bodyguards, from Jalalabad to Mitarlam, to meet some tribal elders, when a wandering Soviet helicopter spotted them and fired a missile at the car.'

'That must have hurt!' he said, pulling a face.

'Yes, the driver and one other were killed instantly. Noorzai and the other passenger somehow survived the strike and were found by locals, staggering along a road. They provided help to the men and a local group, aligned to AQA, took them to a nearby doctor who did his best, bearing in mind he had few medical supplies and anaesthetics. Their injuries were horrendous and the men had lost a lot of blood. Noorzai's companion died during treatment, but he managed to survive, even though he had sustained broken limbs, severe burns and lost a lot of blood. He probably should have died, but someone was watching over him that night. Anyway, once he was better, he was smuggled over the border, probably by a donkey train, and ended up in Peshawar, where local Islamists gave him a safe place to fully recuperate. After a while, he took a house in the town and kept a low profile, although we know that he directed his energies in supporting AQA's activities, primarily in Afghanistan, but also Pakistan itself.'

'Dodgy place Peshawar, I would think?'

'Extremely! I went there once to carry out surveillance on a British subject who was based there, collecting money from around the world and channelling it to extreme groups in the Tribal Areas, the 'wild west' of Pakistan.'

'From day one of watching the target, I felt that it was me being watched and a few times, men wandered up to me and asked what I was doing. I was dressed poorly and pretended to be a vagabond, but one day, after only being there a week, this tall Afghani with fierce, haunting eyes, approached me and told me that if I didn't leave, he would cut my throat.'

'And did you take the hint?' David asked, breaking into a smile.

'Take the hint? I was out of there like a shot and took the next bus out! If I had stayed, I would be lying in a shallow grave right now, no doubt about it. Since then, we have run operations up there, but we need backup groups for backup groups, it's that dangerous. Pakistani intelligence, the ISI, has people there and they occasionally share information with us, but I reckon their assets are really in deep and have lived there for years.'

'Well, I'll take your word for it and cross it off my 'places to travel' list,' he joked.

Tariq smiled, stretched and stood up. 'Fancy some lunch? We've been at it all morning and could do with a break.'

'Great idea!' he replied, suddenly feeling hungry.

'I know this great place around the corner that serves the best chicken biryani you have ever tasted. Their samosas are pretty good too! Let me shut down things here and we'll take a stroll.'

Later, he took the pistol out of the safe and lovingly took it apart, examining every piece as he did so.

The storeman had been right, as it was in prime condition with hardly any wear. Probably only used on the ranges, he thought.

He cleaned and lightly oiled the weapon and pulled the moving parts back and forth to check the workings. Satisfied, he fitted the suppressor, screwing it tight and looked along the barrel, aligning the iron sights. It felt good to have it in his hands again and he wondered if he would need it that night. Although it was only a pistol, the 9mm rounds were deadly, particularly at close range.

He remembered training with one a few years before, when he was still in the Regiment. It had been on the Nanyuki ranges, in the shadow of Mount Kenya. They had been practicing quick firing drills and had hung up some pig carcasses on wooden frames as targets. The animal was perfect in representing the human body.

After the firing and walking over to the carcasses thirty metres away, he remembered the sight that greeted them. At the front, the targets were pockmarked with small holes, but stepping to the rear of each animal, the skin was shredded, with blood oozing slowly to the ground through the large exit wounds.

Back to the present, he filled one of the magazines and placed all the items back in the safe. With time to kill, when Tariq was on the phone to England again, he borrowed his laptop and brought up the mapping software used by SIS. He zoomed in on the Almond House Hotel, studying the building and surrounding gardens in great detail.

He then zoomed out a little, looking at the surrounding streets and familiarised himself with the layout, particularly key buildings, open spaces and crossroads.

Next, he zoomed out further, until he was looking at a ten kilometre square on the screen. It was mainly urban sprawl, but there were main road arteries passing through it, from bottom left to top right and middle left to top right. He retraced the route with his finger, from the hotel back to the embassy, noting the turns that had to be made and distances covered. Several times, he closed his eyes and ran through the route in his head, until he was sure that it had stuck.

'Enjoying yourself?' asked Tariq amusedly, as he sat down at the table.

'Yeah,' he laughed. 'Just looking at the maps to make sure I can get home if there's a problem.'

'Good idea. I did the same earlier.'

....

It passed six and David prepared himself mentally for what was to come. Earlier, he had changed into casual clothes and his favourite footwear, light brown desert boots. They had been with him since his time in the Paras and had stories to tell. He had also brought his fleece jacket, partly because the evenings were cool, but more importantly to help conceal the Sig Sauer, which was going to be tucked into the back of his trousers.

'We still leaving at 6.30?' he asked Tariq, sitting opposite and flicking through some documents.

Looking up, the agent confirmed that it was.

Standing up, he walked to the safe and retrieved the pistol and other items and placed them on the table. Sitting back down, he closed his eyes for a moment.

'I'll get Bilal to bring the car round,' the SIS man said, interrupting his thoughts.

'Do it,' he replied, opening his eyes.

The two gathered their things and locked up the comms room. They found Bilal hovering by the vehicle, parked near some almond trees. The men jumped into the car, with David in the back. Taking the pistol from his trousers, he laid it on the seat beside him. They set off through the main barrier and headed west towards the hotel. Looking out of the window, he saw locals making their way around town and some no doubt heading home for the night.

The image of Khan came into his mind and he wondered if their plan to snare him would actually work. He thought about the man's integrity level and how far it must have fallen over the years, to make him reach out to Al-Qaeda.

Quicker than he expected, they pulled up about a hundred metres short of the hotel and parked.

'Bilal. You know what to do. Wait here until I call you and then drive to the front and pick us up. We'll be no more than two hours, I would think.'

The driver nodded his head and shuffled in his seat. They had briefed him fully on his responsibilities and David was confident he was the right man for the job, watching their backs. He had tucked the weapon into the back of his trousers and pulled the fleece well down.

'Ready?' asked Tariq, looking over his shoulder.

'Ready!' he confirmed, and the two men stepped out of the car and walked towards the hotel.

They moved steadily along the pavement, both of them casually looking around, to see if there was anything suspicious. On arriving at the building, the agent went straight to reception to check on the meeting room and he walked over to some seats in the lobby.

'Meeting room two,' said Tariq, brandishing a key and sitting down.

He nodded and picked up a newspaper.

Glancing at his watch, Tariq said, 'Thirty five minutes to go,' and he tapped the table in front of him twice, indicating that he understood.

Then they waited, periodically looking towards the front doors. A lone businessman arrived and glanced across at them curiously before checking in, but otherwise it was quiet.

....

Well before the agreed time of the meeting, Tariq suddenly stood up.

'He's here,' he whispered into his hand, before walking towards the new arrival.

David glanced up and saw Khan standing near the entrance, looking around nervously. When he spotted Tariq walking towards him, he smiled resignedly and shook the hand that was offered. They spoke for a few moments, with Tariq casting an arm towards him and the scientist nodded his head.

'Let me introduce David to you, Hamza,' the agent said when they reached him.

Standing, he took the man's hand and shook it, looking deeply into his eyes. He saw a man afraid, confused even. Playing such high stakes was obviously taking its toll, as he noticed the bloodshot, tired eyes and wondered if the man had slept recently.

'Good to meet you, Hamza,' was all he said in his best German accent.

The man nodded, not looking pleased to see him, and turned to follow Tariq, who was pointing the way towards the meeting room. The SIS man unlocked the door, turned the lights on and beckoned them in.

'Why don't you sit here?' suggested the agent, indicating a chair opposite the window.

The man grunted something in Urdu, making Tariq smile and sat down as instructed. Once they were settled, the SIS man began speaking quietly to the scientist. The man looked seriously at him as he spoke, but kept glancing at David, almost expecting him to say something.

After a short time, Khan, who seemed visibly irritated, held up his right hand and spoke in clipped English.

'Forgive me, but can we get on with it? There are important things to discuss.'

'Yes, we can discuss it Hamza, no problem,' replied the agent.

Khan broke into a half smile and looking at both men in turn, and casting his head around the room as if to inspect it, spoke plainly.

'Actually, I'm not happy with this meeting place. I would like to discuss things somewhere more......private.'

'This is private,' assured Tariq. 'We will not be disturbed here.'

Khan stood up and said calmly, 'Let me speak with my driver, to check on something,' and he opened the door and walked quickly out.

'This is not good,' whispered David, after Khan had gone.

'I know,' replied the agent. 'Let me think!'

'We can't let him lead us somewhere that we don't know.'

Tariq breathed heavily, looking straight him. 'I've been working on this for months now and I'm not about to give it up.'

'At least get on to Bilal and tell him that we may be moving location,' he spat angrily.

'OK, OK. I'll call him.'

As Tariq was reaching into his pocket for the phone, the scientist opened the door suddenly and walked in, followed by a towering Pakistani man with a deep scar above his eye. Down the side of the man's jacket was the telltale bulge of a concealed weapon.

David felt calm, but knew that events were overtaking them. He recalled the words of his Platoon Commander at Sandhurst, many years before, talking about battle tactics. 'Gentlemen, no plan survives contact with the enemy!'

'So, I've arranged it,' announced Khan. 'We'll go to another location, where we can discuss things in more......privacy. Please follow me,' he said, as he left the room, trailed by the bodyguard.

The two men exchanged anxious glances, but stood up and followed. Instead of turning left, back towards the lobby and reception, Khan had turned right along a darkened corridor and they could hear footsteps moving quickly along it. They eventually came out the back of the hotel into a courtyard with latticed greenery above. A single bright lamp shone from the corner of the building, casting a ghostly glow on those below.

There were two cars parked, one in front of the other and Khan told the two men to take the front vehicle. David's head was screaming that this was all wrong, as he and Tariq climbed into the rear passenger seats. Glancing over his shoulder, he saw Khan briefing two men, the bodyguard and another who had appeared out of the shadows.

'This is going pear shaped!' he whispered forcefully. 'I reckon we've got about twenty seconds to do something and move, before we end up in a very dark place.'

'This is my operation and I say we see it through,' snarled Tariq through clenched teeth, looking straight ahead.

'It's your call,' he submitted, 'but at least call Bilal, while we have the chance.'

The SIS man surreptitiously pulled the phone out of his pocket and speed dialled Bilal's number, keeping the handset down by his waist.

Just then, they heard footsteps crunching on the gravel outside and Tariq disconnected the call, sliding the phone back into his pocket. The door opened and the driver stepped inside. He wound the window down and Khan's face appeared by his shoulder.

'Go with this man,' he said coldly, 'and we will follow. You are perfectly safe.'

They drove out of the courtyard in convoy and turned right, heading out of the city. He turned to Tariq enquiringly, his eyes wide open, to see if the call had got through, but the SIS man shrugged his shoulders limply, indicating that he wasn't sure.

'Does he speak English, do you think?' he asked quietly.

Tariq questioned the driver in Urdu and after a few words, turned to him and shook his head.

'Ask him where we're going, will you?' he requested, not expecting an answer.

The SIS man spoke to the driver again, a longer conversation this time, and he got the sense that the man didn't want to talk.

'He says we're going to the 'Big House'. I asked him if it was Khan's and he said he didn't know. He says it will take about half an hour to get there.'

Chapter Twenty-three

They drove out of the city, the buildings becoming smaller and less salubrious, and through the dust he noticed that the people looked poorer and more pitiful. He saw a dog with one of its front legs missing, skipping along the roadside with a thin bone in its mouth, avoiding the people around it. The street lights were getting more scarce now and there were sections of road that were in almost complete darkness, save for the occasional light above someone's door or stall. As he sat back in the seat, he felt the pistol sticking into his lower back, pleased it was there and comforted by its strength.

As the buildings receded, they reached flat, open farmland and after a few turns left and right, the traffic disappeared completely. In the headlights of the car he saw a farmer, dressed in ragged clothes, dragging a reluctant cow along the road with rope.

Eventually, they turned off and drove along a rutted, dusty track and came to some large iron gates, made sinister by the spikes running along the top. The driver got out, fumbled with some keys and opened them, pushing them to the sides. Stepping back inside, he drove into a large walled compound, with a grand two storey house facing them. It was dark, apart from the faint glow of a light above the front door.

'Here goes,' whispered Tariq. 'I'm sure it'll be OK.'

'Let's hope,' he replied, still wondering why he had allowed himself to be in such a position.

They exited the car and a dog started barking, annoyed by their arrival. The other vehicle pulled up next to them and he heard the doors begin to open. Hastily looking to his left, he saw a flower bed of sorts, with plants up to his waist, running along the wall. Slowly but surely, with the car hiding his movements, he pulled the pistol out and laid it gently in the flower bed, making a mental note of where it was.

He then strolled towards the light, where the agent was heading.

'Please….,' said Khan, smiling and gesturing them inside.

They stepped into a large entrance hall, with stairs to the left and rooms on either side. Extravagant carpets covered the floor and he noticed old fighting paraphernalia hanging from the walls: swords and spears, ancient iron helmets, wooden shields and old muskets, hanging over an imposing fireplace.

Khan led them crisply through the hall, followed by the bodyguard, into a large sitting room at the rear, with sumptuous furnishings and tasteful landscape paintings on the walls.

'Now, gentlemen,' he began, 'I'm sure you won't mind if my friend here searches you, before we start?'

Stepping forward, the Pakistani patted them down. He was very thorough, taking time to feel the body outline of each man, under the armpits, between the groin and right the way down to their shoes.

He nodded to his master sourly that all was well and took his place by the door.

'Please sit down,' instructed Khan, pointing to the large couch behind them. 'Can I get you some tea before we start?' he offered, almost kindly.

'Tea would be kind, thank you,' replied Tariq, speaking for both of them.

Khan turned his head to the bodyguard, who quietly grunted and left the room.

'Nice place you have here,' muttered the agent, looking slowly around.

'Oh, it's not mine,' protested the scientist. 'I just use it from time to time, when my friend is away. We won't be disturbed here.'

Just then, Khan's phone rang and he spoke urgently in Urdu into it.

'Excuse me for a moment,' he said, standing up and leaving the room hastily.

'What was all that about?' asked David, once the door was shut.

'Something about him having to discuss an important issue outside.'

'Right, I'm going to retrieve the gun,' he stated quietly, avoiding the agent's worried looks.

Moving to the rear door, he pulled aside the thick curtains and peered through the glass.

Total darkness.

He reached down to the key in the door and was relieved when it gave quietly. Stepping quickly outside, he closed the door and moved silently around the veranda.

Stopping at the corner, he waited and listened. Dropping to a crouch, he slowly poked his head around the wall and saw the two cars in the courtyard, weakly bathed by the solitary light. Satisfied that all was quiet, he crouched out from behind the building and hugged the wall, his fingertips scraping along the ancient brickwork.

Stopping once to listen and freezing in his tracks, he heard nothing, apart from the wind rustling the trees above him. On reaching the car, he leant down into the flower bed to where he thought he had left the weapon. His fingers explored the desiccated earth urgently, and he willed himself on to find the gun.

It wasn't there.

'Shit!' he whispered to himself.

He took a deep breath and resumed the search, crouching in the bushes. Suddenly, he heard the sound of a chain clinking behind him and froze. He heard it again and then a low growl from the dog they had disturbed earlier. Keeping still for a few moments, he allowed the animal to settle, pleased to hear the clink of the chain again when the canine lay down.

Conscious that time was pressing, he resumed his search quietly. Moving further along the flower bed and at the limit of his reach, his fingers brushed against something metallic and hard.

He patted the object slowly and smiled. Thank Christ! He picked up the pistol, shaking off the dirt, checked the magazine was still on and flicked off the safety catch.

He stopped to listen and moved stealthily back to the corner of the building. Tiptoeing back to the veranda doors, he placed his ear against the glass.

Satisfied that Tariq was on his own, he opened the door gradually and peered inside, to see him sitting where he had left him. Taking his place again quickly next to him, he slid the pistol under the couch below him.

'Bloody hell!' the agent whispered. 'That was risky.'

'Not as risky as being caught with it! I'm only surprised they didn't search us at the Almond House.'

'What do you think our man is up to?' asked Tariq.

'Oh, I would guess he's getting backup, just in case the meeting goes badly.' Lowering his voice he warned, 'My advice, when he gets back, is to cut to the chase and tell him why we're here. Offer him the deal, get his agreement and we can get the hell out of here. Delay things too long and this place is going to be crawling with the AQA brigade.'

Tariq scowled.

David felt good again, now that he had a weapon to hand. He realised he was actually enjoying the tension, the drama, the fear even.

Without warning, the door opened and Khan walked in, shadowed by the bodyguard carrying the tea. Once he had passed the cups to the guests, the big Pakistani took his place by the door.

'Sorry about that,' Khan apologised, sitting down. 'Now, where were we?'

'Is everything alright?' asked Tariq, trying to put the scientist on the spot.

'Yes, yes,' he replied, regarding him strangely, without elaborating.

'So, we have been discussing a deal for nuclear material,' began the agent, patting David on the shoulder, 'and my friend here, represents the buyer.'

Khan regarded him with interest and smiled half-heartedly.

'I suppose you aren't going to tell me who it is that wants the material?' he asked.

'You're right Hamza. We can't tell you which group, but you can rest assured they will put it to good use.'

He slowly glanced across at the bodyguard by the door and noticed that he wasn't following the conversation, but staring into the middle distance. His hands were clasped together down by his groin, well away from the bulge in his jacket.

'Your fight is not my fight, so I don't care where it goes. As long as the price is right, everyone is happy.' With that, the Pakistani smiled falsely.

The SIS man paused, looked at his host and spoke calmly.

'Before we go any further, there is something I need to cover,' he said.

'What's that?'

Moving slowly, David surreptitiously lowered his arm down the side of the couch and reached for the pistol, his fingertips relishing the touch of cold steel.

Tariq took a deep breath and replied.

'Actually, we're not who you think we are.'

'Go on,' instructed the scientist, slowly sitting up in his chair.

'We are from British Intelligence. We know that you're trying to sell nuclear material to a group hostile to the West, and we have come to offer an alternative deal. A very generous one, where you can remain in Pakistan and work with us.'

Khan's eyes flamed with fury, his malevolent look plain to see.

'What do you think this is, a game?' he shouted.

'We can be very generous. I would like to discuss those details with you now...'

Khan, breathing hard, held his hand up.

'You dare to insult me!' he shouted. 'Do you really think I am interested in working with you? I hate the British and all of the other weak, western countries.'

Composing himself, he looked at his guests for a moment and smiled.

'Shoot them!' he raged.

In a split second, David brought the pistol into the aim. As his finger began to exert pressure on the trigger, a loud, deafening shot rang out from across the room. There was a gasp of pain to his right.

He fired a double tap into the head of the bodyguard, and the man dropped like liquid to the floor.

He stood up, covering Khan, who glared back in anger. Glancing quickly back at Tariq, he saw that he had been shot in the arm, and gasping, was trying to staunch the bleeding.

'How is it mate?' he asked.

'The bastard shot me!' he replied weakly.

'Well, we knew there might be some danger didn't we?' he smiled. 'Keep pressure on it and I'll sort you out in a second.'

Hearing heavy footsteps in the corridor outside, he moved to the side of the room and pointed his weapon at the door. The second driver barged in brandishing a pistol and started shouting something. He fired into the man's head and he too dropped like a stone. Retrieving the pistol, he checked it and passed it to his friend.

'Cover the door,' he instructed.

Walking over to where Khan was sitting, he pistol whipped the man, sending him to the floor. The Pakistani groaned and got back to his feet groggily. Sitting back down, he held his hand to a bloody wound on his cheek.

'How many?' he shouted.

Khan looked up at him slowly, hatred in his eyes.

'I asked for more people when you arrived. They'll be here soon.'

'Fair enough. Take off your shoes and socks,' he instructed calmly.

'What?' asked the man, obviously in pain.

'You heard. I won't ask again.'

The scientist leant down and untied his shoe laces, dripping blood onto the carpet as he did so. Once his shoes were off, he placed them in front of him. Working quickly, he took the laces and tied the man's hands together behind him. He then tied the socks together, placing the makeshift gag over the man's mouth and tying it off.

'Now, you stay nice and quiet,' he instructed, patting him on the shoulder.

He walked over to Tariq, who had unbuttoned his shirt and pulled it over his shoulder. He was holding a cushion against the wound and grimacing in pain.

'Let's have a look,' he instructed, pulling the cushion away.

'We need to get away,' the man pleaded. 'Now!'

'Yes, I know, but I'm just going to sort this out and we'll be away in a jiffy. Don't worry…' he smiled, '…and keep an eye on the door!'

Looking at the wound, he saw that the bullet had passed through the upper arm, missing the bone.

'You'll be alright,' he said confidently. 'It's passed cleanly through. It's going to hurt a lot, but you'll survive. Trust me, I know!'

The SIS man grimaced and nodded slowly.

'Now, all I need is a tourniquet,' he said, looking around the room.

Walking over to the body of the driver and undoing the buttons, he removed the shirt. He then began ripping it into lengths and discarded what he didn't need. He strode back to Tariq and making a ball of the shirt material, placed it over the wound, tying it tight as he did so.

'How does that feel?' he asked.

'Not bad' replied the agent wincing. 'A little tight, but it'll be fine.'

He lowered his head to the man's ear.

'I'm going to check outside. Be sure to keep an eye on our friend,' he whispered.

The SIS man nodded and pointed his pistol at the scientist, as he stepped out of the room. He was back in the entrance hall and, resting his back on the wall, stopped and listened.

All was quiet.

He quickly moved from room to room throughout the house, checking that they were alone, as Khan had indicated. Upstairs, stopping briefly in the main bathroom, he rummaged through a cabinet and found some aspirin for his friend.

Walking to the front door, he opened it slowly and peered outside. It was as it had been when they had arrived, hardly lit and quiet.

Striding quickly over to the compound gates, he opened them, pushing them wide. The movement provoked the dog again, who sprang out from the darkness, barking wildly. The crude chain around its neck was almost choking it as it tried to get to him.

Hurrying over to the cars, he was disappointed to see that the keys weren't there.

'Bollocks!' he said aloud, turning and walking back to the corner of the building.

He scanned the compound wall at the back and found a water butt up against it, opposite the veranda. Retracing his steps back to the front door, he left it ajar and returned to the main room, where Tariq was still covering Khan. He searched in the bodyguard's pockets for the keys and smiled when he found them.

'All OK here?' he asked.

'Yep,' replied the agent.

'Good. Now, as you're injured, I'm taking over,' he stated.

'Fine,' replied Tariq resignedly.

'And take a few of these,' he instructed, handing over the aspirin. 'They'll help a little, but you're going to have to grit your teeth for a while.'

He strode over to Khan, standing by his shoulder.

'Give me your phone.'

The Pakistani glared up at him. 'Fuck off!' he shouted through the gag.

Not impressed with the response, he took his pistol by the barrel and smashed the grip into the top of the man's head. The scientist howled and slumped to the floor. He picked him up and forced him back into the chair, despite his protestations.

'Now, let's try that again,' he said, bringing his face close to the Pakistani's. 'Where is your phone?'

Khan lifted his tear filled eyes and gestured with his chin for him to search his pocket. Reaching down, he tapped the man's jacket and felt the outline of a phone. He pulled it out and placed it into his own pocket.

'There, that wasn't so bad was it?' he said, grinning at his hostage.

He looked down at Khan, still clearly in discomfort and removed the gag.

'So, my friend. When are you due to meet your other buyer?'

The man looked at him with tired eyes.

'Next Saturday, in Peshawar. Seven o'clock, in the old schoolhouse. It's at the foot of the Bala Hissar fort,' he muttered.

'Do you know it?' he asked Tariq.

'Yes. It's easy to find.'

Just then, they heard the screech of tyres on gravel outside and he turned to the SIS man.

'You stay with him!'

He dimmed the lights and moved to the door, crouching down and pointing his weapon at the main entrance. Hearing doors banging and loud voices outside, he was glad he had left the door open. He saw shadows in front of the door and then two men barged in, looking around the hall. They wore traditional dress, shalwar kameez, pakol hats, leather sandals and both had full, dark beards. In their hands, they carried AK-47 rifles, which pointed to the floor. It looked like they were unsure of themselves, somehow waiting for instructions.

Aiming his pistol at the man closest to him, he fired two rounds into his chest. The figure slumped to the floor and his rifle slid along the carpet. Changing his aim quickly, he fired into the chest of the second man, whose surprised expression stayed with him as he dropped to the ground. As he fell, his weapon fired off a burst into the floor, as his finger held on to the trigger.

He dashed out, into the hall and picked up the dropped weapons, quickly taking the magazines off and checking there were more rounds inside. Selecting a rifle, he charged the magazine with the rounds from both weapons and took up a fire position by the fireplace. Just then, a burst of gunfire ripped through the open door, striking the floor and wall behind, showering him in dust. He waited, trying to predict their next move.

He didn't have to wait long.

Long bursts of automatic fire raked the front door, sending glass and wall fragments flying everywhere. He kept his head down and returned fire, only using a few rounds at a time, hoping to keep the attackers at bay for a while. He heard angry cries from outside, as the attackers shouted to each other, making their assault plans.

'Time to go,' he said aloud, as he turned and sprinted back into the living room, giving Tariq warning that it was him.

'Fucking hell!' cried Tariq, when he saw him crouching by the door. 'Sounds like World War Three out there.'

'Maybe it is,' he replied wryly. 'We need to go! I've only got half a mag left for the AK and the pistols aren't going to be much use at distance.'

Tariq struggled up.

Walking over to him, he whispered in his ear. 'Go out the back door and wait for me.'

Before he could protest, David pushed him towards the rear door and strolled over to the scientist, manhandling him out of the chair. He noticed the wound on the man's face and wondered for a moment how painful it must feel.

'Right matey, I've got a job for you!' he said loudly, dragging him towards the door and peering into the hall.

'What do you want of me?' the man protested. 'I've given you everything you've asked for.'

'Not quite,' he replied, looking hard into the man's eyes. 'I want you to negotiate with your friends outside, to let us go.'

'But they'll kill me if I go out there' he pleaded, jerking his head towards the entrance.

'You'll be fine. Just shout your name, before you run out and I'm sure they won't shoot.'

He reached down and untied Khan's bonds, thrusting him towards the door.

'Get going!' he instructed.

The scientist looked back at him unsurely and turning, sprinted for the door as fast as he could go, shouting his name repeatedly in Urdu.

As he reached it, there was a long burst of gunfire that ripped through his body, snapping his head back and spraying crimson blood on the carpet where he fell.

Candidate 44 was dead.

Chapter Twenty-four

'Unlucky,' muttered David wryly, surveying the carnage. 'You almost made it.'

Firing a few shots through the front door, he ran back into the living room, closed the door firmly behind him and jammed a chair under the handle. Stepping over to the rear door, he shouted to Tariq that he was coming out.

He jogged over to the agent, who was sitting behind some bushes, clutching his arm.

'C'mon mate, let's go,' he encouraged, handing him the rifle and walking over to the water butt. 'I'll go first and tell you when to follow.'

He checked that the surface was stable and climbed on top, moving his hands up the wall as he did so. More firing and angry voices from the front of the house could be heard. His fingers reached the top of the wall and he flinched sharply when he felt the shard of glass slice deeply through his palm.

'There's glass on top, so be careful,' he whispered down.

Taking the pistol, he smashed away the fragments until he was satisfied they wouldn't cause any more harm. He levered himself up and sat astride the wall, seeing only darkness below. Taking the rifle from his friend, he lowered himself to the ground, landing on soil and glanced around anxiously.

'Come on over,' he instructed, as he tied some material around his hand.

He heard Tariq climb onto the butt and then groan when he was reaching for the top of the wall. His head appeared and gingerly, he pulled himself up and lifting his legs over, lowered himself gently to the floor.

'Well done!' he whispered. 'Now, follow me. We're going to sprint a few hundred metres, to get away from these idiots, and then jog for a kilometre or two to get some distance between us. OK?'

'Yeah,' whispered the SIS man weakly.

He listened for one last time and heard loud voices and a few shots from the building. Satisfied that it was safe to go, they sprinted directly away from the wall, across open farmland.

From the moonlight, he could make out the ground in front of him, as he heard Tariq labouring behind. After a few hundred metres, they reached a stream bed which they stepped through, before pushing on. The agent was breathing hard, but he knew they couldn't rest.

He turned to face the way they had come and saw that all the lights in the house had been switched on, casting bright light into the edge of the field. There were occasional shots now, as the intruders were going room to room, no doubt expecting to find the two somewhere in the building.

'Great stuff,' he encouraged, hearing that the agent's breathing had settled down. 'Stay close.'

They set off once more at a jog, heading roughly forty five degrees to the left from their original course.

The farmland they were on had recently been cut and apart from the odd stubble of vegetation and boulder, the ground was firm and easy to move across.

They came to another stream across their path and waded through it, flinching at the smell of the rancid water. After jogging for another five minutes, they came to a small copse in the corner of a field and he instructed his friend to take a quick breather.

Looking back at the building in the distance, he heard someone firing into the night, probably from where they had climbed the wall.

'Gotta keep going,' he whispered. 'You alright?'

'Yeah, fine' said the agent tiredly, 'but my arm is bleeding again. I can feel it soaking into the shirt.'

'Hang in there. When we get some decent distance from the building, I'll tape you up again.'

As he was turning to start running again, some light caught his eye. Glancing over his shoulder, he saw a pair of vehicle lights pointing in the direction they had originally taken.

'Shit!' he muttered. 'We've got company.'

They set off, their frames bent over to reduce silhouette. After a few minutes of steady running, they came to a small mud hut on the edge of a field.

Quickly climbing on to the roof, he lay flat and watched the lights in the distance. The car was moving slowly and every now and then, it stopped. Figures dipped in and out of the headlights, searching the ground relentlessly. He heard a dog barking and wondered if the mutt in the compound had been pressed into service.

His hand throbbed from the cut and he clenched his fist a few times, trying to alleviate the pain.

Even though they were still some distance from the car, he was glad he had deviated the route, otherwise they might have been caught in the lights.

Jumping down from the roof, he urged his friend on.

Looking to his left, he could see what looked like a small village, several kilometres away, lit by a few gloomy streetlights. They set off again, fast for the first few minutes and then slower, settling into a steady jog. They were just crossing another small stream, running parallel with the track, when he noticed headlights approaching fast.

'Quick, in the stream,' he hissed. 'Get as low as you can!'

The two men slid into the fetid water, lying flat with only their heads exposed.

'Get some mud on your face and rub it all over,' he instructed, as he placed his weapons in some undergrowth on the bank in front of him.

Reaching down into the stream bed, he brought up a handful of gooey mud, spreading it on his face rapidly. He noticed Tariq doing the same, although less enthusiastically.

By now, the car was a hundred metres away and hurtling along the track towards them.

'Head down!' he urged, as it closed the distance.

The car swooshed by in a cloud of stones and dust.

'Stay down!' he urged, seeing his companion start to raise his head.

Glancing back at the car, he saw with dismay that it was slowing down.

'Fuck it!' he cursed quietly.

'What's wrong?' asked the agent.

'See for yourself.'

By now the car had stopped and was idling a few hundred metres away.

Slowly, he pulled the rifle from the reeds and into the aim, towards the driver's door.

Time stood still.

'What are they doing?' the SIS man whispered nervously.

'Probably discussing what to do next. Just hold tight and we'll be fine.'

Just then, the doors opened slowly and four figures emerged. In the gloom, he could just make out that they were wearing loose-fitting clothes, turbans and armed with assault rifles. It looked like they were scanning the countryside and one produced a torch, which he was shining at the stream. He could hear agitated shouting and saw some arm waving, as one of them issued instructions.

Two of the figures started to walk purposefully along the stream towards them, whilst the others headed away from the car in the opposite direction.

'Keep your head down, as things are about to get serious,' he warned.

When the figures were a hundred metres away, they stopped suddenly and peered towards the hiding place.

Satisfied, after an exchange of words, they continued on, scouring the ground around them.

He tracked them with his rifle and when they were closer, he fired at the figure nearest the stream. The man crumpled to the ground with little sound, as the other raised his weapon and fired towards the two. Rounds fizzed over their heads, as David took aim again. He fired at the figure, who screamed and dropped to the floor. The man, though obviously wounded, brought his weapon to bear and fired a burst of automatic at his prey. Taking careful aim again, he shot the pursuer in the head and the figure slumped on his side.

'Be ready to bug out along the stream, that way,' he whispered.

Taking aim at the tyres, he fired off a few rounds.

Just then, muzzle flashes appeared far to their right and a line of bullets hit the ground and water metres from them.

'They're trying to outflank us!' he warned, as he fired back. 'Keep low and follow me!'

He turned and raced along the stream, with Tariq close behind. Rounds were still being fired, but they seemed to be towards their original position. After a few minutes of running, they came to a small flat bridge and ducked behind it.

Observing for a few moments, he whispered, 'I reckon they've gone back to the car. Let's go.'

They continued along the stream for a few hundred metres, until they came to a line of trees perpendicular to them.

He signalled for the agent to follow. Keeping low, they jogged along the hard ground until they reached a small wood of thin trees, where they took a moment to rest. Tariq was breathing hard and looking anxiously around him.

The sound of more rounds being fired back at the stream pierced the stillness.

'Right, we need to put more distance between us and the nutters. Let's get a shift on to that village,' he urged, pointing to the lights in the distance. 'Keep your eyes peeled for more headlights, as this ground is as flat as fuck and we might not have a stream next time to save us.'

They set off, their wet clothes clinging to their skin, as they ran along the treeline and only once had to lie down on the hard ground, when they spotted more headlights. Eventually, they reached the outer edge of the village and slipped out of sight, into a crumbling wooden barn.

'Let's have a look at that wound,' he instructed, getting out his phone to give some light.

Tariq undid his sodden shirt and pulled it open, so he could see. The wound looked nasty and although the bleeding had slowed, fresh blood was seeping out through a thin layer of bloody crust. He applied a new bandage, making sure it was tight.

'How's that?' he asked his patient.

'It's OK,' replied the agent, wincing through gritted teeth. 'You could be a nurse when you grow up!'

'It's time we got away from here' he urged, walking over to the barn door and peering outside. 'It's only a matter of time before those lunatics pass through here. Can you call Bilal?'

'Sure,' replied the SIS man, pulling out his phone.

He had an animated conversation with the driver and gave directions, as best he could, on where they were hiding.

'He'll call me when he's closer. He did get the call earlier and tracked us close to the house.'

'Good. Why don't you rest up for a bit? I'll keep an eye on the road,' he promised.

'Thanks. I will,' he replied, sitting on the floor and resting his head against an old metal trough.

....

Time seemed to pass slowly and once or twice, he felt his eyes began to close from the exertions and fear of the ordeal. He pinched himself hard and opened his eyes as far as they would go, only resting them when he felt awake again.

Pacing impatiently around the barn, his night vision picked up strange objects around him. He stretched his muscles and had a look at his aching hand. Using the phone for light, he saw that the wound was ragged and deep and would require multiple stiches. He tied the remaining length of shirt around the cut and felt the blood begin to soak into the material.

As he was doing so, he heard the unmistakable sound of a car, moving slowly through the village towards them.

'Bilal!' he murmured to himself.

Remaining in cover, he looked along the street at the approaching vehicle, wondering why it was going so slowly.

It had been over half an hour since Tariq had called the driver and he was convinced that their ticket out had arrived.

Clutching the rifle, he waited.

The car passed under one of the few streetlights and to his horror, he saw that it was full of bearded men, scanning left and right. Keeping dead still, and holding his breath, he watched the vehicle pass, metres from him. It seemed that one of them in the back, looked straight at him in the darkness, but the moment passed and the car moved out of the village.

He strode over to where his friend was resting and shook him on the leg.

'Wake up!' he whispered.

The agent opened his eyes and got to his feet wearily, asking what the matter was.

'We've just had our AQA friends drive past the barn. Who knows when they'll come back?'

'Bloody hell!' the agent whispered, pulling out his phone.

He called the driver once more, asking him where he was and urged him to get a move on. Describing the barn and where they were hiding, he told him to call the clinic that supported the embassy, to tell them to prepare for some new patients.

'How far out is he?' David asked, peering into the darkness.

'Quite close.......I think.'

Ten minutes passed and another ten, before he saw headlights in the distance, closing fast.

'This might be him,' he warned, as the vehicle drew closer.

The car shuddered to a stop outside the barn and a man got out, standing by the door. He studied the figure hard from the darkness and satisfied that it was Bilal, called Tariq to leave.

'Good to see you Bilal!' he said, grinning from ear to ear.

The driver smiled back and ushered them into the car, as if he was collecting a fare.

Once they were bouncing along the road, he drew breath.

'That has got to be one of the longest nights of my life!'

'Me too!' smiled the SIS man.

They drove on in silence, thankful they were safe. Eventually, they pulled up outside the clinic, near to the embassy, and the two men staggered up the stairs like a pair of old drunks.

....

A few days later, when David was sitting in the comms room one morning, putting the finishing touches to his incident report, Tariq walked in with his arm in a sling.

'How's the arm, mate?' he asked.

'Not bad thanks. It's a little stiff, but the surgeon has done a good job, and these painkillers do the trick!' he grinned.

'Good to hear!' he replied, standing up and patting the man gently on the back with his bandaged hand. 'You did well out there. It was touch and go for a bit, but we got out alive, which is the main thing.'

The agent nodded and raised his eyes to the ceiling.

'And I think we both learnt an important lesson about getting into cars with strangers!'

'Very lucky, we were. Anyway…' he said, his face brightening, '…I wanted to let you know that I'm going to put you forward for a commendation. You saved my life out there and I'll always be grateful.'

'You don't need to worry about that.'

Tariq smiled again. 'No, I'm grateful.'

'We should work together again, although let's give Al-Qaeda a rest for a bit. What do you say?'

'Deal!'

……….

The following morning, after meeting the COO of the Punjab Petrochemicals Company, David sat at his desk at the embassy, tapping away at his laptop.

The meeting had been useful, at least as a cover for his visit to the country, but it had been more than that.

He had learnt so much about the country and the COO, Yasir Rana, had been generous with his time, explaining how the oil and gas sector operated in Pakistan. Of course, he had done some research before leaving England, but nothing beat hearing about the industry from someone who lived it.

Yasir had worked in oil and gas all his life, ever since graduating from university and now in his fifties, he could look back on a long and illustrious career serving his country. He had spoken of the old days, when the industry was in its infancy and the country had been heavily reliant on western help to extract the resources from the ground.

He had also explained how the sector had progressed and how after a time, been able to employ its own people and look after itself, shrugging off western expertise.

It had been tough, he had chuckled, but in the end, they had made it into what it was today, a player on the world stage, making billions for the country.

He had pressed him about openings in the company that he could potentially work on and had been greeted with a wry smile by the oil man. They took the odd westerner, he was informed, senior geologist, extraction specialist or the occasional international lawyer, but hadn't had anything for him that was current. They had agreed to keep in touch and shook hands warmly when he left.

'Maybe I'll return to this country in the future?' he mused, back to the embassy.

His thoughts were disturbed by Tariq entering the room, carrying a box wrapped in paper under his arm.

'I wanted to thank you again for saving my life and I've brought you a little momento, to remind you of your time in Pakistan,' he said, handing him the box.

'Thank you,' he replied, holding the box. 'Can I open it?'

'Sure, go ahead.'

He pulled the paper off and found a neat wooden box underneath. Carefully opening the lid, he saw a beautifully crafted knife inside, sitting on a bed of soft red silk. Picking it up reverently, he held it in his hand, marvelling at the work. The blade was about six inches long and curved one way and then another and the handle was made of polished animal horn. Carefully, he ran his finger along the side of the cutting edge, testing the sharpness of the weapon.

'I'm ready to face Islamabad on my own now!' he grinned, sweeping the knife from side to side in mock display.

'You'd be well protected with that on your side. It comes from the north of Pakistan, where my family originated and where knife making is still an art.'

'It's beautiful. I'll keep this in a special place when I get home and you're right. It will remind me of this place and the adventures we had.'

Hours later, when David was sitting on the plane heading west, he reflected. He had been in some tight spots in the past, particularly with the SAS, but this action really had been a close run thing.

He shook his head slowly, thankful that the bodyguard had aimed his first and last shot at Tariq, rather than at him.

He thought back to clambering over the wall and running into the night, dragging the injured man with him. He remembered seeing the headlights in the dark, racing towards them and only having enough time to dive into the stream to hide. Then, fighting them off and running for their lives. Closing his eyes and clenching his still sore hand, he knew that the memories of that night would not recede quickly.

As he was starting to feel sleepy, he felt a light tap on the shoulder. Looking up sharply, he saw a British Airways stewardess smiling down at him.

'Can I get you anything, sir?' she smiled sweetly.

He grinned and thought for a moment.

'Your phone number?'

The woman laughed and put her fingers to her lips, as if to correct herself.

'That's a bit forward, sir!' she whispered, lowering her head closer to his own.

She reached for a napkin, looked at him again and hurriedly scribbled, as he admired her figure.

'That's my number. I'll be in the bar at the Hilton with the other girls, around eight. It's the one next to terminal four.'

He nodded and studied the napkin, before slipping it into his pocket.

She looked into his eyes, still smiling, as if she was trying to read his mind.

'I'm Anne, by the way,' she said, before turning on her heel and walking away down the aisle.

Chapter Twenty-five

England

David met James in the Farmer's Daughter pub in London, a few evenings later. It was just off Baker Street, but hidden away by being set back from the road. Rough-hewn benches and tables, damp from the rain, sat unused in the front and large potted plants were placed around tastefully. He pushed open the door and noticed the old wooden bar to the left with personal pewter tankards hanging above. The pub was fairly empty, with a few regulars sitting at the bar and some sweethearts nearby, holding hands under the table.

He saw James sitting at the back in a comfortable old chair, facing the door, with a black Labrador nestled at his feet, chin on the floor.

'Christ, you look five years older!' remarked the man, when he approached.

'I feel it,' he replied, slumping into the chair opposite.

The dog stood up and walked round to inspect the visitor, wagging its tail enthusiastically.

'I'd better get you a drink then. What'll it be?'

'Oh, a lager would be nice,' he replied.

He patted the dog's head and stroked it affectionately along its sleek back, enjoying the welcome from his new canine friend.

Looking around the pub, he liked it immediately. There was a heavy wood presence and prints of old farmyard scenes adorned the walls. Soft lighting gave the place warmth and as he settled into the chair, he thought he might revisit the place sometime in the future.

James returned with two glasses, setting them down on the table and sat back down. The Labrador accepted one last stroke and settled down once more at its master's feet.

'Good health,' James announced, raising his glass. 'And good to see you back!'

As David lifted his glass to reply, James shot him a look.

'What the hell have you done to your hand?'

'Err, had a bit of an accident out there. Nothing to worry about though. Just needed some stiches to sew it up.'

'How was it?' asked his boss.

'I thought it was going to be fairly straightforward, but we mucked up by getting into vehicles we didn't know and moving to another location. It's been a while since I was shot at by AK-47s!'

'Tell me about it,' urged the man, stroking the dog at his feet.

David went through the events in Pakistan. Two hours and a few pints later, he was done.

The older man considered what he had heard for a moment.

'I think you did the right thing with Khan. The man was a menace and better off six foot under. Although you were supposed to only talk to him, I agree with your actions.'

He nodded his head, thinking back to the lives he had taken.

'Thanks,' he said quietly.

The former colonel leant forward.

'Are they going after Noorzai in Peshawar?'

'Yes, they're planning it as we speak. They're putting quite a team together I understand, so hopefully they'll get their man and this 'nuclear material' topic can disappear for a while.'

'Quite. There are plenty of other 'topics' we can get you involved in. Not for a while you understand. You need to recover and get back to your other life.'

'That'll be good for a while,' he conceded, taking another sip. 'It'll be nice to get back into the swing of things again.'

'Oh, incidentally. That chap you worked with in Pakistan. Tariq is it?'

'That's right.'

'Well, he's put you forward for a commendation, of all things!'

'Yes, he told me he was going to.'

'Now, we don't go in for that sort of thing, as you'll appreciate, but VX will acknowledge it and it will sit on a file somewhere, never to be seen.'

'No problem,' he replied, feeling suddenly tired.

'I knew you'd understand.' After a pause, James patted the dog a final time and said, 'Anyway, you need to be back at work tomorrow, bright and breezy, so we'd better call it a night for now.'

Standing up, he reached into his jacket pocket, pulled out a fat brown envelope and handed it to his protégé.

'Another job well done.' He turned and said over his shoulder, 'See you in the office,' before strolling out of the pub with the dog at his heels, nodding to the barman as he went.

David clutched the envelope to him and breathed out strongly. Draining his glass and placing it down carefully, he ripped it open and peered inside, seeing a thick wad of crisp fifty pound notes. His thoughts took him back to Pakistan, where he could almost smell the fields again. Images from the operation flashed through his mind at a hundred miles an hour, until they slowed and finally stopped on the picture of Khan's dead face.

He shook the bloodied image from his brain and stood up, making his way to the entrance. A light spring shower was starting to fall and he pulled up his collar and dipped his head below the old oak doorframe.

He broke into a smile and stepped outside.

Terminology

AK-47. Assault rifle. 7.62mm calibre.

AQA. Al-Qaeda. Sunni Islamic terrorist group.

Artillery Spotter. Someone trained to direct artillery fire on to targets.

Basha. A waterproof sheet used to provide shelter.

Belt kit. Pouches worn around the waist to carry what a soldier needs to fight. Contains ammunition, food, water and personal medical kit.

Bergan. Rucksack. Used by a soldier to carry what he needs for operations.

Browning. Pistol used by some British units. 9mm calibre.

Case catcher. Case to catch a round ejected from the breech.

Check zero. Carried out to confirm the accuracy of a weapon.

Chest rig. Pouches worn on the chest usually for extra ammunition and equipment.

Chopper. Helicopter.

CO. Commanding Officer. Lieutenant Colonel.

C-4. Plastic explosive.

C8. Assault weapon made by Colt, used by some British Army units including the SAS. 5.56mm calibre.

Daysack. Small pack used to carry equipment and supplies for short operations.

ETA. Estimated Time of Arrival.

Fix. Location.

Forward Air Controller. Someone trained to guide aircraft on to targets.

GCHQ. Government Communications Headquarters. Provides signals intelligence to the UK Government.

GPS. Global Positioning System.

Grub. Food.

HAHO. High altitude, high opening freefall parachute jump, used by Special Forces.

HALO. High altitude, low opening freefall parachute jump, used by Special Forces.

Hard routine. The routine followed by soldiers trying to hide from the enemy. Normally includes no talking, no cooking, no smoking and storing human waste.

ISI. Inter-Services Intelligence. Premier intelligence organisation within Pakistan.

IED. Improvised Explosive Device. A bomb constructed and deployed by insurgents.

Laser range finder. A range finder that uses a laser to determine distance to an object.

Lynx. Multi-purpose helicopter made by Westland used by British Forces.

L118A1. Sniper rifle used by British Forces and the SAS. 7.62mm calibre.

MC. Military Cross. Medal awarded for exemplary gallantry during active operations.

Medic. Someone trained in emergency medical procedures.

Merlin. Helicopter made by Augusta Westland used by British Forces. Can carry 24 seated troops and their equipment.

Mozzie Rep. Mosquito repellent.

NCO. Non Commissioned Officer.

OC. Officer Commanding. Major.

OP. Observation Post.

OPSEC. Operational Security.

Platoon. Sub unit within a Company. In the infantry, about 30 men.

RTI. Resistance to interrogation.

Section. Sub unit within a platoon. In the infantry, about 8 men.

Selection. The phases a soldier must go through to be selected for the SAS.

Shemagh. A scarf usually made of cotton that provides protection from the sun.

Signaller. An expert in radio communications.

Sig Sauer P226. Pistol used by British Forces and the SAS. 9mm calibre.

SIS. Secret Intelligence Service, commonly known as MI6, is the foreign intelligence service for the United Kingdom.

SOPs. Standard operating procedures.

Spike strips. A device used to stop vehicles by puncturing the tyres.

Squadron. Sub unit within a regiment. In the SAS, about 70 men.

Squadron Commander. The Commander of a Squadron. Major.

Suppressor. Device attached to a barrel to reduce noise and muzzle flash.

Tab. March.

Troop. Sub unit within a Squadron. In the SAS, about 16 men.

Troop Commander. The Commander of a Troop. Captain.

VHF. Very high frequency. Frequency used for some military radios.

VX. Vauxhall Cross. Headquarters of SIS.

Printed in Poland
by Amazon Fulfillment
Poland Sp. z o.o., Wrocław